The Secrets of Lake Road

The Secrets of Lake Road

KAREN KATCHUR

THOMAS DUNNE BOOKS ☙ ST. MARTIN'S PRESS
NEW YORK

This is a work of fiction. All of the characters, organizations, and events portrayed in this novel are either products of the author's imagination or are used fictitiously.

THOMAS DUNNE BOOKS.
An imprint of St. Martin's Press.

www.thomasdunnebooks.com
www.stmartins.com

The Library of Congress Cataloging-in-Publication Data
is available upon request.

ISBN 978-1-250-06681-7 (hardcover)
ISBN 978-1-4668-7470-1 (e-book)

St. Martin's Press books may be purchased for educational, business, or promotional use. For information on bulk purchases, please contact the Macmillan Corporate and Premium Sales Department at 1-800-221-7945, extension 5442, or write to specialmarkets@macmillan.com.

First Edition: August 2015

10 9 8 7 6 5 4 3 2 1

For my sister, Krista, and our late grandmother, Ann
for their love of the lake

ACKNOWLEDGMENTS

I spent many summers as a kid at a lake in the Pocono Mountains, but not nearly as many as my sister, Krista, and our late grandmother, Ann. It was their love of the lake and its community that inspired this book.

Although this is a work of fiction about made-up people who just happened to inhabit a real place, I would be remiss not to mention the very real lake community, past and present, who are some of the kindest people I have ever known. Thank you for so many good memories.

Also, I would like to thank Joseph Shambo and the Whitehall Fire Department Underwater Recovery Team for being so generous with their time and answering all of my questions about the amazing work they do. Any and all errors with regard to underwater rescue and recovery are mine and mine alone.

I want to thank my agent, Carly Watters, for pulling me from the slush pile and taking a chance on me. Your belief and support overwhelm me. I couldn't have asked for a better guide and advocate. Also, I'm grateful for my editor, Anne Brewer, who knew exactly what I was trying to do and helped make this book so much better than it was originally. My gratitude extends to

St. Martin's Press and their amazing staff for their continuous enthusiasm and hard work.

To Kathy Kulig, Terri Prizzi, and Sylvie Kaye, thanks for being there from the beginning, for reading almost everything I have ever written, and never letting me give up. You ladies rock.

A special thanks to my mom, Johanna Houck, and my mother-in-law, Mollie Katchur, for being such strong women and amazing role models.

And, of course, a huge amount of gratitude to my girlfriends in no particular order, Tracey Golden, Mindy Strouse Bailey, Tina Mantel, Kate Weeks, Karin Wagner, and Jenene McGonigal. I cherish each and every one of you for your warmth, your wisdom, your guidance, and most of all, your friendship.

And last, but certainly not least, to my husband, Philip and our two beautiful daughters, without whom none of this would be possible. You are my heart, my everything.

The Secrets of Lake Road

CHAPTER ONE

No one touched the bottom of the lake and lived. If you were lucky, you'd surface wide-eyed and frantic, babbling at the darkness, the thickness of what lay below. If you were unlucky, underwater recovery dragged the lake for your body.

As Caroline unpacked her duffel bag in the small bedroom where she had slept every summer since she could remember, she wondered who would be brave or stupid enough to try to touch bottom this summer.

The cabin door to *The Pop-Inn* creaked open and closed with a bang. Caroline rushed to the window to see who it was. A warm breeze blew, carrying the dampness of the lake and the smell of a barbecue. The leaves rustled in the hundred-year-old trees. She looked down the dirt road that led into the colony, catching her older brother, Johnny, pass by. If he'd noticed her watching, he pretended he hadn't. He wasn't five steps away when he lit a cigarette, a habit he perpetuated at the lake but never at home. Rules at the lake were lax if they existed at all.

He blew smoke from his lips and whipped his head to the side, sweeping the wavy bangs from his eyes. He walked down the hill with a swagger that was uniquely his, cool and a little cocky, but with enough insecurity that hinted at a sensitive side and, as much as she hated to admit it, a certain charm.

Caroline hoped Gram didn't see the cigarette. "No smoking in front of Gram," their mother had warned repeatedly during the three-hour drive from their home in New Jersey to the lake. But at sixteen-years-old, Johnny always did what Johnny wanted to do, no matter what anyone said. In a way she believed their mother was trying to protect Johnny from Gram's wrath, a disposition Gram reserved solely for Caroline's mother, but apparently her mother was as oblivious to that fact as she was to other things, in Caroline's opinion.

She returned to unpacking, putting clothes into the dresser she and Gram had painted white last summer. Her mother walked into the room and handed her clean sheets. While she made up the bed, her mother leaned against the doorjamb with a far-off look in her eyes. Her long dark hair cast shadows in the hollows of her cheeks, making her face appear gaunt, haunted.

The way her mother looked, her expression, reminded Caroline of the lake. There was a place inside of her mother as vast and as murky. It must be a sad place, because she often heard her cry. She imagined it was also a place where her mother felt trapped. She'd pull at her clothes and hair as though she were tangled in fishing line. Sometimes she'd run out of the house and drive off. Sometimes she wouldn't return home for days.

Gram said we all run from something, whether it was a terrible childhood or a bad marriage, or perhaps we run from ourselves, and Caroline's mother was no different. Caroline understood what Gram was saying, but she couldn't help but wonder why her mother was always running from her.

"All set?" her mother asked when Caroline had finished making up the bed.

"Looks like it." She ran her hand over the new green quilt Gram had stitched, smoothing out the wrinkles.

"I'm going to see what Gram needs from me." Her mother walked away, leaving her alone to finish unpacking.

Caroline unrolled her new poster of the latest boy band and pinned it to the wall. She particularly liked the lead singer, and it wasn't because she was boy crazy. She liked his skateboard. Okay, maybe she liked his hair, toothy smile, and flawless skin. That reminded her. She dug into the bag in search of sunscreen. She felt around and pulled out her cell phone. No bars or messages. She wasn't surprised. She tossed it into a drawer. It wasn't like anyone from home would miss her enough to text. And even if someone did want to contact her for some reason, it was next to impossible, since the lake was nestled deep inside the Pocono Mountains and what was considered a dead zone.

Gram's voice rang out from the kitchen. She paused to listen.

"Why not?" Gram asked.

"I have things to do," her mother said.

"You always have *things* to do. What things, Jo?"

"I don't know. *Things.*"

A cabinet door was closed harder than usual.

"Can you at least stick around for a few days and help me clean out that back closet and porch? I can't do it by myself," Gram said.

Her mother sighed heavily. A second or two passed before she grumbled, "Maybe."

But Caroline knew her mother's maybes were always nos. She had learned at a young age that *maybe* was just her mother's way of putting off the answer you didn't want to hear. Could she get ice cream? Maybe. Could she go to the movies? Maybe. Could she get a skateboard? Maybe.

No ice cream. No movie. No skateboard.

Another cabinet door slammed, rattling the dishes inside, and Caroline figured Gram understood what maybe meant too.

Caroline went back to digging into her bag, pulling out an extra bathing suit and shorts. The cabin's screen door squeaked open and closed this time without a bang. Her heart beat a little faster. Someone was sneaking out and she knew who.

She dropped the clothes onto the bed, raced out of her room, passed Gram in the kitchen, and bolted outside. Her mother waved as she hopped in the car and pulled away from the cabin. Gravel and dust kicked up from the tires of the old Chevy as she headed down the dirt road.

Caroline swiped her eyes. *Crybaby*, she scolded herself. At twelve years old, she should no longer need hugs and kisses goodbye from her mother.

And yet she still wanted them.

Gram opened the screen door. "Are you hungry for lunch?"

Caroline shook her head. "I'm going to see who's around." She dragged her feet, and puffs of dirt covered her sneakers. No matter how many times Gram planted seeds, only sparse patches of grass grew under the shade of the old maple trees.

Most of the cabins in the colony had yards. Very few were able to get grass to grow.

Caroline grabbed her bike from the ground. It was considered a boy's bike, with the bar going across the frame rather than scooping down like a girl's would. She had asked the man who had sold her father the bike what the difference was other than the obvious disparity with the bar. He had said the design of the scooped frame dated back to when girls wore skirts and dresses rather than pants. Otherwise, there was no difference in the performance or the ride. She wasn't about to wear a skirt or a dress, so the boy's bike it was.

She coasted down the dirt hill and crossed onto Lake Road, the main thoroughfare connecting the colony to the lake, and stopped in front of the Pavilion, a big wooden building that served as the hub of the lake community. Nervous excited energy buzzed just below her skin, the kind of energy that bubbles to the surface with the prospect of things to come. The Pavilion was the unofficial meeting place, where her friends gathered, where they hung around the snack stand, bathing suits dripping wet, eating hotdogs and French fries while the jukebox played songs that were older than their parents. She checked her pockets, finding the quarters she always carried when she was there to play the retro pinball machines and arcade games, hoping for a shot at the highest score of the summer.

The lake spread out on both sides behind the Pavilion. The water shimmered and baked in the hot sun. Ducks milled around looking for handouts of crackers and stale bread. Caroline took a deep breath and smelled the faint scent of fish mixed with the earthiness of algae, a distinct smell she associated with summertime.

She dropped her bike on the side of the Pavilion next to her friend Megan's, a pink *girl's* bike, the same bike she had had since they were nine years old. Johnny and a bunch of his friends were sitting on the steps outside the large double doors. He had his arm slung around a girl's shoulder, and a cigarette dangled from his fingers. The girl's breasts spilled out of her tank top, and although Caroline tried not to stare, she did anyway. She couldn't help it. The girl had large breasts, and Caroline knew it was the girl's chest her brother was after. She felt a little sick and a little sorry for the girl. Sometimes her brother was a real jerk.

"What are you looking at?" Johnny asked.

"Nothing much," she said, and approached the steps. She started up on nervous legs, taking her time not to trip or bump into Johnny or his friends. Two girls leaned away as she stepped toward them. She reached for the railing to steady herself, feeling self-conscious, like a little kid, the way she felt whenever she walked by Johnny's best friend, Chris. He was one of the few locals who lived at the lake all year long. Something about his slightly dirty hair and his wide smile made him look as though he was up to no good. The thought gave her a sort of thrill that made her all the more uncomfortable. He was wearing swim trunks, his T-shirt draped over his leg. His skin was bronze and his stomach cut. His one eye was two different colors, half green and half brown, the other solid brown. She couldn't explain how, but his two-toned eye made him that much cuter. Once, she had overheard Mrs. Nester at the Country Store tell a customer his eye made him look as though he were off-kilter, and maybe that attributed to his reckless behavior.

"Something ain't right in there," she had said, and pointed to her head.

Caroline didn't believe this to be true. If anyone bothered to ask her, she would say there wasn't a thing wrong with him. He was perfect.

Chris grabbed her ankle as she passed. He flashed a playful smile and stared at her with his captivating eye.

"Don't let the snappers get you," he said.

Her brother laughed and flicked his cigarette butt over her shoulder. For a split second she thought about telling her brother to screw off. Two summers ago he nearly had his toe chomped off by a snapper and he about cried. *Do you remember that, tough guy?* But of course, she wasn't going to get into a sibling battle in front of his friends, in front of Chris, a battle she was sure to lose.

Chris released her ankle and her skin seemed to melt where his hand had been. She hurried up the rest of the steps and raced inside. The building was dark without the bright sunlight, and it took a moment for her eyes to adjust.

"Caroline!" Megan called, waving her arms wildly. "Get over here."

Megan was standing in front of the old jukebox, and as soon as Caroline was within reach, Megan threw her arms around her and proceeded to jump up and down, jiggling them both. She let Megan twirl her in circles, feeling totally ridiculous and unaccustomed to so much silly exuberance.

When Megan finally released her, she gave Caroline the once-over. She returned the favor and noticed Megan's heavy blue eye shadow, pink shiny lips, and the two new bumps under her T-shirt. As if the pink bike wasn't enough, Megan had gone all girly on her in the last year.

Megan started talking fast, in a rush to catch up on everything she had missed since their last text messages, which turned out not to be much, even when you considered how short and few the texts tended to be. Mostly, Megan babbled about some boy, Ryan, she was crushing on. Caroline told her about playing softball, her struggling grades, and how she was glad summer was finally here.

"I hope there are some cute boys this summer," Megan said. "Maybe someone new. You do want a boyfriend, don't you?"

"No," Caroline said much louder than she had intended.

Megan shrugged. "Why not?"

"I don't know."

"Well, I do."

"What for?"

"Duh." Megan rolled her blue-lidded eyes and turned toward the jukebox. "I don't want to be the only one starting seventh grade who hasn't been kissed." She turned back toward Caroline. "And I mean properly kissed, tongue and all."

Caroline must've made a face as though she had tasted something awful, because Megan's eyes opened wide and she said, "It's not gross."

"If you say so."

"It's not." Megan looked back at the old jukebox. The outside world had moved on in terms of technology, but the lake and its community refused to succumb to any pressure to change. It was the sense of familiarity, of sameness, that Caroline found comforting year after year. She wished she could say the same about her friend.

They were both silent. The air between them felt awkward and strange. She didn't want to think about the things Megan talked about, about kissing boys, but her mind jumped to Chris anyway. Her ankle tingled where his hand had touched her, the skin still warm. She bent down and swiped the feeling away, pretending she had an itch. She cleared her throat. She wanted to say something to make the queerness in her stomach and the weirdness between her and Megan go away.

"Come on," she said, and tugged Megan's arm, thinking if she could get her to jump into the lake, the water would take care of everything else. For one, it would wash the paint off Megan's face and she would look more like the Megan from summers past. Two, it would rinse away the heat from Chris's hand on her skin—and whatever feeling that came with it, the one that squirmed in her stomach, would drown.

Caroline continued to pull Megan through the Pavilion and out onto the beach. No one stopped them to check for swim passes. No one cared. Caroline tossed her baseball cap, kicked off her sneakers, and stripped from her shirt and shorts to the one-piece bathing suit she wore underneath. The sand was hot to the touch. The girls hurried past the chain-link fence with the sign SWIM AT YOUR OWN RISK, and stepped onto the pier.

Caroline looked around for anyone she might recognize, and spotted Adam. His family was one of the regulars who rented a cabin on the lakefront. He was a few years younger, at ten years old. His body was thin and birdlike. His summer buzz cut made his ears appear too big for his head. On either side of Adam were the Needlemeyer twins, Ted and Ned. They were one year younger than she and Megan, and as they walked toward them, she could've sworn she heard Megan call the boys *babies* under her breath.

The twins ribbed Adam, bumping him in the shoulder. Adam shoved Ted back. "I'll do it when I'm ready," he said.

"Do what?" Caroline asked. Behind Adam was the high dive, and beside it the low dive and the one most used.

"We dared him to jump off the high dive and touch bottom, but he's too scared. Chicken. *Bwack, bwack, bwack.*" Ted flapped his arms.

"Am not." Adam shoved him again, which only coaxed Ted into flapping his arms faster.

"Let's see you do it," Megan said to Ted.

"What? You don't think I can?" Ted folded his arms, puffing up his chest.

"I think you're just as scared as Adam," Megan said, and lay down on the pier, positioning her body under the sun's rays.

"I'm not scared," Adam said. His face paled, and he looked as though he might cry.

Caroline stepped in front of him to shield him from the others. She didn't want Adam to cry, nor did she want them to see if he did.

"Go on," Ned said to his brother. "Let's see you do it. I *dare* you."

Ted glared at his twin and then turned toward the ladder and started to climb. For as long as Caroline had known them, neither brother would ever back down from a dare. It was a brother thing, or maybe a twin thing, always trying to one up each other.

Caroline watched Ted ascend. She had to shield her eyes from the sun when he reached the very top. "This is stupid," she said.

Ted walked to the end of the board. His brother called up to him, "Pencil jump."

He dropped his head as though he were hoping no one would suggest how he had to do it, but of course his brother did. "Fine," he said, and hesitated, head bowed, staring at the water below.

"*Bwack, bwack, bwack.*" Ned flapped his arms.

Ted wavered. Ned kept squawking, taunting him. Until he jumped.

Caroline pulled in a sharp breath. At the last second Ted spread his arms wide to prevent a deep plunge. He hit the water with a slap.

"Chicken!" Ned called when Ted surfaced. Then he turned to Adam and said, "Your turn."

Caroline looked at Adam, whose face was no longer pale, but more ash gray. "Don't try," she said to him. "It doesn't mean you're a chicken. It means you're smart." She climbed the ladder to the low dive, but everyone knew you could never touch bottom jumping off the low dive. The lake was just too deep. Still she said, "Watch this, Adam," and pencil jumped clean into the water. At first it was cool and refreshing, but the farther she sank, the temperature dropped to near freezing. And although she kept her eyes closed, the darkness of what lay below deepened. She kicked her long legs wildly, her arms paddling at a frantic pace, and propelled to the surface, relieved when her head broke above water and her lungs breathed in air.

"Doesn't count," Ned said when Caroline climbed the ladder and stepped back onto the pier. "You have to do it from the *high* dive."

Caroline made a face at him. Ned resumed flapping his arms like a chicken. A little girl poked her head out from behind him. She was maybe six or seven years old, with blond braids and bright blue eyes. Her bathing suit was yellow with pink polka dots. She must be new to the lake. Caroline had never seen her before.

"Hi," Caroline said, pushing Ned out of the way. "Is this your first summer here?"

The little girl smiled and nodded.

"What's your name?" she asked.

"Sara," she said.

"I'm Caroline." She pointed to Megan, who hadn't moved from sunning herself. "That's my friend Megan. And the boys, well . . ." The boys had stopped teasing one another, and they jumped off the pier, splashing around in the lower end of the lake. "Don't listen to them. They're not very smart."

Sara's eyes widened. "Why not?"

"Because they're not. They were just being stupid."

Sara twisted her mouth to one side as though she was considering what Caroline was telling her.

A woman wearing a wide-brimmed sun hat was standing on the beach waving her arms at them. Caroline waved back. "Is that your mom?"

The little girl nodded.

"I'll just be a minute," Sara's mother called.

"Okay," Caroline called back.

"What are they up to now?" Megan interrupted, pointing to

Adam and the twins. Adam was holding something in his hand. The twins were hunched over him, looking at whatever he had found.

Megan stood. "I'm going to find out what it is."

Caroline hesitated, wanting to follow her. But Sara's mother had turned her back, and Caroline couldn't just walk away from the little girl.

"So," Caroline said, looking over her shoulder at her friends. The circle they made around Adam tightened while she tried to think of something to say to Sara. "Do you like to swim?"

Sara smiled and nodded again.

"Me too." Caroline looked toward the beach, where Sara's mother was struggling with a beach umbrella. "Did you feed the ducks yet?"

"No," Sara said.

Caroline used to love feeding the ducks when she was Sara's age, although she couldn't remember the reason why she had thought it was so fun. "Ask your mom if you can feed them." She glanced at her friends again. The twins were holding whatever Adam had found, and Adam looked upset. "The ducks like it when you do," she said absently, wondering what the twins were teasing Adam about this time.

Megan motioned to Caroline. "Come here!" she called.

But Sara's mother still had her back turned as she continued to fight with the beach umbrella. Caroline glanced at her friends again. Adam's face was flushed.

"Did you ever touch bottom?" Sara asked.

"What? No," Caroline said. "Never."

Megan continued waving her over. Caroline shifted her weight from her right foot to her left, gazing at her friends. Sara stared at the diving boards.

Finally Caroline couldn't stand it any longer. She had to know what her friends were up to. Sara's mother had said she would only be a minute. She reasoned Sara wouldn't be left alone for long. She bent down so she was at eye level with the little girl. "Wait for your mom, okay?"

Sara nodded.

"Okay," she said, and in the next moment she was racing down the pier. "And remember," she called, "the boys were just being stupid!"

CHAPTER TWO

Jo fooled herself into thinking she didn't know the reason she had hopped into the old Chevy and sped down the dirt road away from the cabin. She rolled down the window. A warm breeze blew her long hair from her shoulders. "Three Times a Lady" by the Commodores crackled on the radio. You couldn't get a decent radio station within twenty miles of the lake. With the Pocono Mountains surrounding you on every side, reception was scant, and the outside world as distant as outer space.

She was stuck in a time warp, and the year was 1978, when the lake was at its finest if you listened to the old-timers tell it. Vacationers were attracted to the sense of familiarity, simplicity, sameness. It was the lake's charm and the reason you came back year after year. The place and the people and their desire to cling to the good old days were what pissed Jo off. There wasn't anything good about the good old days, at least none that she could remember.

Still, the song wasn't bad, and for awhile she sang along as she drove around the colony and fought the urge to turn onto the highway and leave the blasted lake and everything that came with it behind.

Tired and worn from years of battling with Gram, her

mother—whom she had stopped calling Mom when Johnny had come along—she sunk farther into the driver's seat. Her right hand lay limp in her lap while she loosely gripped the steering wheel with her left. Everything caught her eye as she passed by, the cabins and screened-in porches, the fishing poles and tackle boxes left outside front doors, the maple tree she had stood under the first time she had kissed Billy.

She turned the corner and looped back around. The smell of sun baked earth filled her head, and the dampness from the lake clung to her skin. The sights, the smells, the feel—all of it reminded her of Billy.

If only Gram knew what she was asking, demanding she stick around for a couple of days, but then again maybe she did know and she just didn't care. "You can't change the past," Gram had said. "All you can do is live with it."

But the hardest part for Jo to understand was the disappointment in Gram's eyes whenever she looked at her. It had become a thing between them, this look of disappointment, separating them through the years. Neither one knew how to bridge the gap nor did it seem that either one wanted to try. Too many years had passed. Too much had been said or not said for either to back down now. It was as though both mother and daughter had given up on each other.

"I'm disappointed in you, too," she whispered to herself in the car as the Commodores crooned about love.

Subconsciously, or maybe consciously, she steered toward Lake Road and headed down the hill, taking it slow, maneuvering the Chevy around the potholes nobody bothered to fill. She spied Johnny and his friends hanging out on the steps of the Pavilion. He cupped the cigarette he wasn't supposed to be smoking in his hand and pretended not to recognize their car. As she drove past, she kept her eyes straight ahead.

Pretending not to see each other had been their unspoken agreement since Johnny had turned fourteen two years ago. She didn't ask the typical questions a mother might ask her teenage son about where he was going and who he was going with mostly because she understood his desire for independence, for freedom. She believed Johnny appreciated the trust she had placed in him, and so far he hadn't given her any reason not to. She understood better than anyone his need to stray.

After all, he was a lot like her.

He even looked like her—dark hair, full mouth, high cheekbones. The way he looked and behaved, it was easy to forget he was half of his father, too. More times than not she thought of him as solely hers. She didn't rag on him about things like smoking and drinking as long as he didn't do it in front of Gram. Besides, he only did those things while he was here. She understood that, too. There was something about this place that brought out the best and worst in you, pushing you to extremes.

"There's something in the lake water," she had often joked, but she never laughed. A part of her believed it was true.

Caroline had always been a different variety of kid. From the moment she had entered the world, she had made demands Jo struggled to meet—the feedings every hour, the crying, the fussing, the tantrums when things didn't go her way. "Mommy, you stay here," a three-year-old Caroline had said, stomping her foot whenever Jo had tried to leave the house.

The image of Caroline standing in the yard outside of the cabin cut across Jo's mind. The way she had looked at her, the yearning in her eyes, had scared Jo. A part of her felt threatened by Caroline's demands of constant love and attention. No matter what Jo said or did, no matter how much of herself she felt she gave, it was never enough. It would never be enough.

For a long time she tried to give her daughter what she could, all the hugs and kisses and affection she demanded, but somehow she'd always come up short. Her biggest fear, her failure as a mother, was simply that she didn't have anything left to give.

At thirty-two-years old, Jo felt used up.

She continued driving past Johnny and his friends, and parked on the other side of the Pavilion. The lake poured out in front of her. It was beautiful on the surface, glimmering in the hot summer sun, the water dancing in rhythm against the shore. And yet, underneath all that refreshing sparkle, deep in its belly, its true form lay waiting, where its cold dark reality lurked.

Laughter drew her attention to the beach on her left. Already she could see it was crowded. Families spread out on blankets and chairs. Kids jumped off the low dive and raced to the floating pier in the middle of the lake. Younger kids stayed in the shallow water closer to their parents, where it was safe.

The lake had been her summer haunt since childhood. Gram and Pop had bought the cabin in 1984 at a time when the resort was considered one of the hottest vacation spots in the Poconos. It was at a time when the beach had been overcrowded with vacationers, and a young Jo had to race through hordes of people with her towel and Gram's beach chair just to get a spot near the water. Pop had to reserve even the smallest of rowboats two weeks in advance if he wanted to do a little fishing.

The lake had held the Trout Festival, the largest festival in the county. But it was the Pavilion that Jo had loved best as a kid. It was always bustling, the second-floor bar hosting concerts with some of the biggest local names in the music industry. Sometimes late at night, when she should've been asleep, she'd sneak out of the cabin to listen to the band. She would press her cheek and palms against the Pavilion's outside wall, the whole building vibrating with sound as though it were alive and dancing with the occupants inside.

Over the years the lake's popularity had waned and the crowds had thinned, with new vacation spots opening for competition. But the regulars—the cabin owners and locals—kept coming, and together they remained loyal. Once you fell in love with the lake, the Pavilion, it was unlikely you'd fall out.

After tucking her hair behind her ears, Jo climbed out of the Chevy. A delivery truck pulled into the lot. She waited while it backed up to the stairs leading to the second-floor bar. A man in a gray uniform emerged with a clipboard in his hand. He opened the back door of the truck where the kegs and cases of beer were stacked.

Jo hustled past and trotted up the steps. Inside, the heat smoldered like an oppressive cloud. Eddie leaned on the bar, looking over a stack of order forms.

"We're closed," he said without looking up.

"Hey, stranger." Jo sat on the stool in front of him.

He lifted his head and smiled wide. "Hey, Jo. I thought that was your boy I saw earlier. When did you get in?"

"This morning."

"You look good." His dark eyes settled on hers. His long hair was tied in a ponytail, and a sweat-stained red bandanna was wrapped around his head. "Do you want a beer?"

"I thought you were closed."

"Not to you." He popped the cap off a cold bottle and set the beer down in front of her. She took a long swallow before reaching for a cigarette. He was quick with a light, and when she leaned into the flame, she couldn't help but notice his missing thumb tip, the one the snapper had bitten off when they were sixteen years old.

He glanced at his thumb, and she was embarrassed to have

been caught staring. After all these years, she struggled to shake the image of him flapping that turtle through the water, screaming, splashing, and later, sitting on the beach, staining the sand black with his blood, his then girlfriend, Sheila, holding him.

She had been Billy's girl back when it had happened. Everything in her life, good or bad or in-between, always led back to Billy.

She polished off the bottle of beer and set it on the bar, raising her pointer finger, signaling to Eddie for another. She couldn't remember the last time she had gotten drunk in the middle of the afternoon. Maybe as far back as last week when she had split a bottle of wine with one of the other maids while they were scrubbing the floors in the half-a-million-dollar mansion they were hired to clean back home in New Jersey.

"So are you planning to stick around for a few days?" Eddie asked.

"It looks like it." She didn't have much choice. Gram was adamant about needing her help, although she still had to clear it with Rose, her boss. She raised the bottle to her lips. "Apparently, I have chores to do around the cabin," she said before taking a long drink.

"Is Kevin joining you?" he asked.

"He had to haul a load to Arizona." Although he was most likely on his way back by now. Kevin drove a big rig for a trucking company. He was on the road more than he was home, and she was okay with that. She understood it was easier for him to be away. He had given up so much, sticking by her when she became pregnant at sixteen with Johnny, marrying her when he could've walked away. She loved him for it. Sometimes she loved him so much, it hurt.

The delivery guy made an appearance with several cases of beer stacked on a dolly. Eddie rushed to help him. While the guys unloaded the order, she continued to smoke and drink, wondering how she was ever going to get through the next couple of days.

By the time Eddie returned to the bar, she was feeling dizzy from the heat. Frank Heil, the owner of the Pavilion, the bar, and the beach, was too cheap to leave the air conditioning on when the bar was technically closed. Eddie had to work in the heat until the sun went down and the doors were opened to customers.

"Here." He opened another cold bottle and set it in front of her. "You know, I didn't want to say anything earlier, but your boy was all over one of those Chitney girls."

"So soon? It didn't take him long." She picked up the cold bottle and placed it on her cheek.

"Those Chitney girls are, well, you know what I mean. I'd make sure Johnny knows what he's getting into. The oldest sister, she's got two kids, and she doesn't even know who their father is." He was about to say something more but then stopped.

People were shouting on the beach below. Their voices traveled through the open balcony and to the second-floor bar. Eddie looked at her. "That doesn't sound good, does it?"

"No, it doesn't," she said.

A woman screamed.

CHAPTER THREE

Caroline crashed into the circle her friends made on the beach. She peered at the object in Adam's hand. It looked like two pieces of rusted metal joined by an even rustier circular ring.

"What do you think it is?" Adam asked.

"It's definitely old." Ted picked it up and turned it over.

"If you're cut," Ned said to Adam, "you're going to need a tetanus shot."

"I told you, I'm not hurt," Adam said.

"Where did you find it?" Caroline asked.

"Right there." He pointed to the area near the pier where the water was shallow. "I did the pencil jump," he whispered. "And my foot got caught on it." He stammered and looked around for his mother, who was always yelling at him to be careful.

Megan took the metal object from Ted. "I think I know what it is." She squinted in an ominous way. "I think it's a horse's bit," she said. "From the horse in the legend."

They huddled in close as they passed around the new-found treasure, an expression of awe on their faces. In hushed voices they agreed that yes, it certainly looked like a horse's bit and appeared to be very old. Yes, it could be from the horse in the legend. More mention was made concerning tetanus shots. Adam kept shaking his head and saying over and over he didn't get cut.

"What's this about a horse's bit?" The woman wearing the wide-brimmed sun hat, Sara's mother, stepped forward. She had obviously been eavesdropping on their conversation.

"Didn't you ever hear of the legend?" Megan asked.

Caroline hit Megan in the arm as a way of shutting her up. The mention of the legend, something the kids talked about in private, wasn't something a newcomer to the lake would have heard about. Heil and many of the other members of the lake association forbade anyone to talk about it and scolded kids when they did. The legend brought back bad memories, a link to a past drowning most people wanted to forget. Any mention of the legend between Caroline and the younger kids was discussed in the privacy of clubhouses and dugouts, places where parents were nowhere to be found. But Sara's mother appeared amused. She squeezed her way into their circle and stood in front of Megan.

"Go on," she said to Megan.

An uneasy silence fell over the group. Other sounds were magnified: a duck flapping its wings, the water lapping against the pier, the sound of a pinball machine inside the Pavilion.

"We're not supposed to talk about it," Adam said, and glared at Megan. "Besides, I found it and I want it back." He reached for the bit, but Megan held her arm up so he couldn't get it.

"It's his, Megan," Ted said, and tried to pull her arm down. The two danced around in a game of Keep Away.

"Hold on." Sara's mother pulled Ted and Megan apart. She took the horse's bit from Megan's hand. "Tell me what you know about it."

Everyone but Megan stared at their feet.

"A long time ago, like, I don't know, in the early 1900s," Megan said, "they used to cut the ice on the lake for refrigeration and stuff. But one time the ice cracked and a horse and carriage fell through. Legend says the horse and driver drowned, and their bodies were never found. On certain nights during a full moon some believe you can hear a horse whinny." She lowered her voice. "Others claim they've heard the sound of the horse's hooves clip-clopping across the ice."

"And you think you found the bit from this horse?" Sara's mother's thin eyebrows raised and disappeared underneath her sun hat.

"Maybe," Adam said, and wiped his hands where the rust from the metal had stained his skin orange.

Everyone stopped talking when Adam's mother crossed the beach to where they were standing. "Hi, I'm Betty, Adam's mom," she said to the young woman.

"I'm Patricia." Sara's mother stuck out her hand.

"It's mine, Mom," Adam said. "I found it."

"What is it?" Adam's mother asked.

Patricia handed the metal piece to her. "The kids were just telling me about the lake legend." She smiled as though she had conspired with them, and tilted the wide-brimmed sun hat just so.

"Were they now?" Adam's mother wasted no time and jumped in to explain that the legend was a myth told around campfires. "Something the kids made up a long time ago and nothing more than folklore."

"Is that so?" Patricia looked at Caroline as though she just now recognized her. Then she eyed the rest of the kids. She looked all around them and past Adam's mother as though she were searching for something. She continued looking around the beach, turning in circles.

Adam's mother gave the bit back to him. "Take this to Mr. Heil. It's his beach, and whatever it is, it belongs to him."

"But I found it in the lake," Adam said.

"Go," his mother said. "All of you."

Adam sulked but did as he was told and headed toward the Pavilion. They all followed him, dragging their feet in the sand. Behind them, Caroline heard Adam's mother ask Patricia if everything was all right.

Inside the Pavilion, Heil was standing in-between two pinball machines, hanging a sign that read PLAY MACHINES AT YOUR OWN RISK. Although the space between the two machines was wide enough for two people to stand side by side, he was wedged in tightly, his large stomach hanging over the waist of his shorts. His tube socks were pulled high on his calves, covering the lower half of his pasty, tree-trunk legs.

"What do you have there?" he asked, talking through the nail pinched between his lips. With some effort, he got himself out from between the two machines. Adam handed him the bit.

"He found it in the lake," Ted said.

Heil turned the metal over in his hands. "What is it?"

No one spoke. Not even Megan.

"Well?" he asked. "It looks like a piece of garbage. People shouldn't litter in our waters. It's a crime." He tried to sound authoritative, but the waver in his voice confirmed he was just as anxious as they were about their treasure. "I'll just hang onto this. It's not something you kids should be playing with."

"If it's garbage," Adam said, "why can't I have it back?"

Heil took a step toward Adam, who shrank under Heil's large belly. "You shouldn't be playing with a scrap of metal. And don't you kids be telling tall tales. Do you hear?" He pushed through the center of their circle, taking the horse's bit with him.

Adam's shoulders drooped. "Now what?"

"It was nothing but junk anyway," Ted said.

"But what if it wasn't junk? And there's other stuff out there," Ned said to his brother.

"Like what?"

"I don't know," Ned said. "Other things like an old saddle or horseshoe or maybe even a horse's skull." He then turned to Adam, excited. "Show us again where you found it."

"I don't know," Adam said. They went around in circles this way for several minutes, trying to coax Adam into showing them the exact spot where he had found the horse's bit.

Megan took off her sunglasses and inspected her face in the lens. "Can you still see my eye shadow?" she asked Caroline.

"What? No," Caroline said absently, not paying attention. She could've sworn she heard someone scream. By this time, the twins had convinced Adam to show them where he had found the metal. The boys started heading back outside.

"You didn't even look," Megan protested.

"Shhh," she said, bringing her pointer finger to her lips. "Listen."

The second shriek had both she and Megan turned toward the open doors that led to the beach and lake. The twins disappeared outside. Adam was a step behind them and still in the Pavilion. He turned back and looked at Caroline as if he was asking if she heard it too.

Two guys shooting pool put their sticks down. A family at the snack stand looked over their shoulders. There was another scream, this one higher pitched and more frantic. A man standing near the counter touched his wife's arm before jogging toward the open doors that led to the swimming area. The guys shooting pool quickly followed.

There was more hollering, followed by another screech that pierced Caroline's ears. Terror pounded inside her chest. She was afraid to move.

She was too afraid not to move.

Caroline grabbed Megan's arm and pulled her through the Pavilion, down the stairs, and onto the beach. They joined Adam and the twins. A crowd had gathered—men, women, kids, toddlers. Through the crowd, she saw the woman in the wide-brimmed sun hat—Sara's mother—wading in the water up to her waist. She was screaming a name at first Caroline couldn't understand. Adam's mother stood on the pier near the high dive, also calling a name. It sounded like "Sara."

The man from the snack stand reached Sara's mother in the water. Her arms flailed as she talked with him. He nodded a few times before he also started calling Sara's name.

Caroline searched the beach, weaving in and out of the crowd, stepping over blankets, scurrying past beach chairs, and looking for the little girl with the blond braids and bright blue eyes. Her gaze stopped on the sign posted on the chain-link fence: SWIM AT YOUR OWN RISK. She glanced at the empty lifeguard stand, where someone should've been sitting, watching. But of course no one was, and an overwhelming feeling of guilt backed up in her throat. She shouldn't have left the little girl alone. She should've stayed with her. She should've been watching.

Johnny and his friends stormed onto the beach. Chris ran straight for the lake, shouting at the hysterical woman, "How old?"

"Seven," Sara's mother cried out. "She's seven."

Caroline watched as Chris dove under. Johnny bumped into

her arm as he pushed past her through the crowd. He ran into the lake, diving into the water near Chris. The hair on her arms stood up, and a chill climbed up her spine even as moisture gathered on her forehead in the hot sun.

"Johnny!" she yelled, suddenly terrified for her brother's safety.

A woman in the crowd asked, "What's the girl's name?"

"Sara," another man said.

Someone called out, "I'll check the Pavilion. Maybe she wandered off inside."

Other men in the crowd began peeling off their shirts and rushing into the lake. Some did a surface sweep, looking for signs of the girl above the water. Others dove like seals, plunging into the murky depths, popping up to the surface, only to plummet once again. Bystanders collectively held their breath. When either Johnny's or Chris's head emerged from the dark ripples, Caroline allowed herself to breathe with them.

Heil joined the group on the beach. "Help is on the way," he said to the few adults nearby. His face was grim. Sweat stained the navy blue T-shirt pulled tight across his expansive stomach. He wiped his brow.

Caroline stared at the lake and laced her arm through Megan's, needing to hold onto something, someone. The sun glared, scorching the top of her head. Sweat trickled down her back. She made a promise to herself that if Sara was found, she would play with her, swim with her, watch over her, and never let her out of her sight for the rest of the summer.

"Pavilion's empty," a woman said.

Caroline recognized the woman as one of the cabin owners in the colony. She had two boys, four and six years old. Caroline had watched them learn to swim in the shallow end of the lake last summer. Now their mother wrapped her arms around their shoulders and pulled them close. She kissed the tops of their heads, and Caroline imagined she was grateful they were safe by her side.

Several long minutes passed.

Some of the men who had started out strong in their search slowly swam toward the beach. Their breathing was heavy, and their faces lined with defeat. Johnny and Chris were still out there, diving down, trying to reach bottom. Searching. But too much time had gone by. Sara had been under too long. The crowd had grown quiet. Caroline's entire body shook from the inside out.

A siren cut the silence. The sheriff's vehicle pulled into the parking lot. In the next few seconds an underwater rescue and recovery truck pulled into the lot, towing a boat. The spectators parted as Heil opened the gate for the sheriff and the recovery team to enter the beach area. A diving crew worked hard to unload the watercraft. More sirens shattered the air, and an ambulance pulled alongside the truck. Medics jumped out carrying first aid gear.

The man from the snack stand grabbed ahold of Sara's mother and led her to shore. Medics rushed to her side. She rocked back and forth, back and forth. A shrill moan escaped from her lips. One of the medics guided her to sit in the sand and wrapped a blanket around her shoulders. A man from the recovery team, the one who looked to be in charge, asked her questions about Sara, trying to determine the last time she had seen her, the possible location in the water where she could have disappeared.

Two other members on the recovery team asked the crowd to back up. Johnny emerged from the water and dropped onto the beach. Chris followed a few seconds later and collapsed next to Johnny. Some of Johnny and Chris's friends joined them. "Man, that was brave," one of them said. Tank-top girl hugged Johnny.

A part of Caroline wanted to hug him too, tell him he was stupid and brave and how proud she was to be his little sister. The other part knew he'd only blow her off in front of his friends. And still, another part, a deep down unreasonable part, felt as if he had somehow failed her for not finding Sara alive.

The sheriff and the underwater recovery team talked with parents and potential witnesses. A man stood at the top of the high dive, surveying the lake. Four men on the recovery team, two in dry suits, loaded the boat and began searching the swimming area around the pier and diving boards. The process was slow, methodical. Caroline knew they had to search with zero visibility. And Sara was small, so small.

She had told the man from underwater recovery, the one who appeared to be in charge, she had last seen Sara on the pier. What she had wanted to tell him but somehow couldn't, was to search deep where the diving boards were located, where Sara had overheard the boys daring each other to try to touch the bottom of the lake. But how could she tell him what she was afraid had happened without sounding guilty? When had adults ever listened to kids?

An hour passed.

The crowd gradually dispersed, or at least the regular crowd who had witnessed a similar scene in summer's past. First-timers to the lake hung around, never having seen a drowning before. It sounded cruel, but sometimes it was hard to look away from something so horrifying. No one passed judgment on the onlookers. Let them look. Let them know what could happen. Let them understand that these were the dues collected by the lake in its splendor.

Megan pulled on Caroline's wrist in an attempt to lead her back into the Pavilion. Caroline yanked her hand free. She wasn't going anywhere. She couldn't tear her eyes away from the divers. After twenty minute shifts they'd surface, shaking their heads. She wondered if they could even reach the bottom. She didn't believe anyone could.

She had witnessed a drowning three years prior, the man's body gray and gorged in death. It had been a boating accident. He had fallen and hit his head on the side of the fishing boat when he went overboard. He was knocked unconscious and drowned. It was awful and sad, but this was different. This was a young girl swimming near the beach where other kids swim. People were around. Parents were watching. And bad things weren't supposed to happen to kids.

Another hour passed.

Skillfully, the underwater recovery team continued their systematic search in the area where they believed Sara most likely went under. With zero visibility, they used a side scanner for the localized search, but it became apparent they would have to branch out and cover more territory.

Caroline's stomach dropped and swayed with their every movement. From the gossip on the beach, no one could say for sure exactly when Sara had entered the water. No one had been paying attention. The part-time lifeguard had been on break.

Johnny and Chris and friends retreated to the beach steps to watch and smoke their cigarettes. No one talked. Megan stayed with Caroline as the *whop, whop, whop* of a helicopter sounded overhead. It circled the length of the lake a half dozen times. And then it was gone. The sun's rays faded. Storm clouds had started gathering over the mountain, growing increasingly darker, blacker. The wind started to blow. But otherwise, the lake was silent except for the occasional splash from a diver emerging from what lay hidden below, coming up empty.

Megan's parents, Mr. and Mrs. Roberts, appeared. Mrs. Roberts placed a hand on Megan's shoulder. "Come on, honey. It's time to go."

"Are you coming?" Megan asked Caroline.

"No," Caroline said, and kept her eyes on the watercraft. She wasn't ready to make the walk back to the colony where the news was sure to have traveled. The gossip would start as early as this evening, and she would learn more about the family who had lost a daughter to the lake than she had known about her own family. It seemed wrong. All of it was wrong, and she felt a deep sadness that left a dark and empty space inside her heart.

Perhaps this was how her mother felt, how it felt to be a grown-up. And she wanted no part of it.

CHAPTER FOUR

Jo stood next to Eddie on the balcony of the bar overlooking the beach and lake. After hearing the screaming and rushing outside, they had remained quiet in the hours they had watched the scene unfold, unable to turn away, knowing the intimate details of each practiced step of underwater recovery by heart.

Shadows moved across the water, typical and somehow remarkable at the same time. A warm wind blew, and in the near distance thunder rolled. Eddie untied the red bandanna from around his head and replaced it with a black one.

"Look at him down there," Jo said about Heil. "He acts like he's king of the lake."

Heil was directing his staff to clean up now that most of the onlookers had fled the beach when the storm clouds started moving in. Earlier he had ordered two of his workers to cook hotdogs and hamburgers for the underwater recovery team. No charge. He took care of the men as they had gone about their job, making sure to offer an endless supply of food and drink. A drowning wasn't good for business, but it was even worse for business if Heil failed to show compassion and cooperation. He was president of the lake association and made damn sure everyone knew it. He walked around as though the entire lake community's survival rested upon his shoulders. He was a large man, a fat man, an ever-so-loud man. It was impossible to ignore him.

Maybe Jo didn't like him for these reasons, but she believed it had more to do with a gut feeling telling her not to trust what others deemed were his good intentions.

Eddie looked down at Heil and shrugged. After all, Heil was his boss.

"They should be coming in off the water," he said of the underwater recovery team. It was too risky for divers to search in the dark, particularly with the threat of a storm looming. But at the last minute there was activity on the boat and another diver went under.

Jo leaned farther out on the railing, the muscles in her neck and shoulders tightening as each second passed. She spotted her daughter at the lake's edge, but it was Johnny who was foremost on her mind. She had watched as he attacked the water, diving down and popping up, covering as much area as he could in his efforts to find the girl in time. He moved through the water, graceful and fearless as if the lake was an extension of his body, a part of his flesh and bones. Sometimes, long after the summer had ended and they were settled in their home and in their lives, Johnny would breeze by in his nonchalant way, and she would catch the smell of the lake on his skin and in his hair. It was as if the lake lived inside of him, what was good, cool, and refreshing, but tangled with something dangerous, too.

Lightning lit up the blackening sky in a one-two flash. The sheriff's deputies appeared and cleared the beach of stragglers, including Caroline, forcing them to seek shelter.

Eddie ran his hand down his face. "Lots of new renters this summer," he said, and returned his gaze to the recovery boat, the visibility fading in the waning light.

"Why doesn't anyone warn them? Why don't they tell them about the dangers of swimming here?" she asked, thinking about the diver, wondering whether he could feel the temperature drop through the dry suit as he dove closer and closer to the bottom. He would start at the farthest point from the boat and systematically work his way back, sweeping the area with his hands into a center line and then outward, double searching each section at a time, kicking up silt, making it that much harder to navigate, searching blind.

"The signs are posted," Eddie said. "And advertising three drownings in the last sixteen years wouldn't be good for business."

"Posting signs on the beach and in the Pavilion isn't enough."

"No matter what you do, it's never enough."

She supposed that could be true, but she would never accept that it was fair. Then again, what in life was ever fair?

After a long pause he added, "They found something. It's the only reason they'd still be out there."

She agreed.

The diver emerged and handed something to the three men on the boat. It was much too small for a body, even a child's body.

The sheriff, Dave Borg, appeared on the beach. He stopped and talked to Heil. Heil nodded continually to whatever the sheriff was saying, rubbing his chin and appearing troubled about something.

Thunder continued to rumble. The men on the boat moved quickly. They looked to be securing their equipment, no doubt eager to get off the water. The wind picked up, bending the branches of trees and scattering leaves. The sheriff and Heil made their way onto the dock, waiting for the recovery team to come in.

"I'm going to find out what's going on," Eddie said. "Watch the bar."

"Yeah, okay." She turned around, but there was no one in the bar to watch.

She stood alone on the balcony. Thunder clapped. The recovery team reached the dock where the sheriff and Heil waited. From where she stood, she couldn't tell what was passed to the sheriff, but it was definitely a bag, and she believed it contained whatever they had found on the lake bottom. One of the deputies charged onto the dock, taking orders and then dashing away, passing Eddie on the beach.

The recovery team finished securing their watercraft and rushed for cover from the storm that was quickly making its way over the mountain. Eddie met with the sheriff and Heil when they stepped off the dock. Heil was shaking his head, hiking his shorts over his expansive waistline. Thunder roared across the sky. The wind whirled, whipping Jo's hair across her face.

The men were talking, arguing. Heil was waving his stumpy arms around. Eddie stood between them. He was hunched over, looking more and more uncomfortable as time passed, covering his stomach as though he'd been sucker-punched. Heil pointed at him and motioned toward the Pavilion and bar. A few more words were exchanged, the men shouting as the storm moved overhead. They hurried into the Pavilion. After another minute or two Eddie returned to the balcony.

"You're never going to believe it." He gripped the rail. The wind continued to howl. The first few drops of rain sprinkled her cheeks.

"Is it something from the little girl?" She had to holler over the wind.

"No." He shook his head. "It's got nothing to do with the girl."

"Then what?" A bolt of lightning split the sky.

Eddie took ahold of her arm and pulled her off the balcony and into the bar just in time. The rain came pouring down, blowing sideways in the wind, hammering against the building. Thunder cracked. Something in Eddie's eyes frightened her. "What is it? What did they find?"

"Bones," he shouted. "They think they found Billy's bones."

CHAPTER FIVE

The air was thick with humidity, fermenting what was rotten in the lake. At times it smelled like dead fish, dank and feral. Other times it smelled like a thousand decaying lily pads and plant life, sodden and moldy. Tonight it smelled a little bit like both.

Caroline breathed into the palm of her hand to keep from getting sick. She was standing under the overhang on the top step of the Pavilion. The sheriff's deputy had chased her off the beach, forcing her inside and out of the storm. She had backed up slowly at first, breathing into her cupped hand, unable to move her eyes away from the water. A loud crack of thunder had felt as though it shook the ground beneath her feet. When she had turned, she caught sight of her mother on the bar balcony. Even in the dark she could see the haunted look on her mother's face, the one that thrashed her insides and kept her hidden inside herself. It could be days until her mother surfaced.

Lightning flashed. Thunder stomped and bumped across the sky. One of the deputies escorted Sara's mother to his vehicle. She was in for a long night. The underwater recovery team had packed their gear and gone home. They weren't expected to return until morning.

"There you are." Gram pulled Caroline into her arms. "You didn't come home for supper. You know you're supposed to check in and let me know your plans."

"Didn't you hear?" She stepped back and searched Gram's wrinkled and worn face, her thinning white hair, and her eyes, where the youthful spirit sparkled even in dark times. It was the sparkle Caroline relied on and looked for, a sign to tell her everything was going to be all right.

"Yes, I heard," Gram said. Rain poured onto the roof of the Pavilion, battering the old building with its onslaught. She yelled over the storm, "Let's go home. You must be starving."

Gram had told her once that she had seen enough death in her lifetime, and she didn't like to talk about it. She had said, "It is what it is, and there's nothing anybody can do to stop it." She told Caroline it was something everyone had to live with, and Caroline often wondered if Gram had been referring to something more personal, someone in her past other than Pop.

She followed Gram through the Pavilion. The pool table and pinball machines stood empty. The jukebox remained quiet. A few people milled around the snack stand, but the loud rain halted any conversation they may have otherwise had. They hurried through the wind and rain to Gram's big Oldsmobile parked on the other side of the Pavilion, far away from the beach. They were soaked by the time they reached the car. Caroline was wet and cold. Goose bumps prickled her skin.

Back at the cabin, Caroline ate two helpings of Gram's infamous homemade macaroni and cheese, a favorite comfort food, before curling up in her new hand-stitched quilt in her bedroom. She tucked her hands under her chin. The storm had been fierce but quick, lasting thirty minutes or less. A welcomed breeze blew through the open window. The cool air swept over her sun-kissed skin, sending shivers up and down her arms and legs.

"I'm scared," she said to Willow, the name she had given the big weeping willow tree outside her bedroom window. In response it brushed its branches against the side of the cabin and scratched at the screen.

Ever since she was little, she had talked to Willow, her imaginary friend who just happened to be a tree. It was silly really to think of a tree in this way, but Willow was one of the constants during her summers at the lake. He listened when she couldn't find the words to talk with her mother or Gram. He never rolled his eyes or sulked the way Megan sometimes did when they'd disagree over something stupid. He didn't pick on her or make fun of her like Johnny did. Willow was there when she closed her eyes at night, every night. She imagined him standing guard while she slept. He wouldn't let anything bad happen to her. He would protect her. And he was always there the moment she opened her eyes the next morning.

Although she hadn't talked to Willow much over the last few summers, tonight she fell into past habits, needing to feel secure. As always he was there, towering high above the cabin, watching. His branches reached toward anyone who paused long enough to gaze at his splendor. Sometimes she'd climb into the crook of his arms and listen to his leaves in the summer breeze. Other times she'd read to him from one of her mystery novels. She imagined he liked mysteries as much as she did.

"Her name was Sara," she whispered to Willow. A knot clogged her throat, and she swallowed hard. "She's still missing."

She had overheard one of the men from underwater recovery talking about a typical scenario, how they'd normally pull a body from the lake within the first six to eight hours. But they still hadn't found Sara.

Only one other time did she recall hearing a story about someone named Billy, a boy who hadn't been found right away. It had happened years before Caroline was born. She had overheard Gram talking to Pop one night when they had thought she had been asleep. Her mother had taken off and hadn't returned, and they had been worried. Caroline remembered feeling scared and angry, although she didn't understand why.

She had crept out of her bed and entered the hall that separated her room from the bath and kitchen. She pressed her back against the yellow painted wall and hid in the shadow of the door. It was then she had learned that the boy named Billy had been missing for five days, how every waking hour had been spent dragging the lake for his body.

"It's always been Billy," Gram said. "And somehow she blames herself."

Pop shook his head and smoothed his gray beard. "Well, something went wrong." He covered his neck as if he were choking. "They shouldn't have let it go on for five days."

Caroline wasn't exactly sure what they had meant, but it had been as if her mother had somehow played a part in it—the lake and the drowning. She had asked Gram only one time about the boy named Billy. Gram pinched her lips and told her never to mention his name again.

Caroline never did.

Now, as she whispered to Willow, she wondered what Sara had in common with Billy. Why hadn't she been found? What did it mean?

CHAPTER SIX

Dee Dee pulled to the side of the cabin and stopped, the head-lights resting on a large tree limb blocking the only parking space. Tired after another long shift at the hospital, she sat staring at the limb, the car idling. The storm earlier that night had been a bad one. Twice the lights on her floor had flickered but never went out, although they had a backup generator if they did. Chris, her son, had been able to get a text through—the service was always sketchy at the lake—letting her know the cabin's power had gone out but was quickly restored and that a little girl had drowned.

She threw the car in park and got out, leaving the headlights glaring on the massive limb. She was late getting home. At the last minute Mrs. Hopper in Room 303 had needed help to get to the . . . well . . . hopper. She recently had her second knee replaced, both joints giving out under her considerable weight. The charge nurse, one of the RNs on the floor, had asked Dee Dee to help Mrs. Hopper, who had asked for her specifically.

"Come on," she said, taking the big woman under the arm and helping her stand. "Try to put your weight on the walker," she instructed. "I got you. You won't fall."

Slowly, the woman rose, grasping the walker in front of her. "Oh, I won't fall," she said. "But if I did, you're the only one I trust to catch me. Those other nurses are too skinny. They should take a lesson from you and lift some weights, put some muscle on their bones. How much can you lift anyway? My grandson used to be a body builder. Did I ever tell you that?"

"No, I don't think I heard about him before," she said, having heard about everyone else in Mrs. Hopper's family. She might as well hear about the grandson, too. "Try to lift your feet." It was better for her to bend the new knee to get used to it, rather than shuffle along.

Mrs. Hopper went on and on about her grandson's muscles and only stopped when Dee Dee stepped out of the bathroom to give her privacy. She checked the clock. Her shift had ended twenty minutes ago—not that it mattered. There wasn't anyone at home waiting for her, which was just as well. She helped Mrs. Hopper back to bed and explained she didn't lift weights. She credited or cursed, depending on how you looked at it, genetics.

"Chris," she called after stepping through the cabin door, letting it slam behind her. No answer. "Chris," she called again. It was close to midnight, but she really didn't expect he'd be home. Living at the lake year round, Chris had waited all winter to see his summertime friends. And at sixteen years old, what boy his age wouldn't still be out with them, out with Johnny and whatever girls had latched onto them for the night?

She dropped her purse onto the kitchen counter and slipped off her white sneakers. She was an LPN, a licensed practical nurse. It didn't pay much, not as much as a RN, but a little more than an orderly. She liked her job and the patients, like Mrs. Hopper, helping her to and from the bathroom, and helping the weak with her strong arms. Besides, patients, especially the really sick ones, could be trusted to tell you the truth. They had nothing to lose. It was everybody else Dee Dee had a problem with.

"Chris." She poked her head into his room, double-checking. His bed was empty.

She changed clothes, shoved her feet into work boots, and went back outside to the shed in search of a handsaw. It was too late at night for the chainsaw, which was too bad because it would've made the work that much easier. The door to the shed stuck, and she had to yank hard to get it open. She heard a small animal scurry to the corner when she stepped inside. She pulled the string to the bare light bulb and looked around. She found the handsaw hanging on a nail above the workbench. Underneath the saw was an old, deflated inner tube, the one Chris used to ride on behind their boat, the same inner tube her father had used to pull her and her brother, Billy.

She lifted the tube, and the unmistaken smell of rotting rubber wafted through the air, the scent unpleasant to most but not to her. It was the scent of happier times. She remembered not only the times when Chris was a young boy riding the tube, but also, more sharply, the times with her brother. When Billy was young, well before puberty, he'd sit between her legs and grip the handles. "Hold on!" she would yell as they sailed across the water. It had felt like flying.

And one time when their father had made a particularly sharp turn, the tube had flipped, sending both her and Billy jetting across the lake, their bodies slapping the water, their laughter filling the air. On the pier not far from where they were thrown, a group of girls around fourteen years of age, Dee Dee's age at the time, jeered and poked fun at her. Even then her strong body and large frame evoked ridicule.

"Come on," an eleven-year-old Billy had said, tugging on Dee

Dee's arm, pulling her away from the sneering girls. "I'll race you to the boat."

The endless summer days on the lake with her brother had been some of the best days of her life. He had been her best friend.

She grabbed the handsaw and slammed the door to the shed and the memories. She walked around the tree limb, careful not to trip over the smaller branches. It was thicker than she had originally thought. It split from the old oak tree next to the cabin. They were lucky it didn't hit the roof. On the bright side, it would make good firewood. She tried lifting the end, grunting at the heft of it. "Well, shit." Nothing was ever easy.

She set to work, sawing off the smaller branches and tossing them aside. She worked for another thirty minutes, her back and arms tiring from the labor. When she sawed off most of the smaller pieces, she began the arduous work of sawing the limb in quarters, her thoughts on the drowned little girl. She hoped she was found before the storm hit. The lake bottom was treacherous, formed by a glacier thousands of years ago, leaving behind shelves and caverns and ravines. It would be anyone's guess where the strong current in a storm would take a little girl— anyone's guess where she would be hidden.

After another thirty minutes or more she dragged the last piece of the limb to the side. She pulled the car into the opened space, cut the lights, and sat down on the porch step in the dark to wipe her brow and catch her breath.

She heard footsteps, recognizing at once who it was by the shape of the hat on his head. "Just like a blister," she had said to Sheriff Borg when he had been within earshot. "Showing up when the work is done."

He walked over to where she was sitting and placed his foot

on the step, resting his forearm on top of his thigh. "We need to talk."

Her first thought was Chris. "Is it my boy?" she asked, and pulled herself up, her muscles exhausted. It wouldn't be the first time the sheriff had paid her a visit: minor stuff Chris had been involved in, graffiti, peeling out in the Pavilion parking lot, pissing in public. The sheriff always had brought Chris home rather than slapping a fine on him—or worse, locking him up in jail for the night. He was willing to help her out, knowing she was raising Chris on her own.

"No," he said. "It's not about Chris."

"Well, then come on in." She was thirsty, and whatever it was he came to tell her, it could wait until she had a drink. She went over to the door and held it open. He stepped inside and removed his sheriff's hat. His gray hair was clipped close to his scalp. His brow was furrowed. He followed her to the small kitchen where she offered him a glass of lake water. He declined.

When she finished drinking and set the glass down, she noticed the blister the size of a quarter on her hand. It was almost funny given her earlier comment. She poked at it, the fluid inside squishing around. *Man hands.* The thought reminded her of an episode on an old sitcom about a guy breaking up with a woman for having man hands.

"So what's this about?" she asked.

"It's about what happened today." He was tall like her. If any man at the lake could match her height and strength, he was the one.

"You mean the little girl? What does she have to do with me? Did they find her?"

"No, they still haven't found her." He started playing with his hat, kneading the edges with his fingers. "But they did find something else." He paused.

"What?" She had no patience for bullshit. Whatever it was, she wanted it straight-up.

"They recovered some bones today while they were searching for the girl."

She eyed him, skeptical about what he was telling her. "What bones?" she asked.

"I'm no medical examiner, but they looked to be bones from a forearm."

She stared at him, wanting to believe what he was telling her was true.

He stared back. "Of course, they'll need to be sent to the lab. It will be a couple of days before we have any definite answers."

Her breathing was shallow, her spine rigid. "What does this mean?" she asked. The bones had to be her brother's, Billy's. The sheriff wouldn't be here otherwise.

"I'm not sure it means anything. Just that we may have found what we couldn't before."

"But it could prove something, right?" She never believed Billy's drowning was an accident, although that was how it was ruled, an accidental death, even though his skull had been cracked. At the time they had explained it, justified it with excuses, how he must've fallen, hit his head, and drowned. There hadn't been any witnesses to prove otherwise, although Dee Dee didn't believe that either. Billy had left the cabin that night with his girlfriend, Jo. Where the hell was she when it happened? Why wasn't she with him?

There was something off about that whole night from the moment Jo had set foot inside their home. She had been distracted, waiting for Billy to finish dinner so they could go out for the night. Billy had asked Jo a question twice, although Dee Dee no longer remembered what the question was, something innocuous. But Jo wasn't paying attention, and that was the strangest part. Jo *always* gave Billy her full attention. For three summers since Billy was thirteen years old, Jo was a permanent fixture by his side like a lake leech stuck to his skin.

But that week, that particular night, Dee Dee was certain something had changed. It was as though she felt the fracture in their relationship as sure as if the earth's fault lines had shifted beneath her feet. Of course, it was impossible to know exactly what had changed. And she had never gotten the chance to ask him.

And then there was Heil, how hard he had pushed to have the case closed when witnesses confirmed Billy had been drinking underage, the alcohol supplied by Heil's bar. As for the missing bones from Billy's forearm, they were thought to have been clawed off by snappers, gone forever.

So no, she never believed her brother's drowning was an accident. There were too many unanswered questions.

"Look," the sheriff said. "I know you're hoping they'll find some evidence, something new to suggest it wasn't an accident."

"You know I am," she shot back, letting her anger and frustration show. She was nineteen and already knocked up and alone, deserted by her boyfriend, when she had lost Billy. She was just a kid. And yet the sheriff had always been willing to listen to her, to the possibility there was more to the story about her brother's disappearance than he was ever able to prove.

Tonight he stared at her as though he was unsure whether or not to continue. He knew her well enough to know there was no reasoning with her when she was agitated.

"Go on. Spit it out," she said.

"Not a lot of people know about the bones. Heil wants to keep it quiet. He doesn't think it's a priority under the circumstance.

All he's concentrating on is the current situation with the girl. He doesn't want to remind people there were other drownings around here."

"What Heil does or doesn't do makes no difference to me." All she needed was someone in a lab somewhere to prove what she had known all along.

"Fair enough. Just don't get your hopes up." When she didn't respond, the sheriff put on his hat. "You should wear gloves next time." He pointed to her hands, referring to the blister. "I'll be in touch," he said, and showed himself out.

After the sheriff left, Dee Dee grabbed a six-pack of beer from the refrigerator. She turned off all the lights and stepped outside to sit on the porch swing in the dark and think. She often sat alone deep into the night, staring out at the lake, drinking beer with nothing but her thoughts to keep her company. Some might say she had a problem, drinking alone in the dark undercover. Maybe she did. But she had stopped caring what other people thought a long time ago. So what if she drank herself numb most nights? She wasn't hurting anyone and how many people could say the same thing? Not many by her estimation. Not many at all.

A cool breeze blew from the water. The storm broke the humidity at least for a little while. She popped the tab on the can. The sheriff was right. She needed to keep things in perspective and try not to put too much into a pair of bones. It could prove to be nothing. But what if it proved to be something?

She downed the beer and crushed the empty can in her hand, the blister screaming in protest. She reached for another can.

CHAPTER SEVEN

It was early evening the next day, and the little girl was still missing.

Jo stepped out of the bathroom with a towel wrapped around her head. She was wearing her favorite low-rise jeans and a white T-shirt. She felt a little better after showering, but the pack of cigarettes she had smoked while sitting on Eddie's dock that afternoon in the hot sun had added to her already pounding head.

It had taken two hours for the text message to go through to Kevin telling him he needed to get to the lake, that they may have found Billy's bones. She wasn't sure what it meant, if it meant anything, but she wanted him here. While she had fiddled with the phone, she watched the underwater recovery team search the lake to no avail.

She rubbed her brow.

Gram walked past, her purse slung over her shoulder. She was wearing one of her staple outfits for special occasions—a pair of blue cotton pants and matching blouse.

"Where are you going?" Jo asked, and removed the towel from her head. The thick tousles draped over her shoulders, soaking her T-shirt almost instantly.

"Frank Heil called an association meeting." Gram shot her a sideways glance and continued for the door.

"I'm coming with you." She tossed the towel onto the kitchen table and ran her fingers through her hair.

Gram stopped and stared at her. "Why? You were never interested in these meetings before."

"Well, I am now."

They piled into Gram's Oldsmobile, a big green four-door sedan Pop had bought her before he had died. He had joked about how Gram couldn't hurt herself if she happened to bounce off a few trees in what he nicknamed the Loch Ness, a battle-ax of a car. It had been five years since he had passed of heart failure right there in the cabin in his bed, sleeping peacefully next to Gram. It wasn't until the next morning that Gram had become aware he was gone. Since then, the Loch Ness endured several run-ins with posts, curbs, and Jo's bumper, but so far it had stayed away from any trees.

Jo smiled on the inside, remembering Pop, the father she loved. He had been a good man, a solid man who had been grounded in his beliefs of right and wrong, who had tried not to judge her or her decisions, although in the end, he had done just that. And still, at times like now, she missed him all the more.

Gram backed out of the parking space, nicking the fence post. "Holy crow's nest," she said, and threw the car in drive.

Jo held onto the *oh shit* handle as Gram ran over every pothole on the way to the Pavilion. She blew past the stop sign on Lake Road and slid into the parking lot. Her usually open face was closed in a stern expression, a look she typically reserved for Jo. Then again, Frank Heil and his association meetings had that kind of effect on Gram and most people around there.

They got out of the car without talking. Jo followed Gram in silence up the steps to the second floor, where the meeting was being held. Eddie was behind the bar. He squeezed Jo's shoulder and leaned over to give Gram a peck on the cheek. For a second Gram's face opened to him, but just as quickly it closed.

"He's fired up," Eddie whispered loud enough for both her and Gram to hear.

Heil was on the other side of the barroom with his cohorts. One was a man by the name of Stimpy, who owned the rental boats on the lake. The other two were local fishermen, and Jonathan, who owned not one but five cabins in the colony. They all had something to lose if the beach and lake remained closed.

Other cabin owners filtered in and took their respective seats around scattered tables, leaving Sheriff Borg to sit alone. It was a known fact that Heil had the sheriff in his back packet. Freebies at the Pavilion—swim passes, rounds of drinks at the bar— kept the sheriff on Heil's side when it came to association matters and community affairs.

Small town politics sucked, and Jo was reminded why she avoided such meetings. She hated public debates and narrow-minded people. But she was here because she had to know if there was any news about the bones. She had to know if they were in fact Billy's. She could hear Kevin's voice inside her head telling her it didn't matter whose bones they were, to get out of there, to leave the lake. But he had to know she couldn't. Her guilt wouldn't let her.

She took the seat next to Gram and scanned the crowd, concerned she might see Billy's sister, Dee Dee. About thirty people gathered. She recognized each and every one of their faces, locals and seasonal cabin owners. Much to her relief, Billy's sister wasn't among them.

Heil took his position at the front of the room. He held up

his hand and, like obedient children, they quieted in their seats and waited for the next command.

"We all know why we're here. Tragedy, I tell you. And no one is more upset about this than I am."

The people nodded and murmured in agreement.

Heil pulled his pants up high to cover his large belly. He rolled onto the balls of his feet in a power bounce. "But we must make a living in spite of what has happened here."

"Are you planning on opening the Pavilion and beach tomorrow?" one of the cabin owners asked.

"Of course he is." Jonathan spoke for Heil. "I've got renters who expect the full vacation experience on the lake, and that includes the beach and swimming. Hell, that's all they're here for."

"He's right," someone said from the back of the room.

The crowd started talking at once. Jo tried to follow the outbursts, catching bits and pieces. "Besides, it's gruesome, all this waiting around, watching them drag the bottom looking for that little girl's body."

"What's taking so long?"

"Why can't they find her?"

"And those poor parents, having to wait."

"It's not our fault. Why should we be punished?"

"We're paying to swim and fish."

"That mother should've kept a better watch on her kid."

"You can't blame the mother."

"Why not? Where was she?"

"It was an accident."

"Tragedy."

"We're losing money."

"What about the bones?"

"Yeah, I heard they found some bones."

"All right," Heil said. "Everyone, calm down."

Sheriff Borg stood and put on his sheriff's hat. He rapped his knuckles twice on the table. The action caused the mob to settle down.

"Law enforcement is looking into the bones." Heil shot the sheriff a look, and the sheriff nodded. "But that's not our immediate concern. What we need to focus on is the business at hand." He continued. "And that's finding that little girl and getting the beach and lake reopened. What we need is to speak to the recovery team."

"That's right," a woman from the corner bar piped in.

Heil turned to Stimpy. "Get out there and bring one of them fellows in. I have an idea."

Excitement buzzed around the room. Everyone wanted to move forward, for summer vacations to continue as planned as if nothing bad had happened. The community at the lake, the locals and regular summer vacationers, had been through this kind of thing before. Tragic, yes, but no one sitting in Eddie's bar ever thought it could happen to them, to their family, to their child. You never thought it could happen to you.

Gram sat perfectly still. Jo's own spine was rigid, although her foot wagged at a ridiculous pace.

One of the men from underwater recovery climbed the stairs and entered the bar. He was average height with dark brown hair and eyes. He wore a black T-shirt and jeans. A yellow safety vest was strapped to his chest. He carried a matching yellow hardhat. He scanned the crowd of people, and by the time he finished, he was scowling.

Heil slapped his hand on the man's shoulder and turned to his co-conspirators to quiet them down. All eyes focused on the two men.

"We have no doubt you're doing everything you can," Heil

explained, sounding much like a politician. "But it's over twenty-four hours that we've had the lake and beach closed. People pay for the lake experience. They expect to take their boats on the water and fish. Families expect their kids to swim."

"I understand," the man said. "We're working as fast as we can." He then added, "For the little girl and her parents."

"Yes, for the girl and her parents," Heil said. "But I have an idea that may help both the lake community and the family to move things along."

"I'm listening," the man said.

"Now, keep an open mind. She's dead. We all know she's dead. No one can survive underwater for an entire day and night." Heil looked around for consent. "So what I'm proposing is a sure way to recover the girl. Although it may seem gruesome, I assure you it's not. Not really. It's practical. It's using our very own resources, and it won't cost the taxpayers or community any money." He paused, a pleased expression on his face. "It's free."

"What is it?" someone asked from the crowd.

Another shouted, "I know what you're suggesting."

A woman said, "I don't understand. What is he talking about?"

"Now, calm down." Heil beckoned the group. "We can find that little girl by ourselves and quickly. We've done it before."

The crowd collectively gasped, but nodded, understanding what Heil was suggesting. "It's like when that Hawke boy drowned. What was his name?"

"Billy," someone said. "Yeah, that's right. Billy."

Jo opened her mouth and closed it again when Gram squeezed her thigh.

"There are reasons we use the technology we have," the man from underwater recovery said, his face now etched in a perma-nent frown. "We don't want to jeopardize any possible forensic evidence." He looked to the sheriff, and once again the sheriff nodded.

He continued. "We have the side scanner. If you just give us a few more hours, my guess is that we should be able to find her by tomorrow afternoon at the latest."

The crowd began to rumble their dissent.

"That's another day the beach stays closed."

"What about the fishing boats?"

"It's costing us money."

"Find her now by any means possible."

"It's best for everyone."

Gram's hands were curled into two tight balls, her knuckles white. She turned to Jo. "Barbarians. Every last one of them."

Heil held up his hands in an attempt to quiet the crowd yet again. Sara's mother appeared in the doorway, and a hushed silence spread throughout the room. Her face was drawn and hollow. She looked much older than she was. The man from underwater recovery rushed to her side.

"I want you to find my baby girl," she said to him. "I want you to get her out of that damn lake."

"We will, ma'am." He took her arm, and before she could address the crowd, if she even wanted to address the crowd, he ushered her out the door and down the stairs to avoid a scene. The sheriff followed them out.

The mob stayed seated with their eyes cast down, unwilling to look at one another. Several seconds of an uncomfortable silence ensued until one of the women, Mrs. Hofsteader, stood to leave. She and her husband, Cal Hofsteader, owned one of the cabins on the lake directly across from the Pavilion. She tapped her husband's shoulder, and he followed her out the door. Other women began to gather themselves, collect their purses, accepting it would be another day of waiting. Most of the men followed, but Stimpy and a few other fishermen huddled in the corner of the bar.

Jo turned to Gram and motioned in the direction of Stimpy and the fishermen. "What do you think they're up to?"

Gram stared at the men. Their heads were bent together, and they were whispering. "I think they're going to take matters into their own hands," she said.

CHAPTER EIGHT

Caroline was sitting at the kitchen table with a glass of milk and cookies when Gram stomped through the door. Caroline's mother marched in behind her. Both were in a huff over something, and Caroline stared at them, making a quick mental list of her actions in the last few hours, trying to determine if she was to blame for their foul moods.

Looking back and forth between Gram and her mother, and not coming up with anything she might have done to make them mad, she hoped they weren't fighting with each other. She had been aware of a rift between them ever since she was little. She couldn't remember a time when it wasn't there, this thing she couldn't name. She couldn't always see it in their eyes or hear it in their words, but she felt it, an invisible storm rumbling in the air around them.

"So now what?" her mother asked.

"Now nothing," Gram said. "We wait like the rest of them."

Her mother crossed her arms. Gram poured a glass of lake water from the jug in the refrigerator. Her hands shook when she raised the cup to her lips.

"What's going on?" Caroline asked, startling both women. It was as though they hadn't seen her sitting there.

"Nothing for you to worry about," Gram said, and shot Jo a look.

"Is it about Sara? Did they find her?" Caroline had spent the day with Megan, sitting on the public docks and watching underwater recovery, waiting. Initially, she had gone to the Pavilion but the sign tacked to the doors read CLOSED.

Gram sat next to her and patted her arm. "Not yet, but they'll find her soon."

Johnny waltzed into the kitchen, the screen door banging behind him. He smelled of cigarette smoke and something else, something funky Caroline associated with a boy smell, wet and doglike. Gram must've smelled it too, and she crinkled her nose at him.

"I'm going to change," Gram said, and stood, leaving them in the kitchen.

"You need a shower," her mother said to Johnny.

He smelled underneath his arm and shrugged but headed to the bathroom anyway. He pushed the back of Caroline's head as he passed by, making her spill milk down the front of her T-shirt.

"Jerk," she said, grabbing a napkin and catching the milk on her chin.

"Would you two knock it off?" her mother said.

"I didn't do anything." Caroline hated the whininess in her tone. "He started it."

"Baby," Johnny called.

"Am not!" she yelled back at him.

"Enough, Caroline."

"Why don't you ever yell at him? Why is it always my fault?"

Her mother sighed and covered her face. "It's not always your fault, okay? And you're right." She dropped her hands and smiled.

"Your brother can be a real jerk sometimes." She brushed the hair from Caroline's face.

Caroline's chest opened as she looked up at her. Her mother was so beautiful when she smiled. She wanted to tell her, but she was too afraid she would take it the wrong way. Everything she said, good or bad, her mother misunderstood.

"What?" her mother asked, and furrowed her brow. "You're looking at me funny."

Caroline opened her mouth to talk, not knowing what words would come out. There was so much she wanted to say now that she had her mother's attention. She was scared and feeling so alone. "I should've watched her," she said about Sara. "She was on the pier, and I knew her mother wasn't paying attention." She looked down at her hands and waited for her mother's reaction.

Without saying anything, her mother sat next to her and wrapped her arms around her. It was a rare embrace, and Caroline clung to her, elated to gain her mother's affection even though the reason for it made her feel terrible. "I shouldn't have left her alone."

Her mother pulled back and took Caroline's face in her hands. "She wasn't your responsibility."

She nodded. "I know," she said, but still, it felt that way.

Gram walked into the kitchen, now wearing polyester pants and matching cotton shirt. She yanked open the refrigerator door, not realizing she had interrupted a rare mother-daughter moment. "Who wants dinner?" she asked.

"I have an errand," her mother said, and stood. She touched Caroline's shoulder, pausing to give it a squeeze before she fled for the door.

———

Caroline lay on her bed and listened. The cabin was quiet except for the murmur of the small TV coming from Gram's bedroom. She closed her eyes and tried to sleep, but it was too early for bed. And it was too late to be out with friends. It was the time in-between when she was either too old for certain things or too young for others, a time when there was nothing for a girl her age to do. She wondered what was happening down at the lake, if people had gathered or if everyone had stayed home. Where was her mother?

She sat up and swung her legs to the floor. She looked out into the night. Leaves rustled. Willow's branches swayed in the breeze. Her mother said it wasn't her fault, what had happened to Sara. Maybe she was right. But she couldn't just sit here feeling they way she did. She had to do something. At the very least, she wanted to know what was happening down at the lake. She was still wearing her T-shirt and shorts, so why not go and find out? Carefully, she lifted the screen out of the window and slipped through.

She had figured out how to crawl out the window undetected when she was ten years old. She'd had a bad dream about a wolf scratching at her bedroom door and trying to get inside to bite her throat. She had been so scared, she had wanted to flee, to climb in Willow's branches, the one place a wolf couldn't reach her, and hide. She had been surprised at how easily the screen had lifted away, but in truth, the cabin was old and in need of repairs.

Ever since the night of the wolf dream, when she wanted to escape, she'd crawl out the window and up the willow tree. No one ever thought to look for her there, and she felt safe. Once, she had spied her brother making out with a girl on the corner of the dirt road. She had stayed hidden in the tree and watched her brother slide his hands underneath the girl's top, the girl batting his hands away, but eventually giving in. She felt guilty watching her brother do these things, and she felt dirty, too, but she couldn't stop herself from staring. No way she'd ever let a boy touch her in that way.

Tonight, instead of curling up in one of Willow's branches, she jogged down the dirt road toward the lake, keeping to the edges near the trees. She felt a strong pull toward the water, and it was more than curiosity about the progress of the search. She knew she had to be at the lake, to see whatever there was to see.

Rather than take the Lake Road and risk running into anyone, she turned right, sneaking between two cabins that led to a small trail through the woods. Voices echoed from the ballpark, possibly Johnny and his friends drinking in the dugout far away from the recovery team and law enforcement.

She continued slipping through the shadows as quietly as possible. A dog barked and she froze. She looked left and right. The dog stopped and after a few moments, she started moving again. She didn't stop until she reached the parking lot on the other side of the Pavilion. The lake was deserted. The Pavilion was dark and empty but for the upstairs bar. She made her way closer to the dock, and from there at the far end of the lake she saw two large spotlights and a boat, but no sign of the recovery team.

Voices near the dock drew her attention. She took a few steps back under the cover of the trees. Stimpy and two other men she recognized from the Pavilion sat on the fishing pier with a couple of empty traps, hard at work tying lines. She inched closer.

"What do you have for bait?" one of the men asked.

"Crappies," Stimpy said. "What did you think I had?"

"Are you sure Heil knows we're doing this?" another man asked.

"He knows this is the best way to find that girl."

A twig snapped under her foot.

"Shhh," Stimpy said. All three men looked around. She didn't dare move.

"Shit. We're getting jumpy, and all we're doing is helping. There's no way they're going to find that girl their way. It's been too damn long. Too damn long."

"How many snappers do you think we're going to need?"

"At least a dozen. Maybe more."

Caroline understood what the men intended to do. The idea frightened her, and she backpedaled farther into the trees before turning on her heels. When she reached the cabins near the trail, she paused, peering at the lake over her shoulder, feeling as though she was playing some obscure part in a horror movie.

In the next second, she shot through the woods, no longer caring about making noise, about being seen, about being chased by a dog. She thrashed through brush and tore up the hill, slowing only when she reached the dirt road that led to the colony. She tiptoed as she got closer to the cabin, her stomach twisting and turning. She slipped under Willow's branches and crawled through the window before putting the screen back in place and curling into a ball on her bed.

Everyone on the lake knew about snappers and what they were capable of. Snappers bit off fingers and toes, chewed through fishing lines and nets, fed on dead and decaying flesh.

She pulled the covers over her head and tried hard not to picture Sara's body at the bottom of the lake covered in mud and grime. And bite marks. But no matter how hard she tried, the image flashed in her mind's eye over and over until she thought she might scream.

CHAPTER NINE

Jo walked through the colony, checking her phone every few minutes, searching for a signal. Slivers of moonlight sliced through branches of trees, lighting bits and pieces of the dirt road. She sidestepped potholes, the ones she could see, and kept walking.

The colony consisted of roughly thirty cabins. Most were named after birds that populated the area—*Wren, Sparrow, Meadowlark*. Gram caused a commotion with the lake association when she named her cabin, *The Pop-Inn*. Heil and a few other cabin owners claimed she had broken tradition and interfered with the continuity of the summer rental properties. Gram argued that she owned the cabin and could name it as she pleased.

Besides, Gram enjoyed the play on words—"popinjay" named after the bird, although not a local bird, "pop-in" visitors coming and going as they wished, and her favorite, "Pop's" Inn, the idea that amused Pop immensely. But the most compelling reason Gram fought hard to name the cabin *The Pop-Inn* was to piss off Heil and let him know she couldn't be controlled the way he manipulated the other members of the lake association, the community, and even the sheriff.

Gram had gotten her way.

Jo continued walking and searching for a signal, her thoughts on Caroline, regretting rushing out on her when Gram had walked into the kitchen. But Jo had found herself shying away from Caroline. Sometimes the way her daughter looked at her made her uncomfortable. It was as though her daughter could see through her, as though she could see straight through to Jo's own guilty heart.

She kept moving, not having any luck getting a signal in the colony, so she decided to walk down by the lake. Across the parking lot, the first floor of the Pavilion was dark, but the second floor bar was lit up. Voices were hushed. Under the circumstances, it was a slow night for Eddie. Heil must be losing a whole lot of money. She checked her phone again and finally had a connection.

"Hello, Rose," she said. "Sorry to call so late, but something's come up and I'm going to need a couple days off."

"Oh no, you need to give me more notice. Who am I supposed to get to cover for you this late?"

"I know. But this is important." *It's Billy. They may have found his bones.* But she couldn't say this so instead she said, "My mother needs my help."

Rose continued as if Jo hadn't spoken. "I've got a full workload. People want to come home from their vacations to a clean house. And I'm already down two maids this week."

"I wouldn't normally ask."

"Then don't." Rose was a fair boss, but she demanded a minimum of two weeks notice if you needed time off.

"But I only need a few days," she said. "Can't you make an exception this one time?"

"If I make an exception for you, then everyone else will expect the same kind of treatment."

"I understand. I do. But just this one time. I swear, I won't do it again. Rose?"

The other end was silent.

"Hello? Rose?" She shook her phone. "Can you hear me? Rose?"

The line was dead.

It wasn't as though she liked cleaning houses—hers or other peoples'. Far from it. It was mindless, unrewarding, and more often than not, disgusting. But it was a job, and no one could fault her for that, not even Gram. She looked at her phone. She held it in front of her and continued walking, searching once again for a signal.

She wound her way around the dock, passing the fishing boats tied and tucked for the night. She was coming up on *Hawkes'* cabin, Billy's cabin, spelled after his last name rather than the bird, but it played into the theme of the other cabins just the same.

The closer she got to his place, the stronger the feeling in her gut told her to turn around. She shouldn't be seen near his home. It was a stupid risk. But she was always drawn to do the very thing she shouldn't, powerless to stop herself. Besides, the cabin was dark, and it appeared as though no one were home. Otherwise, she would've kept moving. But she allowed herself to linger and gaze at the place she had once known so well. It had been years since she had seen it. Even in the shadows, it looked taken care of, recently sided, a sign the Hawkes lived here year-round.

She took a small step forward.

There were countless times when she had scrambled up these same steps, banged on the screen door, called for Billy. He was always there waiting, grinning in that crazy silly way he had. A part of her wanted to believe if she bounded up the steps right now and knocked on the door he would be there, and she could fall into his arms as though nothing bad had come between them. She liked to think it could happen, but of course she knew it could not.

The porch swing creaked, pulling her from her thoughts. Its chains rattled. She jumped at the sight of Billy's older sister.

"Jo? Is that you?" Dee Dee walked toward her. There was something off about the way she moved, a kind of clumsiness in her stride.

Jo instinctively backed up. "I—I didn't know anyone was home." She diverted her eyes from Dee Dee's face. It hurt too much to look at her straight on. The resemblance to Billy, what he might've looked like had he aged, was too much to bear. She stuffed the phone into the back pocket of her jeans, looking for a way out. She never should've stopped here. Why didn't she turn around? Why was Dee Dee sitting on the porch in the dark anyway?

"It's been a long time since I've seen you around here." Dee Dee was wearing cut-off jean shorts, a black T-shirt with a JACK DANIELS decal stamped across the front.

"I'm helping." Jo's words got mixed up. "For a few days. Cleaning out closets." Although Gram hadn't gotten around to it yet. "I should get back," she said, taking another step away.

"What's your hurry? You don't have a few minutes to talk to an old friend?"

Jo almost laughed at the idea that they were ever friends. For as long as she had known Dee Dee, they never had been. When she was young and had first started dating Billy, she hadn't understood why his sister hadn't liked her. But she knew the reason now, knew why Dee Dee had treated her with so much disdain.

"I really should get back," Jo said, taking another couple steps backward before turning away.

"Chris said he tried to find that little girl." Chris's father had taken off before Chris had been born, leaving Dee Dee to raise him on her own. The fact that Kevin had stayed when Jo was pregnant around the same time had always left Dee Dee a little bitter. "And Johnny tried to find her too," Dee Dee added.

Jo stopped at the mention of Johnny's name. *Leave Johnny out of this*, she heard herself say in a whispering voice. By the time she turned around, Dee Dee had caught up to her.

"What did you say?" Dee Dee asked.

"Nothing," she said, trying to sound calm. The last thing she wanted was to provoke her. "I didn't say anything."

Dee Dee grabbed Jo's bicep with her large hand and squeezed. "Do you hear that?" she asked.

"Hear what?" She tried pulling her arm free, but Dee Dee held on tightly.

"Shhh," Dee Dee said.

There was no telling what Dee Dee heard, but Jo listened anyway, believing it had to be something because Dee Dee always had these crazy animallike senses. She'd turn up wherever Jo and Billy were, appearing suddenly whenever they were fooling around no matter how quiet they whispered into each other's ears, tugged at each other's clothes, moaned into each other's shoulders. It was as though she could not only hear their bodies coming together, but also smell their pheromones.

And one time when they were lying on the dock, Billy's face buried in her chest, she spied Dee Dee watching them from the doorway of *Hawkes'* cabin, the little girl she babysat every summer clinging to Dee Dee's leg. She had glared at Dee Dee over the top of Billy's head. In a way she had been challenging her, daring her to try and come between them.

But all Jo heard tonight was the buzz of crickets, the water lapping against the bank near their feet.

"The water. The lake. It flows through our veins, and there's nothing we can do about it," Dee Dee said. "We can't stop it. It's like venom."

"You're not making any sense." Jo tried again to pull her arm free, but there was no way she could out-muscle her. Dee Dee was tall and strong and angry.

Dee Dee moved in close. Her breath reeked of beer. "It runs through our veins. Our family. Our kids. It gets inside you, and it's so goddamn beautiful, you can't help but drink it up."

"Yes," Jo said, wanting to sound agreeable if only Dee Dee would let her go. "It can be irresistible."

"It was for my brother. I wish he would've stayed the hell away from you."

Dee Dee was no longer talking about the lake; rather, she was referring to Jo, blaming her for what had happened to him.

"Did you hear they found his bones?" Dee Dee continued, squeezing Jo's bicep.

"So it's true? They're Billy's?"

"Don't be stupid. Of course, they are. And I should have a report soon to prove it."

"Right," Jo said, thinking out loud. "The sheriff would've had to send them to a lab or something."

"That's right." Dee Dee moved in closer, her sour breath warm on Jo's face. "Do you want to tell me what they'll find now? Or later?"

"Nothing. How should I know? It was ruled an accident." Her upper arm was stinging, her lower arm nearly numb.

"It wasn't an accident," Dee Dee said. "And you know it." She shoved Jo and stumbled. Jo caught her. Somehow their arms and legs entwined. They took an awkward step backward and sideways as though they were stepping to some kind of strange dance. It took all Jo's strength to keep from falling, or maybe it was

Dee Dee's sturdy body that kept them off the ground. It happened so quickly, Jo couldn't be sure. But once they found their footing, they couldn't get away from each other fast enough. They broke apart and stared at each other. A moment of silence stretched between them.

Finally Dee Dee said, "You were his *girlfriend*. He trusted you."

I know he did! Jo wanted to scream.

CHAPTER TEN

Caroline woke with her sheets damp and sticky. Already the day felt warm and muggy, but it was the dreams of Sara that had kept her tossing and turning through the night, making her break out in a cold sweat. Her mouth was dry, her throat sore. She remembered yelling in the last dream, screaming really, for Sara to swim faster lest the snappers in the water drag her down. In the real world, snappers didn't behave as predators, but rather more like scavengers, eating what was dead at the bottom of the lake. In dreamland, of course, rules of nature were broken and all bets were off.

She threw back the covers and shuffled into the kitchen in her pajamas in search of a cool drink. Her mother was sitting at the table with a cup of coffee. Her eyes were cast down, but she looked up when Caroline opened the refrigerator door and removed the jug of water that had been pumped from the well. Lake water.

"Don't drink that," her mother said, and grabbed the jug from Caroline's hands.

"Why? What's wrong with it?" she asked.

"Just drink something else for once, will you?" Her mother

stood and poured the lake water down the drain in the kitchen sink.

"Why?" Her mother was acting as though Caroline wanted to drink poison.

"Have some milk or orange juice," her mother said.

She yanked open the refrigerator door for the second time and pulled out the pitcher of juice. Sometimes it felt as though everything she did annoyed her mother, including her choice of beverage.

She poured a glass of OJ and sank onto the bench at the table. Her mother picked up her coffee and rather than sit next to Caroline, she stood at the sink with it.

Last night her mother had held her; this morning she had pushed her away. She wondered what it was about her that made her mother treat her this way. What did she do wrong?

"Is Gram still sleeping?" she asked. At least Gram could stand to be around her even if her mother couldn't.

"I don't know, Caroline." She put the cup into the sink. "I'm getting a shower."

In the next minute, Caroline heard the bathroom door lock and the pipes clank as the water turned on. She stood from the bench seat. Somehow the cold treatment from her mother always stung more after the times she had shown her the slightest bit of affection.

Well, she'd show her. She picked up the empty water jug and carried it back to her bedroom. She sat on the edge of the bed and twisted the cap on and off, debating whether or not she had the courage to go through with what she was thinking about doing.

The well was located on the other side of the lake, and Caroline had been filling jugs with water for as long as she could remember. When she had been little and too weak to carry them on her own, Gram had accompanied her, and the two of them had made the trek. Her job was to hold the jug steady under the stream of clear cool water while Gram pumped. Gram said it was the best tasting water around. After all, the lake was one of the few freshwater lakes in the state of Pennsylvania, and she felt lucky to have a summer cabin next to it.

Caroline was sure Gram had other jugs of water in the pantry, and she'd replace the one in the refrigerator soon enough, but this wasn't about replenishing their supply. Her mother made her feel bad about herself all over one stupid drink, and that in turn made her angry. She chewed on these emotions, biting her bottom lip for a minute more. She decided she would refill it. She'd take only the one jug for no other reason than for spite.

After a quick change into shorts and a T-shirt, she stuck her baseball cap on, grabbed the jug, and slipped out the screen door, making sure not to let it bang shut.

When she reached Lake Road, she paused, thinking of the best route to take without being seen. She didn't think she could bear another day watching underwater recovery on the lake, and she certainly didn't want to risk bumping into Johnny or Chris or anyone else for that matter. She wasn't sure, but she imagined her eyes looked as if she had been crying. Her face was probably pink and blotchy. Her mother had told her once she wore her heart on her sleeve—right before she had advised her to toughen up.

Thinking about her mother's words enraged her more, and she stomped through the woods, taking the same path she had the night before. She wasn't halfway down the narrow trail, staying clear of the poison ivy that covered most of the area on her left, when the same dog started barking again. *Darn dog*. She spotted the mutt through the oak and maple trees. He was tied to a dog coop on the side of a cabin. She recognized him: Cougar, a name that mocked the poor animal before it ever stood a chance. No wonder he barked incessantly. He was looking for attention and, knowing his owners, Stimpy and his wife, he was hungry, too. She made a mental note to bring poor Cougar some food at some point during the day.

When she came to the edge of the parking lot, she spied the underwater recovery team's vehicle. Two of the men stood next to the truck, drinking coffee. Three other cars were parked in the lot. A couple sat on the hood of a sedan parked closest to the truck and men. Caroline recognized Sara's mother. She was wearing the big sun hat she had worn on the day Sara disappeared. Her knees were pulled close to her chest, and she was hugging her legs tightly. A man sat next to her, presumably Sara's father, hunched over with his feet propped on the front bumper. Both parents' shoulders slumped, but Caroline could tell solely from the way they held their heads, necks craned forward and chins lifted, that their eyes had never left the water.

She turned away from the scene, her stomach feeling as if a thousand minnows swam back and forth in it, making her seasick. She wound her way unnoticed to the far side of the Pavilion. The sign on the door was the same from yesterday: CLOSED.

Turning at the sound of a car coming down Lake Road, she took off in the opposite direction of the beach and the recovery team, deciding on the longer route to the well. She'd have to walk in a near full circle around the lake, but the idea appealed to her. She wasn't in any hurry to return to *The Pop-Inn* and face her mother, or Johnny the Jerk for that matter. Nor was she in any mood to listen to Megan's obsessive talk about makeup and boys and kissing.

She stuck close to the back of the cabins alongside the lake, smelling bacon and eggs as she passed. Sometimes she'd hear voices and the clinking of silverware inside. When she came to the last cabin before a stretch of woods, she saw Adam sitting on the pier all alone, holding a fishing pole.

"Hey, Adam," she said. "Catch anything?"

He looked up. "Just a couple of sunnies."

There were a few slices of bread next to him. He was using dough balls, sticking them on the end of the hook, the perfect bait to catch sunnies. She had done the same thing so many times, she couldn't keep count. All the kids fished for sunnies at some point during their time at the lake. Of course, you tossed the small fish back as soon as they were caught. They were too small to eat, and she was certain they wouldn't taste good if you could.

She sat next to him. Several fish had gathered around his hook, sneaking pieces of bread before darting away. A half dozen ducks were making their way across the water looking for handouts. Underwater recovery loaded their watercraft, preparing for another sweep.

"Do you think Heil will ever give the horse's bit back to me?" Adam asked.

"I doubt it," she said, and tossed a few bread crumbs to the ducks.

"Yeah, I didn't think so." He rolled another dough ball and stuck it on the end of the hook. "Can I ask you something?"

"Sure."

"Do you believe in the lake legend?"

She had never really thought hard about it. It was one of those things you heard, and being a kid, you accepted without question that it was true. "I believe in it," she said. "Do you?"

"Yeah," he said. "You know what I think?" His voice was serious. "I think you have to be a kid to believe in stuff like legends."

Caroline smiled, thinking he was right. She picked up the water jug. "Do you want to come to the well with me?"

They walked single file with Caroline in the lead, ducking under low branches and jumping across muddy patches where the lake water receded. They walked a good stretch in the woods following along the lake's shoreline, until they came to a private beach and stopped.

"Should we go around?" Adam asked.

Caroline looked at the cabin not twenty yards away. It looked dark and quiet. "Let's cut across. I don't think anyone's home."

They jogged across, kicking up sand onto the backs of their legs. They were halfway to the other side when someone yelled out a window, "What do you think you're doing?"

"Run!" Caroline shouted. She dashed to the next patch of woods and didn't stop until she was under the cover of trees.

Adam caught up to her, huffing and puffing. His cheeks were flushed. The excitement and exertion caused them both to burst out laughing. "Holy moly," he said. "That scared the crap out of me."

"Me too," she said, thinking if Megan had been with her, they would've gotten caught. Megan was terrible at anything physical, especially running. "Come on."

They continued to follow the meandering path around the lake, passing several more cabins with private beaches. Each time they stopped, counted to three, and darted across. No one caught them. No one yelled for them to keep out. Only once were the cabin owners outside, and they had to walk around rather than cut across the property. Caroline had to admit, she was having fun, the first bit of fun she had had since the summer had started.

It wasn't lost on her that she was enjoying hanging out with a ten-year-old boy more than any of the times she had spent with Megan the last few days. She wondered again if there was something wrong with her. She would be turning thirteen in the fall. Surely, other thirteen-year-old girls preferred doing the kinds of things Megan liked to do. She doubted any of them wanted to run through the woods, attempt trespassing, play silly games with a boy Adam's age. Maybe this was what her mother saw when she looked at her—an oddball for a daughter, one who enjoyed sports, received poor grades, and dressed like a boy.

It was true. Caroline didn't fit in at school. Even the girls on her softball team weren't exactly friends. They were big girls, tough girls, and more times than not, they were surprised when she threw someone out at first base or caught a line drive, although they shouldn't have been.

She was a good ballplayer.

She wore the dirt stains on the knees of her uniform with pride. She took raspberries on her thigh sliding into home plate. And still the other girls teased her, laughed at her skinny arms and legs, her lanky build, all the while hiding behind chuckles.

After an hour, she and Adam reached the well. Some of the anger she felt toward her mother peeled away as time elapsed. And for a few minutes she had forgotten about the little girl Sara and the underwater recovery team on the lake. But when she remembered, she crossed her fingers hoping Sara would be found soon and not because she wanted the public beach opened, but because the image of Sara's parents sitting on the hood of a car was the saddest thing she had ever seen. Even at her age, she understood the scene would forever be imprinted on her mind. It was something she would never forget.

"I'll pump. You hold the jug," she said to Adam. He held the jug under the spigot. Caroline lifted the handle up and down, up and down until a steady stream of water flowed.

Once the jug was filled, she screwed the cap on tightly. They decided to make the trek back, but this time they'd take the shorter route. Adam was worried his mother would be looking for him. Caroline assumed he didn't tell his mother initially where he was going since she was always quick to say no. His mother constantly worried about him, keeping close tabs on him, more than the other mothers around the lake. In a way, Caroline envied Adam. At least his mother showed she cared.

They approached *Hawkes*' cabin, where Chris lived. She hesitated, anxious about passing by his front door. If he saw her carrying a stupid water jug and hanging out with Adam, she thought it somehow made her look like a baby.

"Let's walk around back," she told Adam.

"But it's quicker this way," he said in that high-pitched voice of his.

"We don't want to bump into my brother." Partly true, and she knew Adam would agree. He took enough teasing from the older boys as it was.

They circled around the back of the cabin. She quickened her pace, but Adam made her stop so he could tie the laces on his sneaker. She leaned against an oak tree to wait. She wished he'd hurry up. Birds fluttered in the branches, crying at the intrusion. She looked up and thought of an old silly rhyme Gram had taught her. "Birdie, birdie in the sky, why'd you do that in my eye? I'm sure glad that cows can't fly."

She laughed and pushed off the tree. Not far from where she stood she noticed a ring of rocks around an old campfire site. It wasn't unusual for campfires to burn deep into the night, but this one hadn't been used for some time. She wasn't sure what exactly drew her toward the abandoned site, but she stepped in for a closer a look. Painted in white on a large rock that could have been used as a seat near the fire were the initials *J+B* surrounded by a heart. The paint was old and faded and nearly rubbed out, but there was no mistaking the letters.

"Ready," Adam said.

"Yeah, okay," she said absently, turning *J* and *B* over in her mind. Maybe they were Johnny's and his big-boobed girlfriend's initials, but that seemed unlikely. Their initials would've looked freshly painted, not old and faded.

Her mind jumped to other possibilities, to her mother, Josephine, and the mysterious boy named Billy. It was unsettling, almost frightening to think of her mother with anyone other than her father. But really, what did she know of her mother's life other than that she had married young and soon after, her brother, Johnny, was born? It was an uneasy feeling, realizing for the first time her mother had been someone else before she had married Caroline's father, before she had been Johnny and Caroline's mother.

Caroline didn't mention the painted rock to Adam. Instead she hurried him away from the abandoned sight and *Hawkes*' cabin. She wanted to forget she ever saw it, but at the same time she knew she wouldn't.

They reached the dock where she had seen Stimpy and his men setting traps. They stopped and looked around. They were alone, although Stimpy's cabin was only a few feet away.

"Let's pull up the lines," she said, and set the water jug on the pier.

Adam's eyes darted around. "What if we get caught?"

"We're just looking to see if they caught anything." She squatted next to the post where the line was attached. She pulled. The trap felt heavy. "They got something."

"Isn't it against the law to mess with a fisherman's line?" Adam asked, but he crouched next to her and peered into the water.

"We're not messing with anything. Not really." She braced herself against the post and tugged harder. The trap lifted from the bottom. She kept pulling, leaning back to use more of her weight. "Anyone coming?" she asked.

Adam looked around. "No. Let me help you." He grabbed farther down on the line and yanked.

Slowly, the trap rose to the surface.

"I see two snappers." Adam's voice lifted with excitement.

It was the second time today she was doing something she shouldn't be. And it was thrilling. "I see them," she said in a voice just as excited as Adam's.

The trap could just about hold the two snappers. One looked to be the size of a Frisbee and the other was much larger, almost twice the size of the first. The big one stretched its neck and snapped. She and Adam jumped and dropped the line. They both watched as the trap sank to the bottom. The water was shallow enough for the turtles to come up through the holes in the trap to get air, to keep them alive.

"Let's get out of here," she said, and picked up the jug.

They jogged along the path beside the dock, dodging fresh droppings left by the ducks. The sun burned the tops of their shoulders and backs as the morning wore on. Adam's face was flushed. Caroline's T-shirt was wet under her arms. She had caught a whiff of her own body odor when she had pulled on the fishing line. She had started shaving under her arms a few months back, but sometimes she plain forgot to put on deodorant.

Once they were a safe distance from Stimpy's pier, they slowed to a steady walk.

"What are they going to do with those snappers anyway? Eat

them?" Adam scrunched up his face as though he had bitten down on something tart.

"No, I don't think they want to eat them." She switched the full jug to her other hand. "I think they want to tie lines to them and see where they lead." She was giving him a roundabout answer. The dreams from the night before were still fresh in her mind, and the idea of the snappers feasting on little Sara's body made her shiver.

"Oh." He kept his head down. After a few moments he said, "You mean, they think they can find that little girl's body by following the snappers."

She paused, thinking about how to answer. She hated when adults held back the truth because they thought she was too young to hear it. Like the time she had overheard her father and mother talking about a procedure, a V-something or other. Her mother had been the one pressing for him to get one, and Caroline believed her mother was trying to hurt him. She had been worried and imagined all kinds of horrible outcomes of what this V-thing would do to her father, when she finally broke down and asked. Her mother had said it was none of her business and she wouldn't understand anyway. So Caroline turned to Johnny. He had laughed at her, of course, but he had explained what a vasectomy was and why their father was getting one. She endured Johnny's relentless ribbing and teasing for weeks after, and she chastised herself for always thinking the worst when it came to her mother. For once, she had been on her mother's side, not wanting a baby brother or sister. Johnny was enough.

Adam looked up at her, his eyes round and innocent, but in them Caroline could see he wanted the truth, as all kids do. "Yes," she said. "They're hoping the snappers will lead them to Sara."

"Yeah." He nodded. "That's what I figured."

A few more steps and they reached the parking lot where the

recovery team gathered in what appeared to be a break in the search. Their watercraft was docked. They drank soda pop and ate sandwiches. Caroline looked toward the Pavilion and, sure enough, one of the doors was flung open. Maybe the snack stand had opened to feed the men. Sara's parents were positioned on the hood of the car in the same position Caroline had found them hours earlier. A man dressed in recovery gear was talking with them. But other than the team and Sara's parents, there wasn't anyone else around.

"I better get home," Adam said. "See you later." He walked on the outer rim of the parking lot, staying far away from the scene.

Caroline took the same path through the woods to avoid the recovery team as well. Cougar announced her presence with a round of barking. She vowed to bring him a treat on her next time through.

When she reached *The Pop-Inn*, jug full of lake water in hand, she spied her father's blue pickup truck parked alongside the cabin. She raced around back. He was sitting on the steps, wearing blue jeans and a gray T-shirt. His messy brown hair fell haphazardly across his forehead. Her mother was sitting next to him, her hands folded in her lap.

"Daddy!" she squealed, and dropped the jug to the ground as she launched herself into his arms.

"Hey there, Caroline." He laughed and gave her one of his bear hugs. "I missed you, too," he whispered into her ear.

She pulled back to look at him just in time to see her mother point to the jug at the bottom of the steps.

"What's that?" her mother asked.

Caroline lifted her chin. "Water from the well."

Anger flickered across her mother's face but disappeared as quickly as it came. "Of course it is," she said, and stood.

Caroline watched her mother cross the yard, walking like a person who had lost her way, drifting without any purpose. Her mother dropped into the hammock under the apricot tree. And Caroline found herself wondering if the trip to the well had been worth it, made purely out of spite, making her mother angry for a brief moment, and in the end, only pushing her mother further away.

She turned toward her father. "When did you get in?"

CHAPTER ELEVEN

Kevin watched Jo walk away. It seemed to him, she was forever walking away. Even after all these years, the sway of her hips and the toss of her long dark hair jump-started his heart and stirred him below. He often had to remind himself that she was no longer sixteen, young and free, that she was a grown woman and she was his. Well, legally she was his wife, but although she had been loyal as far as he knew, she would never really be his. Her heart and soul seemed to be elsewhere, and he didn't let himself think too hard or too long about where that might be.

They were kids when they first met, barely thirteen, about the same age as Caroline was now. Jo had the same lanky arms and legs as his daughter, but that was where the likeness ended. Caroline had his brown hair and deep brown eyes where Johnny looked more like his mother with his hair as dark as night.

But Jo at thirteen was a sight to be seen with her hazel doe eyes, dark hair, and golden sun-kissed skin. She had been attached to Billy's side even then, following his lead, hanging on his every word. She was smitten, and Kevin had hated him for it. The way she had looked at Billy had soured Kevin's stomach until he had tasted bile on his tongue. What he wanted more than anything back then was for her to look at him that way.

But in the end he had never blamed her.

There was something about Billy that even Kevin had found irresistible. Billy had that "it" factor, whatever "it" was. He was charming with the girls and laugh-out-loud funny with the guys. He was quick with a joke and a smile. His pale blue eyes penetrated you when you had his attention, making you feel as if you were the only person in the world who existed. And to gain Billy's interest, to have his eye-locking stare directed at you, made you feel special, made you feel like you mattered, like whatever you had to say was important. How was Kevin ever supposed to compete with that?

One night they had been standing alone under the steps of the bar at the Pavilion drinking beer and smoking cigarettes. Jo had taken off to pee in the woods across the parking lot. Eddie and Sheila had wandered to the pier, their silhouettes visible in the sliver of moonlight. And Billy, well, he had directed those piercing blue eyes at Kevin.

"Do you have a thing for my girl?" he had asked.

"What?" Kevin had shuffled his feet, swaying a little on his drunken legs. "What makes you think that?"

"I see the way you look at her." Billy's voice had had an edge Kevin had never heard before, and it had made him uneasy. He had immediately wanted to make things right between them, to put his best friend's mind at ease, no matter if what he had said was a blatant lie.

"No way, Billy," he had said. "You're wrong." He hadn't known whether Billy had believed him that night, but looking back, it hadn't mattered. In the end Billy's suspicions had been confirmed.

When Jo was settled on the hammock, head turned away, he

looked back at his daughter. "So, what have you been doing with yourself?" he asked.

Before Caroline could answer, Gram appeared behind the screen door. "Are you three hungry? I've got pork barbeque on the stove."

"None for me," Jo mumbled.

Kevin rubbed his stomach and elbowed his daughter. "How about you?" He hadn't had a home-cooked meal in a long time, even if it was only pork sandwiches. On the occasional nights when he was home and not on the road, Jo rarely cooked. She was more of the takeout or frozen dinner kind of wife. She didn't think too much of slaving over an oven, preparing meals for her family, when the fast food place down the street could do the job for her. "Besides," she had reasoned. "I spend an hour making dinner, we sit at the table all of ten minutes, and then we're finished. Everyone gets up and leaves, and I have to spend another hour cleaning dishes. What's the point?"

Gram felt differently, however, and Kevin supposed it was a generational thing. Gram believed her position was to take care of the home and her family. She walked around with an apron tied at her waist most of the time, cooking and baking, cleaning up after the kids. She was happy in her role.

But Jo was a different breed of woman, questioning society's ideals about who she should be, challenging everything from sexuality to family to the work force. If Jo hadn't gotten pregnant at sixteen, Kevin firmly believed her life would look much different than it did today. He often felt he was to blame for proposing, for holding her back, and for being the very reason she didn't become the woman she was meant to be.

She often wore a retro red T-shirt with the Virginia Slim cigarette slogan, her favorite brand that read YOU'VE COME A LONG

WAY, BABY. She'd stomp around the house complaining about picking up dirty laundry and vacuuming crumbs off the living room carpet, cursing that she hadn't come a long way at all. Kevin attributed these occasional outbursts to PMS, but that was a sexist thought and one he wouldn't dare say out loud. The truth was, he wouldn't mind if she quit her housecleaning job—at least the one outside their home. It wasn't like she was good at the whole cleaning lady thing anyway, but they needed the extra cash. Why Jo didn't bother to look for a better job or think about some kind of a career was beyond his understanding. And in the end, sexist or not, he liked to imagine her wearing a little French maid's uniform while he was hauling freight across country alone in his rig even though her work attire was really jeans and T-shirts.

Sitting at the kitchen table in front of a steaming pulled pork sandwich and homemade potato salad made his stomach rumble. "This looks amazing."

Gram beamed. "Then eat," she said.

During lunch Caroline remained unusually quiet, but every now and again she stole quick glances back and forth with Gram. Kevin attacked his sandwich, waiting for one of them to bring up the news from the lake. Jo had told him again about the bones and the drowning before he had both feet out of the pickup truck and on the ground. They had been discussing it right before Caroline had turned the corner and thrown herself into his arms. At the time all he could think about was that at least one of his girls was happy to see him.

When he finished eating, he wiped his fingers on his napkin. "Well, I already heard about what happened," he said, figuring he'd make it easier on them. "I'll head down to the lake and see what I can find out."

"Can I come with you?" Caroline asked.

"Why don't you stay here and help Gram clean up?" He kissed her forehead. "I'll let you know if there's any news."

Caroline looked disappointed, but she nodded and reluctantly said, "Okay." Gram kept her thoughts on the matter to herself. He wondered what she might've said to him about the bones if they had been alone.

Kevin followed the dirt road down the hill. He crossed onto Lake Road and continued downward toward the Pavilion. The doors were closed and the place looked deserted. The sight gave him pause. There was only one time in sixteen years that he remembered the Pavilion closing its doors to the public. He hadn't expected all the memories the scene would conjure. All the emotions he had kept in check for so long stacked up inside him. His chest tightened, and he was having a hard time breathing. He wiped the back of his neck where moisture had gathered. The sun was hotter than usual, maybe because cooling off in the lake was no longer an option. The thought made him shiver despite the heat.

Pull yourself together, he told himself. But now he understood the look in Jo's eyes when he had first stepped out of the truck. She looked haunted, much more than usual. He stared at the CLOSED sign on the door. He suspected Heil planned on opening tomorrow no matter the outcome of the search. He couldn't believe he had kept the Pavilion closed for three days as it was, and he couldn't fathom the amount of money he had to be losing. Heil loved his money.

Kevin gathered himself and willed his legs to keep moving. Each step he took around the building felt as though he were stepping back in time and what awaited on the other side would seize his heart all over again. When he turned the corner, he half expected to see Billy's parents and sister, Dee Dee, crying, cursing, and a sixteen-year-old Jo, face drained of color, paralyzed by the scene unfolding in front her. But instead he saw the underwater recovery team standing around the watercraft. He recognized one of the men and slowly walked toward him.

His tongue felt thick and clumsy, but he managed to say "Jim" in his normal voice, and he extended his hand. He had known Jim through Eddie; he was one of the regulars who frequented Eddie's bar whenever he wasn't volunteering for the local fire department.

"What's the situation?" Kevin asked.

"We think she went down near the diving boards. It's a fifty-foot drop. There's so much muck at the bottom, it makes searching difficult even for the best divers. You can't see shit." He glanced at Kevin. "But you know that. Damn near impossible."

And yet, Kevin wanted to add, they were able to find bones in all that muck, but Jo had warned that Heil meant to keep that quiet, not wanting to remind people of past drownings. For once, Kevin agreed with Heil. "What's the next step?" he asked instead.

"They're going to widen the search area." He lifted his baseball cap and scratched his head. "Some of the fishing guys caught some snappers. They think they have a better chance of finding her with the turtles. You ever hear of such a thing?"

Kevin shrugged. It was how they had found Billy. And in fact, he had heard of other instances where unusual methods had been used. An airplane had gone down in the Atlantic several years back, and divers reported that crabs had unintentionally led them to the carnage. He supposed snappers weren't any different from crabs, feeding on what was provided. People. Humans. We were part of the food chain whether we liked it or not.

Jim situated the cap back onto his head and pulled the bill down low, hiding his eyes. "It might not be a bad idea to try it," he said. "But you didn't hear that from me."

"I hope it doesn't become a circus out there." Kevin thought of Stimpy and his men on boats, following the lines tied to snappers and what that would look like to the little girl's parents. For a second the image of Billy's body flashed in his mind's eye, how the men pulled Billy into the boat and then dumped him onto the beach. His flesh had been shredded to the bone on one of his thighs, his forearm clawed off. The skin on his chin had been torn, and the flap lay on his neck.

"You okay?" Jim asked.

"Yeah," Kevin said. "Sure." He allowed himself a glance at the girl's parents. "Did anybody tell them what to expect?"

Jim looked at the couple and then turned back to Kevin. "Nope. I imagine right now, they just want her found."

"Right," Kevin said, wondering how in the world anyone could prepare them for what horrors finding their daughter would bring. It had been three days. There was no telling what she was going to look like when they managed to pull her out.

He turned to the sound of a car. The sheriff's vehicle pulled into the lot and parked near the girl's parents. Sheriff Borg got out and talked to the couple. He glanced in the direction of the underwater recovery team where Jim and Kevin were standing.

Kevin looked at the ground and turned away from the sheriff. "I'll catch you later," he said to Jim, slinking away, not wanting to attract any attention to himself.

CHAPTER TWELVE

The sun was making its slow descent behind the mountains when Jo climbed the stairs to the second-floor bar. She found Kevin sitting at the far end of the room away from the crowd that had gathered at the tables. Eddie leaned on the bar in front of him. The two had their heads together, and she immediately walked over to them, wanting to know what was going on. She had spent most of the day wandering the colony, avoiding the cabin and cleaning closets.

"Hey," she said, and sat on the stool next to Kevin.

Kevin looked up and caught her eye. He still looked at her sometimes the way he did when they were teenagers, as though he was seeing her for the first time, and his eyes filled with the same deep desire. And like when they were teenagers, her body reacted, her yearning just as strong. But she wished he wouldn't look at her that way now. Ever. It made her feel so damn guilty.

Eddie put a cold beer in front of her. "The vultures are at it again," he said, nodding in the direction of Heil and his crew.

"I heard." She turned in her seat to look at the mob when one of the men with Heil yelled, "It's been three damn days! It's time to take this matter into our own hands."

"I have a family to feed," Nate said. He owned the bait and tackle shop located at the opposite end of the lake. "I empathize with the parents, but a man's got to provide, and I can't do that if no one can fish on that lake."

She turned back around, having heard it all before. It wasn't until Stimpy bounded up the steps and dropped a snapper the size of a truck tire onto the bar, that the crowd hushed.

"This is the biggest one I caught, but I've trapped a half dozen more, and they'll work just as good." Stimpy looked at Heil who nodded his approval.

"What about the sheriff?" Jonathon asked.

"I don't see him doing anything to stop us," Stimpy said, and again looked at Heil.

Heil mumbled, "That's true."

"Any objections?" Stimpy asked.

"No, no," the crowd of men muttered. Jonathon raised his arms, surrendering. The women in the crowd looked away. Jo stared at the beer in her hand.

"All right then." Stimpy picked up the large snapper by its tail, managing to keep the turtle's mouth away from his body. It looked to weigh close to fifty pounds. "Let's do this," he said, and walked out.

In another minute the crowd dispersed. Some left the bar, while others bellied up for a night of drinking to try to forget what they had just agreed to.

"Maybe I should talk to the little girl's mother," Jo said.

Kevin turned on the stool to face her head on. "What could you possibly say to help?"

"I'm not sure, but someone should say something. Don't you think?"

"Why should it be you?"

"Why not?" she asked, and looked at Eddie, who tossed his

hands up as a way of saying he was staying out of it and made his way down to the other end of the bar.

"I don't know," Kevin said, and lowered his voice. "It might sound like you know something about how she feels. Like maybe you're still pining away for someone."

She glared at him. Why did he always do that, say things to see how she would react? He was always testing her. "Take that back, Kevin."

"Why?" he muttered.

"Take it back," she said sharply.

"Okay, okay." He put his hand on the back of her neck and squeezed maybe harder than he should. "Relax. I'm sorry. It was a stupid thing to say. I didn't mean it."

She stared at him a second more. "Yeah, okay," she said, and he let her go. She sensed people watching them.

He turned back to the bar and picked up his beer. She peeled the label off her bottle. The fact that she had been Billy's girl first was something Kevin couldn't, or wouldn't, forget.

They had been sitting on a pile of rocks stacked around a fire pit behind *Hawkes'* cabin. Billy was perched on the rock where Jo had painted their initials, *J+B*, three years earlier when they had been just thirteen years old. They were sixteen now, and Billy had his arm wrapped firmly around her waist. Eddie and Sheila were sharing a joint and whispering to each other. Kevin sat alone, strumming his guitar. He was humming a song, which song Jo couldn't remember. The flames flickered across his face as though they were dancing in tune. His fingers gently plucked the strings, and his foot tapped the ground with the beat. His singular focus on the guitar, the music, the serenity on his face as he gave himself over to the sound, stirred something deep inside her. There was so much more to him than she ever suspected, this boy who had somehow gotten lost in Billy's shadow.

She had talked to Sheila about it later when the guys were out on the lake for a late-night swim. They had been sitting on the floating pier, legs dangling over the side.

"Why do you think Kevin doesn't have a girl?" she asked.

"Oh, he does, but she's spoken for," Sheila said.

"What do you mean? Who?"

Sheila looked at her as though she were dense. "Who do you think?"

"I have no idea."

"You, silly. Don't you notice the way he looks at you? How he follows you around like a lost puppy? How he hangs on your every word?"

"No," she said. She didn't notice, although even as she said it, she knew it wasn't true. She did notice the way he looked at her. She'd catch him staring and once, they had locked eyes, and it was as though he was seeing her as she truly was. She was left feeling raw, exposed, seen for the first time as the woman she would become, and it had frightened her.

Her feelings for Kevin that summer ran as deep as her love had been for Billy the last three summers. Her love for both was real. It was just that it was a different kind of love for each. Billy was a childhood love, a familiar love, one that had roots, strong and lasting. But her feelings for Kevin felt more grown-up some-how, more physical, more filled with lust and desire.

Tonight they continued sitting side by side at the bar for a little more than an hour, not talking, although she was aware, hyper-aware, of the close proximity of his body next to hers. It wasn't until there were voices outside, echoing across the lake that they looked at each other. In an instant they were on their feet, rush-ing down the stairs and racing toward the beach.

Stimpy and two other men in a small fishing boat were calling that they had found something. Another fishing boat used a spotlight to light up the area not far from the floating pier in the middle of the lake. Underwater recovery had long since gone once darkness fell and it had become too dangerous for the divers to search at night.

"Kevin." She grabbed his arm.

He covered her hand without a saying a word.

The crowd from the bar gathered on the beach. All eyes were focused on the fishing boats. No one talked. The only sounds were the murmurs of the men on the lake and the splashing of the grappling hooks hitting the water.

"What's going on?" a woman asked. "Did they find my Sara?" She pushed through the crowd. "Sara." She stopped at the edge of the water.

No one on the beach approached Sara's mother to comfort her or show their support. Perhaps they believed if they got too close, the tragedy would somehow feel more real or that it would somehow become contagious. It was as though an invisible force field surrounded the woman, pushing them away. After all, she was a newcomer to the lake and therefore not one of them.

People liked to believe they were immune to tragic accidents. This sort of thing happened to those who weren't paying attention, who were careless, who didn't take the signs posted along the fence seriously—SWIM AT YOUR OWN RISK.

The fishermen continued tossing grappling hooks and dragging the bottom where the snappers were congregating, feasting. Minutes passed. The waiting was excruciating, more than Jo could bear. She had to warn Sara's mother, prepare her for what she might see when they brought her little girl to shore. It had to be her because there was no one else.

"I'm going to talk with her," she said to Kevin, and slowly made her way across the beach to the lone woman standing at the water's edge.

Kevin called for Jo to come back, but she knew he wouldn't chase after her. He stopped chasing after her a long time ago.

CHAPTER THIRTEEN

The ballpark was the place to be after dinner since the Pavilion remained closed. Clusters of kids and their parents organized an impromptu baseball game. Most everyone's mother came to watch, setting up beach chairs along the first and third baselines. It was, after all, a recreational field for the lake community and not a regulation ballpark where bleachers might have been erected. Families brought their own bats and balls and mitts. The Needle-meyer twins brought the bases.

Megan sat next to her mother, close to one of the dugouts. Side by side you could see the resemblance between the two. Both wore their blond hair parted straight down the middle. Their skin was pink from the sun. Their eyelids were covered in the same blue eye shadow that made Caroline cringe. Their nails were painted pink. Mr. Roberts's dark complexion and hairy arms were a sharp contrast in comparison. He stepped forward. "I'll be the umpire."

Some of the other fathers took up positions as first- and third-base coaches. Johnny was made captain of one of the teams, and Chris the other. Johnny played baseball for the varsity team in high school back home, although he rarely talked about the game or bragged about how good he was with lake friends. "It isn't cool," he said to Caroline once when she asked him why.

In ways it was true what he had said. It wasn't cool. Home was home, and when they were at the lake for a few weeks every summer, well, the lake was the lake, and you didn't mix the two. It was as though they were a part of two separate worlds, straddling a bridge between their school and their lake friends, neither of which were meant to be crossed.

She liked to think she was standing on sacred ground at the lake, where the outside world—in her case, school and home—weren't welcome. Cell phones were shoved in back pockets and forgotten. Video games and the Internet were no longer distractions. "It's how it should be," Gram said. "You kids are doing what you're supposed to be doing—playing outside face-to-face with other kids."

But Johnny was a good ballplayer, better than good, whether he was home or at the lake. There had been talk of possible scholarships to colleges if he was interested. Caroline didn't know how he felt about it one way or the other. They didn't talk about things in their family, even good things, accolades, and achievements. Everything in her family was one big secret.

"Caroline, you're at third," Johnny said.

A couple of the older boys protested when Johnny handpicked Caroline to play. "She's a girl," they said. "Girls can't play baseball."

Johnny looked at her. "You okay with hardball?"

She nodded and adjusted the cap on her head. She was good enough to play baseball with the boys. She knew it, but she was surprised her brother thought so too.

"She can handle it," Johnny said to the other boys. His faith in her ability overwhelmed her. Maybe he wasn't all that bad for a brother.

They were short a few players. "I'll pitch for both teams," the Needlemeyer's father said. Mr. Roberts volunteered to be both umpire and catcher. Yes, there was a potential conflict with a play at home plate, but there was a level of trust between the kids and their parents that the game would be played fairly.

There was one boy, Jeff, who Caroline didn't know. His family had arrived at the lake for the first time that morning. Johnny picked him to be on their team. "Can you play both center and right field?" he asked.

"I can." Jeff was tall, and his long legs could cover a lot of ground. He looked to be around the same age as Caroline.

Megan pulled Caroline aside before the start of the game and laid claim on him. "He's a babe," she said. Caroline rolled her eyes. *Whatever.*

At one point, an older boy on Chris's team smacked a line drive down the third baseline. Caroline got her glove out just in time for the ball to slap her palm in the center of the mitt where she pinched it tightly, the sting tearing through the leather and up her arm. She wanted to throw the mitt to the ground and shake off the pain, jump around, and yell. Instead she tossed the ball to first base like a pro, pretending it didn't hurt, feeling not only her brother's but all the boys' eyes on her, especially Chris's.

Johnny punched his fist into his mitt. "All right. One out. Two to go," he said.

Between innings, Caroline sat with Megan and Mrs. Roberts rather than in the dugout with Johnny and the team, although they stopped bellyaching about her presence once they saw what she could do. She was part of them, but she wasn't one of them. It was the best way she could explain her feelings at the time.

Twice Megan squealed when a foul ball flew her way. She ducked and flapped her hands *like a girl*, Caroline thought. Maybe Megan did it to get Jeff's attention. But it was that kind of behavior that gave girls a bad rap when it came to sports. Johnny hit two balls out of the park. Everyone hooted and hollered. He shrugged.

The game lasted an hour and a half before it became too dark to see the ball clearly. They called it quits before anyone got hurt. Caroline felt good about her performance. She had stopped every ground ball that had been hit her way. She had thrown the ball to first base with accuracy and speed. But okay, her batting needed improvement.

In the end Chris's team had won nine to seven. The sun set, and most of the adults fled to their perspective cabins once the mosquitoes arrived. The kids hung around afterward, reliving the highlights, poking fun at the mishaps, and extending the fun for a few minutes more.

Johnny patted Caroline's shoulder. "Good game, Caroline." She felt an enormous amount of gratitude, and she'd never admit it out loud to anyone, but she really did love her brother.

The Needlemeyer twins collected the bases. The remaining bats and mitts were plucked from the ground. Gram had been right. A baseball game was just what they had needed. They had all but forgotten about the scene at the lake and the drowning girl. At least until Adam walked onto the field. He was out of breath. His hand covered his skinny chest. They gathered around him— Caroline, Johnny, Chris, Megan, the Needlemeyer twins, even the Chitney girls. Jeff, the newcomer, lingered on the perimeter.

"I think they found her," Adam said.

For a moment no one moved. No one uttered a word.

Megan's eyebrows shot up. She looked at Jeff. Perhaps she saw this as an opportunity to talk with him. She stepped away, cornering him really, and filled him in on the events from the last few days.

Caroline twisted a string on her mitt, struggling with indecision to stay at the ballpark or head down to the lake. She supposed it was like a fire or car accident where it was impossible to keep away, to not want to go and look. And still she stayed rooted to her spot among the others.

"We might as well go down and see what's going on," one of the Chitney girls said, and tugged on Johnny's arm.

Johnny and Chris and the two girls headed in the direction of the woods to the path that led straight to the parking lot and beach. Megan stood next to Jeff, obviously waiting to see what he would do.

Caroline hesitated a moment or two before chasing after Johnny, trying to catch up. "Wait for me," she called, yet knowing he wouldn't. It was dark and darker still under the hundred-year-old trees. She ran blindly, using the mitt on her left hand as a shield against the small branches whipping in front of her face. Cougar barked. She cursed herself for not having a treat to toss to him. Once, she looked over her shoulder, wondering if Megan or Adam or the new boy, Jeff, had followed, but she didn't hear anyone behind her. She imagined they decided to take the Lake Road. She'd beat them there.

She reached the parking lot and slowed to a walk. A large spotlight lit up two boats in the middle of the lake. Men's voices, deep and muffled, carried across the water. Crickets buzzed. She made her way through the smattering of vehicles and reached the dock where both Chris and Johnny and the girls stood. Her heart raced from the running, the excitement, the fear.

Johnny glanced at her but turned his eyes back to the water, his arm secured around one of the girl's waists. The other sister latched onto Chris. Caroline stood on the opposite side of him, her arm brushing up against his. He smelled like dirt and sweat and sweetness all at once, making her legs weak.

A crowd formed on the beach. She thought she saw her father. He was taller than most of the other men. Yes, she was sure it was him. His right shoulder sagged whenever he stood for long periods of time. And like everybody else, he stared at the scene on the lake.

She spied her mother at the water's edge, far from the crowd. Her mother's long wavy hair blew in the breeze. Another woman stood next to her. She believed the woman to be Sara's mother. She couldn't be sure. She wondered where Sara's father might be.

Megan, Adam, the twins, and Jeff walked into the parking lot. They headed in Caroline's direction. Caroline took a small step away from Chris before Megan and the others reached the dock and joined them. The last thing she wanted was for Megan to suspect she liked him.

"Did I miss anything?" Megan asked.

Caroline shook her head.

A woman approached their little group on the dock. It wasn't until she was close that Caroline recognized her as Chris's mother. Caroline knew who she was but never had any reason to talk with her. Besides, there was something unapproachable about her that made Caroline shy away. It had something to do with the expression on her face, hard and edgy, but sad, too.

The sheriff's vehicle drove into the lot followed by one of his deputies. They got out of their cars and gestured toward the lake. Someone on the beach shouted, "They got something! They're bringing it up!"

Caroline's breathing came in short spurts. She wasn't sure what she was feeling: fear, curiosity, dread, or some combination of all three. Dried sweat clung to her skin. Goosebumps broke out across her arms and legs. She held her mitt close to her chest as the grappling hooks emerged from the water.

CHAPTER FOURTEEN

Jo crossed her arms against the cool breeze coming off the water. The wet sand stuck to her feet and flip-flops. The mosquitoes buzzed around her ears. Now that she was standing next to Sara's mother, she didn't know what to say. So rather than say anything, she stood in silent support. Somehow it was enough.

When the grappling hooks submerged a second time, the scene on the lake became quiet.

"He had to go to work," Sara's mother, Patricia, said of her husband. "I know how that sounds. Just horrible. Doesn't it?" She shook her head. "Just dreadful."

Jo didn't respond, but it *did* sound awful. What kind of man left his wife at a time like this, knowing his little girl had drowned, that her body was still out there?

Patricia continued. "He's always working. Seventy, eighty hours a week. He doesn't understand what a monster he's being. He doesn't. He didn't even know his little girl. He didn't know how she painted with watercolors for hours. Or how her face lit up whenever she heard the words *ice cream*. Or how, when she wrapped her arms around your neck and hugged you tight, you felt like the luckiest person in the world."

Jo reached for Patricia's hand and held it. Neither one allowed their gaze to stray from the lake. A few seconds passed in silence.

"It wasn't supposed to turn out this way. It was supposed to be the best vacation Sara and I had ever had. It was supposed to be fun for the two of us. But I turned my back on her. I never should've turned my back. It was that damn umbrella. That stupid, broken umbrella. I wasn't paying attention," she said. "I should've been paying attention. It happened so quickly."

Jo nodded but was unable to speak, to offer comforting words. What could she say? What could anyone say? She understood better than anyone about guilt. Regret. If she could go back in time, she'd fix things with Billy. She'd say she was sorry. She had never meant to hurt him.

But you couldn't go back no matter how many times you replayed in your mind the event that brought you to this point, the things you should've, could've, and would've done rather than what you did do. Jo knew that Patricia would rewind those minutes of that day over and over for the rest of her life, how Sara was by her side and then suddenly she wasn't.

There was a flurry of activity on one of the boats. She turned toward Patricia. For a second there was something familiar about her as though Jo had seen her before, and the shadow of a distant memory flitted across her mind.

"Listen to me," Jo said. Her words came out in a rush. "It's not going to be easy to see her. She's not going to look like she did. The snappers." She paused. "She's been in the lake for a long time." Jo couldn't continue. The words caught in her throat.

Patricia nodded. But Jo was sure Patricia didn't understand what she was trying to say. It wasn't that Sara's body would be pale and bloated and lifeless. It was that she was going to look so much worse than Patricia could ever imagine.

The boat veered toward the shore. Patricia took off running toward the pier on the other side of the beach where it was headed. Jo followed at a much slower pace. None of the other onlookers moved. She noticed Kevin in the back of the crowd. She felt his eyes on her, following her every step, but he kept his distance. He was good at keeping his distance when it mattered most.

The sheriff and his deputy strode to the pier, where Patricia was waiting for the fishermen. Jo stood several feet behind them. When the boat docked, one of the men shook his head. "We're sorry."

"No!" Patricia cried out. She lunged toward the boat. The deputy grabbed her arms and held her back.

"No," the fisherman said. "I mean, I'm sorry, it's not your little girl."

Stimpy picked up a six-foot eel and tossed it onto the beach without thinking twice about how it might be received. Jo looked away. *Idiot*, she whispered. The eel's skin was shredded, its flesh ripped and torn and full of holes.

Patricia turned her head away, wriggling free from the deputy. She stumbled. The sheriff caught her.

"What happened to it?" Patricia asked him.

"Snappers," the sheriff said. "Get her out of here," he said to his deputy.

The deputy took Patricia by the elbow and guided her across the beach to the parking lot, far away from the scene. Her sobs cut across the night air.

A few people from the bar came forward now that Patricia had gone. Someone said, "Would you look at the size of that thing?"

"It's a big one," Stimpy said, and nudged it with his foot. "We stock them in these waters, but I've never seen one this big. The biggest I've ever seen is a four- or five-footer."

By this time everyone on the beach came forward to see the fish, even Kevin. He stood next to Jo. His hands were shoved deep into his pockets. Caroline, Megan, and a couple of their friends appeared from across the way. They stopped to stare at the dead fish.

Heil walked onto the pier and stood next to the sheriff.

"I didn't agree to this," the sheriff said to him. "I won't agree to this."

Heil slapped the sheriff on the shoulder. "I'll take care of it."

"You better," the sheriff said, and strode to his car, where the deputy and Patricia were waiting.

Stimpy and the other fisherman fumbled with the caged snappers on the boat.

"How many in there?" Heil pointed to the traps.

"Four." Stimpy scratched his head. "Some of them got tangled, and we had to cut the lines."

"Well, we're going to need more." He motioned to the lake. "You see how big it is out there. We need more boats, too. You tell the other fishermen, I want every last one of them on the lake. We've got to find this girl."

"Yeah, okay, okay," Stimpy said.

"You hear me?" Heil addressed the crowd behind him. "We're all in agreement?"

There was a collective rumble from the group. Jo and Kevin exchanged a look.

When no one else spoke up, Heil spit in the general direction of Stimpy and the mutilated eel. "Now get that damn thing off my beach."

CHAPTER FIFTEEN

Caroline spent another night tossing and turning, tangled in sheets. Her dreams were filled with snakes and eels and disfigured fish. And in the center, amidst the slithering and thrashing prey, was the rock behind Chris's cabin, the one painted with the initials *J+B*.

Somehow the image of the heart, the initials, disturbed her more than the mangled fish. She was certain it was another piece of the puzzle that had to do with her mother and Billy. Maybe if she learned the secret of Billy, she could end whatever it was that haunted her mother. What she wanted most and longed to know was what made her mother run. But her mother wasn't running, not in the dream. She was swimming, farther and farther away, all while Caroline was drowning in the lake.

Her eyes snapped open, and she sat up in bed. A cool breeze pulled the curtains against the window screen. Light from the moon cut across the floor and the far wall. She could hear her father snoring in the room next door, the sound comforting. She had been dreaming. It was only a dream. But it wasn't.

She leaned back against the pillow, too afraid to close her eyes, fearing the images that swam behind them in the dark. She wasn't going to get any more sleep tonight. Willow's branches scratched against the side of the cabin, beckoning her to come out and play.

She tossed the covers aside. After making sure her bedroom door was closed tight, she lifted the screen and climbed out. She crawled into the crook of the trunk between two big branches about a third of the way up the tree. It was big enough for her to fit comfortably, stretching her legs on the thick branch in front of her and maintaining her balance in the pocket. It was better than any deer stand that had been constructed in the woods on the other side of the colony in the open field far from the cabins.

In summers past she and Megan, the twins, and Adam would hike to the field and play games in the deer stands. They'd use sticks for guns and knives, pretend to track animals, play King of the Mountain. Other times they'd hike farther into the woods where a tree had fallen across the creek that fed the lake. They'd swing on vines, balance on the fallen tree, and hang out far away from the jeering of Johnny and Chris's gang and where the grown-ups could never find them. They'd catch crawfish and salamanders and frogs. They'd make mud pies and build stick huts.

Caroline wished they were doing those things again this summer. What she wouldn't give to go back to the way things were between her and Megan, before Megan went all girly and goofy over boys.

She thought about Chris and felt funny inside, warm and icky at the same time. The way he looked at her when she caught the line drive down the third baseline made her heart flutter. It was as though he were seeing her for the first time, and it made her cheeks burn.

She willed herself to think of something else and pulled her legs to her chest, resting her chin on top of her knees. The willow's long fingerlike branches rocked in the breeze. The leaves rustled softly, gently lulling her. She leaned back against the trunk. Her thoughts settled. Her eyelids grew heavy. She fought to keep them open for a moment or two before giving in. What could it hurt to rest her eyes for a few minutes?

She was unaware of time passing. The wind picked up and the swinging branches roused her. She wondered how long she was asleep when she heard the sound of footsteps.

Who's there? she asked.

A twig snapped.

Hello? she said, squinting into the shadows below.

A little girl appeared underneath the tree. She was wearing the same yellow-and-pink polka dot bathing suit as Sara had worn that day on the beach. Water dripped from her braids down the front of her chest. Bits and pieces of her arms and legs were missing as though someone had taken an eraser to her limbs. *Sara?*

Caroline rubbed her eyes. She must be dreaming. Her spine pressed into the cold hard trunk. Her right leg tingled from sleep. The wind blew her hair across her face, the strands sticking to her lips. She swiped them away from her mouth.

What are you doing here? Everyone is looking for you.

Don't let them find me, Sara said in a whispery voice that seemed to blow with the wind.

Who don't you want to find you?

I want my mommy.

Caroline's body shivered from the breeze. She was confused. Was she dreaming? *Wake up,* she told herself. *You need to wake up.*

Sara, she said, hearing her voice inside her chest just before she felt herself falling, the kind of falling that happens in dreams. She hit the ground with a thud. The air in her chest burst from her lungs in a whoosh.

When she opened her eyes, her arms were splayed in front of

her. Her left cheek was pressed in the dirt. Her legs were spread wide. Leaves and twigs stuck to her skin. She sat up, feeling dizzy. She couldn't catch her breath. Her chest constricted. She sucked in, once, twice, and finally, finally, her chest opened and her lungs filled with air.

She looked up at Willow. She had never fallen from the tree before. She had never had the wind knocked out of her. Slowly, she stood and rubbed her sore shoulder before brushing off the debris from her hands and knees. The hem of her nightgown was torn and hanging on the ground.

It was almost dawn. The leaves were covered in dew. She had been in the tree for longer than she had thought. She slipped back through the window, pulled her nightgown over her head, and shoved it into the back of a drawer. Trembling, she put on a T-shirt and shorts and crawled into bed. It wasn't until she was buried under the covers that she curled into a ball and thought about what she had seen and heard in her dream. It had felt so real. The fall had been real. Her torn nightgown and aching shoulder were proof.

She was scared, but she couldn't tell Gram or her parents what had happened. They would be angry with her for crawling out of the window in the first place. They would say she was stupid for falling asleep in a tree. And what if her father insisted on fixing the screen? Or worse, what if he forbid her to ever climb the tree again?

And even though she was frightened, her mind raced ahead, turning over the dream and what Sara had said. She couldn't let Stimpy and his men follow the snappers and do to Sara what they had done to the eel.

She closed her eyes. Somehow, someway she'd help Sara find her mommy. And maybe in the process, Caroline would find her mother too.

CHAPTER SIXTEEN

The lake turned into a spectacle of rowboats, motorboats, and canoes. Every local fisherman and their kin were out on the water. Stimpy and his men must've trapped two dozen or more of the turtles overnight. It was the only sense Kevin could make of the scene.

Day four of the drowned little girl, and all that remained of the original recovery team was the single watercraft and three crew members. The rest of the team was called to another location in the Poconos, another tragedy, this one occurring along the Delaware River. It had been all over the eleven-o'clock news. A couple of teenagers had been tubing down the Delaware when one of them got sucked under by the current. Kevin had been watching TV with Gram in the cramped living room. Jo had already gone to bed. It had been an early night for everyone after the drama on the beach with the fishermen and the eel.

The word at the lake was that the underwater recovery unit from the next county over would've pitched in and covered the Delaware River drowning, but they were tied up in another recovery farther north.

Welcome to summer in the Poconos, Kevin thought, *where the water was refreshing and cool—and deadly.* He shoved his hands into his pockets. He was standing on the dock next to the parking lot for a little more than half an hour. The sun burned the tops of his feet and the tips of his ears. Sweat dripped between his shoulder blades. His T-shirt was moist and sticky.

The lake water rocked with chaos. The ducks honked their grievances. Men shouted when they felt sure they had found something. Stimpy and his crew scrambled from fishing boat to fishing boat, pulling up drudge and carrion off the bottom, but nothing of the little girl was recovered. It was midafternoon, and they had been at it for several hours. All the while, the underwater recovery team went about their search methodically, professionally.

The Pavilion doors were flung open. Songs played on the jukebox, and bells rang from pinball machines. Two or three families sat on the beach and played in the sand with their young children. The floating pier was surrounded by boats rather than teenagers. The diving boards were empty. And yet, the strangest part was that on a day as hot as today, not one person entered the water. Heil could open the beach, but he couldn't force people to swim.

Kevin raked his fingers through his hair. The scene was all too familiar. But he wasn't thinking about why it was familiar. He wasn't thinking about Billy and the five long days of searching the lake for his body. Instead he was thinking about Jo when she was sixteen years old. He had been standing on this same dock under the hot sun. Jo had been sitting alone on the back steps that led to the upstairs bar. Her dark hair glistened in the sunlight. Her head tilted to the side as though she were deep in thought.

When she looked his way, he lifted his hand and waved. At first she didn't acknowledge him and he had been hurt. He considered walking away, heading back to his parents' cabin— to do what? Sulk? Listen to his dad berate him, how he wasn't tough enough, how he was a pansy for playing his guitar all day long, how he'd never get lucky with a girl? Not like Billy. Now there was a boy who would grow to be a man's man.

While he debated his next move, she started walking in his direction. His pulse quickened. He knew Billy was gone for the day, off with his sister, Dee Dee, to visit family in New York. The closer Jo got, the faster his heart raced. By the time she stepped onto the dock, he was sure his chest would burst wide open.

For a moment neither of them spoke. Kevin had never been alone with Jo before. In all the summers he had been coming to the lake, Billy had been a permanent fixture between them. As for Eddie and Sheila, he wasn't sure where they were nor did he care.

Although, now that he had Jo alone, he realized he had no idea what to say to her.

"What are you doing?" she asked.

"Nothing." He couldn't take his eyes off her.

She touched his hand. Her skin was soft and warm. "Come on," she said.

He walked alongside her, aware of her body next to his, the curve of her hips, the rise and fall of her chest, the casual swing of her arms. He supposed he knew where they were heading. He shouldn't have been surprised. The last few days they had stared at each other, sometimes for long stretches of time. He'd catch her watching him, going out of her way to brush up against him. And once, she ran her fingers through his hair while he was playing his guitar. Billy had laughed. "Careful, Kev," he said. "She'll steal your heart."

Billy had never felt threatened by Kevin. Why should he? Why would Jo want Kevin when she had him? Every girl at the lake had wanted Billy. And Jo had never shown the slightest interest in Kevin.

Until now, he reminded himself, walking so close to her, their hips bumped. So what had changed? Or maybe it was wishful thinking on his part. He owed it to himself to find out and Billy, be damned, because it was too late. She had stolen Kevin's heart a long time ago.

Kevin followed her lead and, as he suspected, or rather hoped, she wound her way around the bend on the opposite side of the lake to the private beaches far from the crowd. She slipped behind *Hawkes'* cabin, Billy's cabin, sly and surefooted, and crept through the woods. He followed, pausing briefly when he noticed the painted rock with the initials *J+B*. He felt the first pinch of guilt, but not enough for him to stop and turn around. He had to be alone with her and if not now then maybe never. He had to know what she was thinking, feeling.

Neither one spoke. They stepped onto the private beach in front of the only cabin that wasn't rented for the summer. Jo turned to face him. He opened his mouth to say something, but what? He didn't know. *Jesus*, he thought. She was Billy's girl. What was he doing?

"Jo," he said.

She touched his lips with her finger. "Don't say anything," she said.

He longed to put his arms around her and kiss her. God, the things he wanted to do to her. It took all his strength to keep his hands at his sides. She was his best friend's girl.

She leaned in close. She smelled like suntan lotion and bubble gum. He closed his eyes when she whispered, her breath hot in his ear, "Do you want me?"

He swallowed hard. "Please, Jo," he begged. "Don't tease me."

He was afraid he wouldn't be able to stop himself, that is, if she ever let him start.

"Answer the question."

"Don't." His voice trembled. "Don't do this to me."

"Just answer the question. Do you want me?"

"Yes," he croaked.

She tossed her head back and laughed. "Oh, Kevin." She stepped back, pulled her T-shirt off, and slipped out of her shorts, revealing the red bikini she often wore that summer. He would dream about her in that bikini, waking up drenched in sweat, his erection bursting in his shorts.

She stood still, allowing him to soak up every inch of her, the most beautiful creature he had ever seen. She reached around her back and untied her top, letting it fall to the ground. She slowly edged the bottoms down her hips until they dropped at her feet. She moved to within an inch of him. Her body was so close, so close. He couldn't stop from trembling.

"Jo," he groaned.

The sound of a car door slamming jolted Kevin from the memory, bringing him back to the dock, the hot sun, and the fishing boats on the lake. The sheriff had gotten out of his patrol car, and he was looking out at the water. Heil emerged from the Pavilion, hand outstretched to greet him. The two exchanged words and made their way toward the dock.

The sheriff tipped his hat as he approached. Kevin gave a terse nod.

"Stick around," the sheriff said to him as he walked by. "Something came up, and I may have a few questions for you."

CHAPTER SEVENTEEN

Caroline hopped on her bicycle and sped down the dirt hill. She paused briefly to check for traffic before crossing onto Lake Road and making her way toward the Pavilion. The doors were wide open for business, but the place was deserted by summer standards. Johnny and his gang weren't sitting on the steps like they normally did. She wondered for a moment where they might be. She continued on through the parking lot and stopped at the dock, spewing pebbles when the back tire of the bike kicked out from under her, almost throwing her off.

In a glance she knew she was too late. Stimpy and his men were already on the lake along with the underwater recovery team, although they didn't appear to be working together. Several other fishing boats crowded the area around the floating pier as though they were waiting for orders. Ducks milled around the dock, honking at all the commotion.

The hot sun scorched her shoulders and back as she surveyed the scene. She felt a tightening in her chest, thinking about her dream, somehow feeling as though she had let Sara down. She had overslept, having been awake much of the night. It was well past noon. She vowed not to make the same mistake tomorrow if given the chance, although exactly what her plan was to help Sara still lingered somewhere in the back of her mind, not fully formed as of yet.

She pedaled back to the Pavilion and dropped her bike beside the stairs. Inside was dark and cool and quieter than usual. A family of three sat at a booth near the snack stand. The jukebox finished playing a record. Two men racked balls for a game of pool. A scraping noise came from the side wall near one of the pinball machines. She looked behind it and found Adam.

"What are you doing?" she asked.

"I'm looking for something." He shrugged.

Caroline smiled. "You're still hoping to find the horse's bit, aren't you?" she said. "I'm sure Heil got rid of it. And even if he didn't, I doubt he'd hide it behind a pinball machine."

"I know." Adam shrugged again. "But it was worth a shot," he said. "Besides, I'm not going out there." He pointed outside. "My folks are sitting on the beach. Heil made them. But he can't make me. Not with that girl still out there. No way."

Megan stomped through the open doors. "God, it's hot," she said, and smoothed her blond hair. She was in full makeup, but it looked subdued in the dim lights or perhaps most of it had melted in the heat. "This sucks. What are we going to do?" she asked.

It didn't matter that Heil had opened the beach. The kids had made an unspoken rule that you didn't swim in the lake while Sara was still out there somewhere. Sara had been one of them, whether they had known her well or not. An invisible line had been drawn separating them, the kids, from the adult world. It had always been there since the day Caroline was born, but she never felt it more sharply than now.

And those same adults using the snappers to find Sara seemed cruel, although she couldn't say what they should be doing to make it right. She just knew the way they were going about it was wrong. Opening the beach and expecting people to swim was wrong.

She looked at Megan and Adam. She couldn't do anything about the heat or the fact the lake was off-limits, but maybe she could talk her friends into going for a bike ride.

"I know what we could do," she said. "Let's go to the Country Store." She searched her pockets for change. Megan pulled a couple of dollars from her back pocket.

Adam stared at the folded bills. "Did you rob a bank?"

Megan shrugged. "Babysitting," she said.

They pooled their money. Adam contributed a couple of pennies and a nickel. Caroline had two dollars in quarters. Together with Megan's stash, they had almost nine bucks.

"Get your bikes and I'll meet you by the steps."

Adam took off running. Megan held Caroline back. "Let's ditch Adam," she said. "And ride our bikes past Jeff's cabin."

"What for?" she asked.

Megan rolled her eyes. "God, Caroline. You know what for. To see if he's around. Maybe he wants to hang out with us."

Megan looked so hopeful, Caroline couldn't say no. "Fine. We can ride past his cabin, but Adam's coming with us."

"But he's a baby," Megan whined.

Who was the baby? she thought but didn't say. She should want to do the things Megan wanted to do, but deep down all she wanted was to ride her bike and buy candy at the Country Store, same as Adam. Oh, and read a newspaper or two. "Adam's coming with us. I'm not going to ditch him."

Once they all had their bikes, they pedaled toward the colony. Adam kept asking where they were going, why they weren't going to the store.

"We have to do something first," Megan said in a snotty voice.

Caroline dropped back to ride next to Adam and let him know she didn't feel the same toward him as Megan did. Megan stopped and waited for them to catch up when they were close to Jeff's place.

"You go first," Megan said to Caroline.

"Why? It was your idea. You go first," she said.

"What are we doing?" Adam asked.

Megan sighed heavily. "Let's ride past together."

And off they went, riding their bikes past Jeff's cabin. Caroline couldn't believe she had agreed to this, feeling more stupid as each second passed. It didn't look like anyone was around much to her relief. Megan made a sudden U-turn and rode past again. Caroline and Adam followed.

"What are we doing?" Adam asked for a third time. "Aren't we going to the Country Store?"

"Yes," Caroline said. "We are." And she sped past Megan, heading straight out of the colony and onto Lake Road. Adam's little legs pedaled fast behind her. Megan reluctantly took up the rear.

Lake Road dipped and turned. The old oak and maple trees provided shady patches in-between long stretches of sunny hot macadam. Within fifteen minutes they reached the Country Store. The bell jingled above the screen door. Mrs. Nester looked over the top of her spectacles when they stepped inside. Adam headed straight for the candy aisle. Megan reached for a cola.

Caroline swiped her forehead with the back of her arm and pulled her baseball cap down to hide her eyes. She walked over to the newspaper stand feeling guilty and conspicuous, which was silly. It wasn't like she was going to steal anything. She plucked the latest *Lake Reporter* from the rack and read the front-page news about Sara. Very little was mentioned about her family other than her mother's name, Patricia Starr, and how it was Sara's first time vacationing at the lake. The article went on to mention the warning signs posted about swimming, and the lengths the community was going through to bring closure to the family, but the details about *how* the community was going about it were noticeably left out.

"Can I help with you something?" Mrs. Nester asked.

"Oh no, thank you." Caroline returned the paper to the rack.

Megan wandered down the makeup aisle. Caroline joined Adam in the candy aisle. Together they picked out bubble gum with the baseball cards, butterscotch suckers, and jelly candies. The entire time Caroline kept thinking about the article in the paper and Mrs. Starr. She looked over her shoulder at Mrs. Nester. Hidden behind her spectacles were sharp beady eyes watching every movement they made. Caroline didn't know what made her turn around and approach the woman. Courage? She doubted it. More like an annoying itch she couldn't help but scratch.

"Do you have any old *Lake Reporter*s?" she asked. "Maybe ones from other important events that happened around the lake?"

Mrs. Nester narrowed her eyes. "I might. Anything specific you're looking for?"

By this time both Adam and Megan had approached the counter and stood next to Caroline. It seemed she had garnered everyone's attention. She pulled the visor of her baseball cap down a little more.

"I was wondering about other lake drownings."

Mrs. Nester peered at Caroline over the top of her spectacles. "Now what would you want with that information? Are you looking to cause trouble? Because that's exactly what you'll get, poking around in that kind of news." She glanced over Caroline's shoulder as though she was making sure they were the only customers in the store.

Mrs. Nester continued. "Folks around here don't like to talk about certain things. It's bad for business."

Caroline put the candy she was holding onto the counter in front of her. "Yes, ma'am. I don't want to cause any trouble. It's just—" She stopped, thinking how to explain.

Megan and Adam dumped their loot onto the counter too. Everyone waited for Caroline to continue, but she didn't know how to tell them it had to do with her mother. She had to know why her mother kept running away from her. It made no sense when she put it this way, but she knew her mother had a secret, and it had something to do with Billy and drownings. If she could figure it out, maybe she could help her mother and she would stop running.

Mrs. Nester rang up their order. When she finished, she told Caroline to wait. She must've seen something on Caroline's face—perhaps pity. Whatever it was, she disappeared behind a door at the back of the store, returning a few minutes later with a pile of newspapers.

"Take these around back. I've got a couple of chairs on the patio. Leave the papers on the table when you're done. If anyone asks, you didn't get them from me."

Caroline took the papers and thanked Mrs. Nester repeatedly.

"Go on now, get, before I change my mind," Mrs. Nester said.

As soon as they were outside, Megan complained. She didn't want to read old newspapers. She didn't see the point. It was like doing homework, and it was summertime. She wasn't going to read anything she didn't have to. And Adam was more interested in the bubblegum and baseball cards.

They settled on Mrs. Nester's back patio. The sun blared, but at least they were in the shade under the trees. Megan took out her new lip gloss and smacked her lips while Caroline sifted through the papers. The black print rubbed off on her fingertips. She scanned the article about the boating accident and the man who had drowned, the one she had witnessed three summers ago. She dug farther into the pile and pulled out the last paper in the stack, dated July 1997.

With trembling hands, she shook the paper open, the headline reading: *Sixteen-Year-Old Local Boy Drowns.* She held the paper inches from her nose and inspected the blurry black-and-white photo of a teenage boy. There was something she recognized in him, a look or coolness she sensed in some boys, definitely Chris, maybe Johnny. But it was hard to gauge something like that from just a grainy photo. She continued to read.

Sixteen-year-old William J. Hawke disappeared late Monday night after last being seen on the beach outside the lake Pavilion by his friend Kevin Knowles police said. After an extensive search lasting five days, his body was recovered near the floating pier in the middle of the lake. It is speculated William "Billy" Hawke went swimming alone that night after his friend had gone home. The drowning was ruled an accident. Memorial services to be announced.

The mention of her father's name came as a complete surprise, and Caroline immediately shoved the paper under the pile. She wiped her blackened fingertips on her shorts.

"Are you finished now?" Megan asked, irritated about having to wait.

Caroline nodded, her thoughts reeling.

"What did you find?" Adam asked.

"Nothing," she said, not wanting to talk about it. "Let's go." She left the papers on the table like Mrs. Nester had asked, and walked to the front of the store, where their bikes lay on the ground.

Adam handed her a couple of baseball cards. "Here," he said. "I already have these."

"Thanks." She took them absently and climbed onto her bike.

She did the math and yes, both her parents would've been sixteen in 1997, the same age as Billy. Her father had known Billy all along. They were friends.

A heavy weight settled onto her shoulders, and a sense of betrayal swarmed her chest. Was her father in on her mother's secret too? What were her parents hiding and why?

CHAPTER EIGHTEEN

Dee Dee stepped outside and gazed at the frenzy of fishing boats dragging the lake. *Goddamn Heil*, she thought, and bent down to pick up the empty beer cans from the night before. There were at least a dozen or more scattered across the porch floor. She dropped the first armful into the recycling bin, catching sight of the sheriff making his way across the yard.

He tipped his hat in greeting. "It must have been some party," he said, eying the cans still on the floor at her feet.

"Hardly." She picked up several more empties, not caring whether he believed she had had a party of twenty or the truth, a party of one.

"Well, I'm glad I caught you." He motioned to her white scrubs. She worked in one of the few hospitals where the nurses still wore white. Most wore different colors—maroon, blue, green, hideous flowered prints. She preferred the crisp, clean look of white. No muss. No fuss.

"What brings you by?" she asked. "I hope you're here to give me some good news."

The sun showed the lines on the sheriff's face. He was older than her by at least fifteen years, but not that old that he didn't cross her mind in ways that maybe he shouldn't. And yet, it wasn't so strange for her to think of him in a romantic way. After all, he was as much of an outsider here as she was, him being the sheriff and her being the woman whose brother had drowned. She supposed it was only natural for the two of them to seek each other out.

"I was able to get my hands on a preliminary report," he said, getting straight to business, which she appreciated. "It's what we thought. The snappers took the bones. But they did find something I think is curious." His hand was resting on his sidearm. His hat was pulled low to shade his eyes against the sun.

Her body stilled. The muscle in her right bicep twitched.

He continued. "Did your brother hurt his arm that you know of? Or mention anything to you about injuring it?"

"No," she said, and then took a moment to think. "No." She was certain. "He wasn't hurt. He would've told me if he were. He didn't keep anything from me. Why? What's this about?"

"They found a fracture on the ulna. They're calling it a nightstick fracture. It happens when something hits the forearm, say in a hard fall or when the forearm strikes something with a lot of force. Either way, it was enough to limit the use of his arm."

Her heart tumbled, rolling over inside her chest. "What does this mean? Does this prove it wasn't an accident?"

"It's hard to say at this point, but I think it's worth looking into."

She crushed one of the empty cans still in her hand. She had waited so long for something, anything to prove her brother's drowning wasn't his own doing. He didn't just slip and fall and crack his head like everyone wanted to believe. And now to discover he had a fractured arm, too. "And you think this contributed to his death?"

"Maybe. Maybe not. I think the question we need to ask is

how he fractured it," he said. "I wanted to confirm with you first that he didn't injure it prior to that night."

"He didn't."

"Are you sure?"

"I'm sure."

"All right, I'll start asking around and see if anybody knows anything about how he might've hurt it."

"What makes you think someone is going to talk now?" She tossed the crushed can into the bin and folded her arms, hiding the large knuckles of her fists.

"Maybe someone knew something then and didn't think it was relevant at the time."

"But it is relevant."

"I think so."

"Will you question Jo?" If Dee Dee trusted anything, it was her instincts. She had sensed something was wrong between Billy and Jo before they had ever left the cabin that night. Did they have a bad fight? Was that how he fractured his arm? She had always believed Jo knew more about what had happened than she was saying.

"I'll talk with everyone who had contact with him," he said. "But you have to understand, it's only a preliminary report. I'm still waiting for the DNA results. Once I have that final report, I'll make the decision whether or not to officially reopen the case."

She looked away from him, not wanting him to see the agitation, the anger she was sure showed on her face. She was sick to death of waiting.

Perhaps he knew what she was thinking because he said, "I'll poke around to see what I can find out, but I'll need those results to make it official."

"What do you think happened to his arm?"

"I have a few guesses, but I can't build a case on conjecture."

"Right." She didn't like what he was telling her, where this was going. "So what happens if no one *opens up*?" She couldn't keep the sarcasm from her tone.

"Then we're back where we started more or less."

"So you're saying that finding my brother's bones only raises more questions about what happened to him."

"Yes and no. It's more information than we had previously." He hesitated. "Listen," he said. "Just be patient a little longer. Let me do my job. I've been doing this long enough to know that sooner or later the truth has a way of surfacing."

There was a ruckus on one of the fishing boats. Both Dee Dee and the sheriff turned to the sound.

"Nothing." Stimpy's voice carried across the water.

"What a goddamn mess," the sheriff said.

"Yes, it is." She checked her phone. "I have to get to work. Is there anything else?"

"That's all for now." The sheriff tipped his hat again and turned to walk away.

She started picking up the rest of the cans from the floor and stopped. "You'll let me know as soon as you hear anything," she called.

"You'll be the first."

Most people at the lake thought she was paranoid, delusional. A drunk. She never believed the sheriff was one of them. "Thank you, Sheriff."

He paused and looked back at her. "Do you think there will ever be a day when you call me Dave?"

She couldn't see his eyes under the shade of the hat, but she felt his stare through to her insides. She shook her head. "I doubt it."

After grabbing the keys from the cabin, Dee Dee got in the car and started the engine. If she didn't get moving, she was going to be late for work. She punched the steering wheel with her palm. *What the hell happened to you, Billy?* She threw the car in reverse and backed out of the parking space, catching sight of the sheriff's broad shoulders and lean stature. He was standing on the docks next to Heil waiting for the fishermen to come in off the water.

Dave. She quickly pushed the thought away. There was no point in daydreaming. It only led to disappointment when reality set in. And yet she couldn't help but think maybe, just maybe, the day would come when she would learn the truth about her brother, a day when she would be able to let go of all the anger she carried.

But until that day the sheriff would be the sheriff. And that was all that he would be.

CHAPTER NINETEEN

Jo slipped past the kitchen door and skirted through the living room, making as little noise as possible. She hoped to escape without bumping into anyone. She woke with a nagging feeling, and it had to do with Patricia, Sara's mother. She sensed it last night while talking with her on the beach. The feeling, or thought, of a memory was there, it was close, but still too far to grasp.

She paused outside the entranceway to the screened-in porch, brushed her hair with her fingers, thinking the back door was the quickest exit to get away, just away, without getting caught. She took two steps into the room and stopped next to a wicker rocking chair.

Gram was sitting in the middle of the floor, surrounded by boxes and odds and ends. Her white hair was messy from sleep. She was wearing her cleaning clothes, an old sweatshirt and jeans, the kind with an elastic waistband. There was a faraway look on her face. She didn't notice Jo standing nearby. Jo took a cautious step backward and turned to leave when Gram caught sight of her.

"Oh, good, you're up," Gram said. "I don't suppose you could stick around for a minute."

Jo closed her eyes before turning around and forcing a smile. "No, sorry. I'm on my way out." She was about to leave when Gram slumped forward, not a lot, but enough to cause concern. She maneuvered around an old lamp, a stack of books, and crouched on the floor next to her. "Are you okay?" She touched Gram's forearm. Her skin was cool.

"I'm a little tired today. That's all."

"Are you sure?" Close up, Gram looked pale.

"I'm fine." She waved her off. "It's just a lot of stuff to go through." Gram looked down at the photo album opened in her lap to a picture of Pop when he was a much younger man. The picture was in black-and-white. He was in a sailor's suit and sporting a crew cut, serving in the Navy at the tail end of the Vietnam War. Gram and Pop had married right out of high school before he had enlisted. She ran her finger over the old photograph. A sad smile crossed her lips.

"Pop was handsome," Jo said.

"He was dashing in his uniform," Gram said. "I remember seeing him in it for the first time." She brought her hand to her chest. "I was so proud and scared for him. That damned war."

Jo gave her arm a gentle squeeze. "But he never saw any action. He didn't have to fight. The war was ending."

"Thank God," Gram said, but she seemed miles away, lost in memories.

Jo envied her parents' marriage, the open way they had loved and respected each other. No marriage was perfect, of course, and there were times when Gram and Pop argued, followed by long stretches of silence, but they had always found their way back to each other. Jo wondered how they were able to balance the good with the bad and keep their love strong for so many years. She supposed it had to do with starting off in the right direction rather than buried in secrets the way *her* marriage had begun.

And yet, she reminded herself that her love for Kevin was just as strong as her parents' love for each other. It was just that sometimes her love was so tangled with guilt, it was hard to separate the two.

Gram continued to page through the photo album. Most of the pictures were taken before Jo had been born. Gram's eyelashes were wet with tears. It had been five years since Pop passed and still, at times like these, his death seemed to catch Gram by surprise.

"I miss him too," Jo said, and wiped a stray tear from her own eye.

She had been close to Pop ever since she was a little girl. She used to follow him around the house while he was doing chores—fixing the kitchen sink, changing the oil in the car, repairing the old washing machine. While he had worked, she would tell him stories, made-up bits and pieces from books or magazines, or she would act out scenes from the playground, or explain in lengthy detail the arts and crafts projects she had worked on in school. He would listen and ask questions as though whatever she was telling him was important when most of the time it was not. It was fair to say she had worshipped Pop and believed he could do no wrong. Even through adolescence, when she and Gram could hardly stand to be in the same room together, through all the arguing, she had maintained a close connection to Pop. That was until the summer she had turned sixteen years old, the summer Pop had learned she had gone ahead and gotten herself pregnant.

She had found out two weeks after Billy had drowned. She had missed her period. At first she had thought the stress she had been under and the grief had made her late. It had been reasonable. But after a few more days had passed and still no period, she had known without having to see the doctor. Her breasts had been sore and swollen more than usual, and her lower abdomen, although normally bloated around that time of the month, had felt different somehow. She had lain awake at night and sworn she had felt a fluttering in her belly as though the baby had already begun to move, to say, *Hey, here I am.*

Terminating the pregnancy hadn't ever been a consideration. How could she have killed his baby when she had been certain it had been conceived out of love? She had owed it to him, to herself, to see the pregnancy through.

Gram had shouted, cursed, and stomped her feet. "How could you do this? What were you thinking? What will people think? My God, do you even know who the father is?"

Jo had handled Gram's outrage with more ease than she had thought possible. Mostly because Gram hadn't asked anything that Jo hadn't asked herself. She could've taken the anger, the name-calling, the judgmental glares from Gram. It had been what Jo had expected from her. Gram was what Jo considered a "good girl," never having said or done anything to raise an eyebrow.

And Jo had known how to fight back against Gram's accusations, her old-school ways and beliefs about how a woman should conduct herself, about how she should understand her place in society, in a man's world. Jo was from a different generation, one that didn't care what men, or really anyone, thought, one that empowered women to be as outspoken as they wanted to be, to own their sexuality. She had wanted to be the one to define the person she would become. She had been free, and yet she had been reckless with that freedom. She had felt as though she had thrown it all away.

But after all the bickering and tough talk, it hadn't been Gram's reaction that had tortured Jo. It had been Pop's. What she had remembered most whenever she thought back to that time was the look of betrayal in his eyes. His faith in her had been shattered. He had said she was no longer his little girl, the girl he had thought he had known and loved. His opinion of his only daughter had changed for the worse. And she hadn't known how to tell him that she had let herself down too. That she had known all her dreams of getting out, living her own life, being free, were over. What she had needed from him was his support, for him to accept she had made a mistake, and that she loved her baby too much to ever turn back.

Gram closed the photo album and put it to the side, along with the memories it had conjured. They sat in silence until Jo slapped the tops of her legs and looked around.

"What are you going to do with all this stuff anyway?" she asked.

"Oh, I don't know," Gram said, and smoothed a white curl from her forehead. "It was just time to clean out the back closets and underneath the porch. No one's touched the stuff in years."

"Well," she said, feeling the day slipping through her hands, knowing she would now stay and help sort through boxes. Seeing Gram tired, the way she was hunched over on the floor, and the moistness in her eyes when she had paged through the photo album, loosened something inside Jo. The compassion had been absent between them for such a long time, but Jo had a sudden urge to tell Gram she was sorry for all the terrible ways she had disappointed her. The words were there on her tongue, and yet she couldn't force them out. She never could say what was in her heart. So instead she said, "Where do you want me to start?"

For the next few hours Jo pulled boxes of old records, books, and photo albums from the closet. She crawled underneath the porch and dragged broken beach chairs and torn umbrellas to the trash. All the while Gram did the sorting, keeping more than she had intended. Maybe it wasn't the right time after all.

Jo tossed the last of a bent plastic chair onto the junk pile in the yard. She was dirty and hot under the glaring sun. She brushed her hands on her shorts and smoothed her tousled hair. What she wouldn't give to jump into the cool lake water. The thought brought her full circle to Sara and her mother and the bones.

She rushed back into the cabin, letting the screen door slam behind her. "Let's call it quits," she said to Gram. She figured she had hauled enough trash for one day, and Gram should rest.

"But we're not done," Gram said.

I am, Jo thought, and left to go jump into the shower.

Within minutes Jo slipped into a clean T-shirt and shorts and made her way onto Lake Road, stopping once to remove a pebble from her flip-flop. When she reached the Pavilion, she wasn't surprised to find the doors wide open. Heil wouldn't keep his precious money-maker closed for four days, not four whole days.

She walked around the back of the Pavilion to the set of stairs that led to the bar. The parking lot was nearly empty, even though the beach was open. Small clusters of families scattered their chairs and blankets on the sand. Their oily bodies baked in the hot sun, but no one was swimming. How could they even if they had wanted? The lake was filled with two dozen or more fishing boats. She scoured the area for Patricia, Sara's mother, and searched the water for signs of underwater recovery. Where could they be? Who was running this crazy show? She groaned at the sight of Stimpy directing the chaos.

Kevin stepped off one of the docks. Something about his expression gave her pause. Slowly, she walked toward him.

"What's going on?" she asked.

"I'm not sure," he said.

Sheriff Borg leaned against a nearby pillar, drawing their attention.

"What the hell was going on out there?" the sheriff asked Heil, and motioned to the pier where the fishermen were now gathering. "They need to do this in a more organized manner."

Heil pulled the waistband of his shorts up around his large belly. "And how do you suggest they do that?"

"They need to be less conspicuous," the sheriff said. "Stick to early mornings or evenings. And make sure those damned fishing boats stay out of the way of the recovery team."

Eddie stepped out of his cabin in a clean shirt and shorts. Heil called out to him, something about Eddie getting his ass in gear. He wanted the bar opened early. But Eddie didn't hear him or if he did, he ignored him. Instead he walked over to the pier and stopped to talk with Stimpy and the other men before sauntering over to Kevin and Jo.

"I told you to get that bar open an hour ago," Heil called to Eddie again.

The sheriff left Heil's side and headed in their direction.

Kevin grabbed Jo's hand and squeezed it tightly, pulling her close.

The sheriff stopped in front of them, eying them. "I wonder if you can answer a few questions for me about your friend Billy around the time he went missing," the sheriff said. "Do any of you know how he might've hurt his arm?" He directed his question to all three of them.

"No," Eddie said. "It's the first I'm hearing about it. I know it's been awhile, but I'm pretty sure I was the only one walking around injured." He showed the sheriff his missing thumb tip. "Snapper got ahold of me around the same time."

"What about you two?" the sheriff asked.

Jo didn't like the way he was looking at her.

"Well?" he asked, waiting for one of them to speak up.

The cords in her neck strained. "I don't remember him being hurt," she said.

"Why?" Kevin tightened his grip on her hand. "What's this about?"

"They found a fracture on his ulna, the smaller bone in the lower arm," the sheriff said. "I'm curious how it might've happened." He directed his next question to Kevin. "As I recall, you were with him that night. Did he fall? Did he get into a fight with someone? Anything at all you can remember, even if you don't think it's relevant."

"No," Kevin said without hesitation. "Nothing I can think of."

The sheriff waited a beat or two, perhaps hoping one of them would offer more information in the silence. When no one spoke up, he said to Kevin, "So there wasn't a fight over anything, say, like a girl?" He looked back at Jo.

"What's your point?" Kevin asked, digging his nails into the back of Jo's hand.

"No point. It's just funny how you ended up with the girl."

Jo concentrated hard on keeping her face neutral. But Kevin, he shook his head, clearly disgusted. "We got together afterward. Not before." His voice was strong, convincing.

"I had to ask," the sheriff said, although it didn't sound like he believed him. "If any of you think of anything that might help clear up this matter, you be sure to let me know." He turned to walk away.

"Do you even know if the bones are Billy's?" Kevin asked, and Jo wished he hadn't. She didn't know how much longer she could hold it together. She wanted the sheriff gone.

The sheriff turned back around, taking his time, looking them over. "Nothing's confirmed. Yet," he said in a low, cool voice.

Eddie set two bottles of beer on the bar. "Don't let the sheriff get to you. He's just being a prick. He's got a hard-on for Dee Dee, and he's just making shit up to keep her happy."

Jo nodded and reached for a beer. She was too shaken to talk, although she didn't lie to the sheriff when she told him she didn't know Billy had hurt his arm. But still, she had a sick feeling in her stomach because she knew how he *might've* hurt it.

Kevin kept his eyes on the bottle in front of him. His body was tense. "It doesn't change anything," he said.

CHAPTER TWENTY

Kevin sat at the bar the rest of the afternoon into early evening. He lost count of how many bottles of beer he'd had, but by the buzzing in his head and the slight sway of the room, it had been a lot. In the time it took to numb his brain, he convinced himself the fracture in the bone meant nothing. It could've happened in any number of ways.

Stimpy and his clowns had gone and come back, their search unsuccessful. They were settling in for the night. They whispered about picking up first thing in the morning. The sole watercraft left on the lake was the underwater recovery team, whittled down to three men, who were also packing it in now that the sun had set.

Jo had gotten off her stool and headed to the bathroom some time ago. She was in there forever or maybe she wasn't. Time became a fuzzy thing. Earlier, after their run in with Sheriff Borg, she had grown increasingly quiet. She became distant, locked inside that place she went, shutting him out.

He turned to look at the bathroom door again. Maybe he should check on her. It seemed like a hard decision to make at the moment; he was unsure how it would play out. She might be appreciative for his concern or agitated with his smothering. He'd give her another five minutes.

Glass shattered behind the bar. Kevin came up out of his seat to find Eddie crouched over a broken mug. "You okay?" he asked.

Eddie waved him off. It was then Kevin noticed Sheila had walked inside with Nick, the drummer from one of the local bands. Heil must've hired them to play for the night.

"Hey, Kevin," Sheila said, and kissed his cheek. She leaned over the bar. "Hey," she said to Eddie, and reached for him. Eddie looked so damned happy, Kevin almost felt sorry for him, because he knew how Eddie felt. He knew how loving a woman could make you so happy one minute and then miserable the next.

The band carried in their equipment and began the process of setting up for the show. Kevin recognized one of the guys: Tony, the lead singer. He had been playing at the Pavilion for as long as Kevin could remember. In fact, when Kevin was playing guitar regularly, Tony used to let him play a song or two to warm up the crowd on the nights Eddie had worked as bar back.

Tony walked over to him, holding a guitar. He shook Kevin's hand. "It's been a long time. Do you still play?" he asked.

"Not much anymore," Kevin said. He had tried to play in the months after Billy had drowned. He'd pick up a guitar, play a few chords, and end up putting the instrument down. At the time it had felt too hard, and he had wondered if he'd ever be able to play again.

Tonight Tony held out his guitar. "Warm us up," he said.

"No, I don't think so."

"Oh, come on, Kevin. What could it hurt?" Sheila nudged him. "Do it for old time's sake."

Maybe it was the alcohol that had loosened him and made him soft, but before he knew how it had happened, he was sitting on a stool on the small stage, tuning the acoustic guitar, warming up his rusty voice. He adjusted the microphone and cleared his throat. *Here goes nothing.*

He started to sing, and the music moved through him as it had in the past, the rhythm familiar and comforting. He moved back in time, swept further away with every pluck of the strings. The crowd, if you could call it a crowd, hushed and turned to listen. He closed his eyes and lost himself in the lyrics, singing an old Goo Goo Dolls song, "Iris," the one song that reminded him of Jo.

She had since returned to the bar, sitting on the same stool she had sat on all day. He didn't have to look to know she was watching, listening. Her eyes burned through him. He kept singing, his fingers remembering every chord. The guitar felt good in his hands.

When he finished, the meager crowd clapped. Tony slapped him on the shoulder. "Beautiful," he said.

Kevin put the guitar in the stand. The music had opened a place inside of him he had locked away a long time ago. He felt vulnerable and exposed, but more than that, he felt a raw need, a yearning so strong, it made his heart ache. He crossed the room to where Jo was sitting. Sheila was sitting next to her. He lifted Jo's chin and kissed her full on the mouth, needing her now more than ever.

She pushed him hard in the chest. He stumbled backward, confused at first, thinking his actions must've taken her by surprise. But then he realized she was looking around to see if anyone had noticed he had kissed her. She wiped her mouth with the back of her hand as though she couldn't stand to have any part of him touch her.

"Goddammit, Jo." He turned and strode for the door.

He didn't make it halfway down the stairs when he heard her call his name. He kept walking, lengthening his stride. The night air was cool on his back. His hands were fisted by his sides. Even now she continued to make him feel the fool.

"Kevin, wait." She chased after him, catching up to him a third of the way across the parking lot. She grabbed his arm and spun him around. "Stop," she said. "Please."

"Why, Jo? Why should I bother?"

Her face was flushed, and she had that crease between her eyebrows she got whenever she was angry. But there was something else in her eyes, a flame he recognized.

"Who are you afraid is going to see us together?" He glanced at the lake. A spotlight from a lone fishing boat drifted across the water, the beam reaching as far as the parking lot, the light crossing them at the knees. It was as though he was reliving the nightmare for the second time. Back then he had to stay away from her to protect her, to protect their secret. But things were different now. The little girl drowning had nothing to do with them, and yet it had everything to do with them. If it weren't for the girl, they never would've found those bones. He grabbed Jo's arms and pulled her to him.

"Billy's dead, Jo," he said. "And you're my wife. *My* wife." He couldn't help himself; he kissed her again, hard, smashing her nose and scraping her teeth with his.

She struggled, twisting her shoulders, trying to free her arms. The more she fought, the more aroused he became. He pulled her closer, her breasts pressed against his chest. He forced his leg between her thighs. She bit his lip.

The sudden pain made him loosen his grip. She punched his chest with her fists and shoved and pushed him until their bodies separated. They both were breathing hard, staring at each other.

"Asshole." She lunged at him, knocking him in the shoulder. He didn't fight back. They had been here before. They had played this game before. Instead he brought his hand to his bottom lip, his fingers coming away bloody.

By the time he looked up again, she was on him. She grabbed his face in her hands and kissed him as hungrily as he had kissed her. He grasped the back of her neck and placed his hand on her low back, crushing her to him. She reached between his legs.

"Oh God," he moaned.

They stumbled to the edge of the parking lot, kissing and fumbling with their clothes. To hell if anyone was watching. He wanted someone to see him have her. He lifted her up and pinned her against the thick trunk of an old maple tree. He clutched a handful of her hair and yanked her head back, kissing and biting her throat. She wrapped her legs around his waist, opening herself wide for him. He pushed deep inside of her, letting her take him to a place only she could take him.

They clung to each other, their bodies slick and warm. His legs felt weak with exhaustion. She sobbed against his chest. He was spent, used, wondering how their love brought out the best and worst in him, how something so sweet could taste like poison.

CHAPTER TWENTY-ONE

Caroline looked over her shoulder not once but continuously. The light of the moon cut through the trees, distorting the shadows of branches on the ground. The lake water looked as dark as pitch, like a sharp, shimmering black hole. She had never been out this late at night, and as if she wasn't paranoid enough, even the Pavilion looked ominous, old and abandoned.

She wound her way to the water's edge, creeping past lake-front cabins, pausing to listen for any sounds. The horse and the legend lurked in the corners of her mind, making the hairs on the back of her neck bristle. She reached Adam's place and slipped around back, stopping in front of his bedroom window. She tried not to think about what would happen if she got caught and tapped on the glass.

"Adam," she whispered. *Tap. Tap. Tap.* "Wake up." She strained to listen for any sounds coming from inside. Nothing. "Adam," she said a little louder. *Tap. Tap. Tap.* A rustling came from in the room. The curtains parted, and Adam pressed his nose against the glass, trying to see outside. She stood back a few inches and waved.

"Caroline? Is that you?"

"Yeah, open up."

He pushed the window up. She could just make out his big ears.

"What are you doing here?" he asked.

"Get dressed. I need your help," she whispered. "And be quiet."

He didn't ask for an explanation. She knew he wouldn't. Adam might be only ten years old, but she knew how to spot a team player when she saw one. He'd help her without question. He'd want to help Sara. Caroline learned in the last few days that Megan was a different sort of friend, although which kind of friend Caroline couldn't say.

Adam was who she trusted with her plan. She stepped into a shadow to hide and give him privacy. He came back to the window. It was a struggle, but they managed to pop the screen off without making too much noise. He climbed out. They stood quietly and listened for any sounds of his parents stirring.

When she thought it was safe to move, she crept back along the water's edge. Adam followed behind.

"What are we doing?" he whispered.

"We're releasing the snappers," she said. She had counted at least half a dozen traps and guessed each one held two or more snappers apiece. The job was too big for one person.

He grabbed her arm so she'd stop walking. She turned to face him. His eyes were open wide. "Why?" he asked.

"So they don't get Sara."

"But don't you want her found?"

She furrowed her brow. It was a complicated question and one with no easy answer. But he had crawled out of his window in the middle of the night, he could get into serious trouble, she could get into serious trouble. It was against the law to mess with a fisherman's traps, and yet he was standing here. She owed him an explanation.

"Yes and no," she said. "I want her found but not this way." It was the best she could do. She didn't know how to explain her dream, how Sara asked not to be found, how she wanted her mommy. The dream had felt *real*. And the least Caroline could do was not let Sara be found by the snappers. She had formulated a plan earlier that evening, lying in bed, too afraid to close her eyes. "She's one of us," she told him. A kid. It was personal. "And we owe it to her."

Adam nodded. On some level, it was personal for him, too. Maybe it was his subtle way of getting back at Heil and the other adults for taking his treasured horse's bit, for not speaking about the dangers of swimming in the lake, its history, what lies at the bottom.

"Are you in?" she asked, giving him one last chance to change his mind.

"I'm in."

They continued to follow the water's edge. Caroline's sneakers sunk in the mud. Behind her, Adam was having the same difficulty. His feet made a sucking sound with each step. And then it stopped. She didn't hear him anymore. She turned around. He was standing still, looking out at the lake. "Adam," she said. "What's wrong?"

"I thought I heard, like, a neighing sound or something." He pointed to the sky. "But I couldn't have. The moon isn't full. You can only hear the horse during a *full* moon."

She looked at the moon. It was a gibbous moon. She had learned about the eight lunar phases in earth science. But was it a waxing or waning gibbous? One occurred before a full moon and the other after. She hoped it was the latter, and that the full moon had already past.

"I checked the calendar the other day, you know, after what I found," Adam said. "It won't be a full moon for another two days."

So it was a waxing gibbous moon. She nodded and looked around uneasily. "Come on," she said, glancing at the moon and lake one last time. "We need to keep moving."

They continued along the water's edge, fighting the mud. When they reached the beach, they had a decision to make. They'd either have to cross the road and make a wide loop around the parking lot, staying close to the woods and possibly waking up Cougar, or they could stick close to the Pavilion but risk running across the open lot without any cover. The direct route was the quickest and also the scariest in her mind. She glanced at Adam. Shadows covered his face, but she sensed his nervousness. Maybe it was best to take their shot in the open and get it over with as fast as possible.

"Stay close to me," she said.

They sneaked along the beach's fence line and reached the Pavilion. The water licked the shore, the crickets chirped, the mosquitoes buzzed around her ears, but otherwise the night was quiet. She took a careful step toward the building, Adam in tow. They kept their backs to the wall, staying in the shadows, creeping slowly toward the stairs. The gravel underneath their sneakers snapped, crackled, and popped like the cereal Caroline ate for breakfast. The sound was much too loud in the silent night. They continued under the steps and around the corner where the lake opened wide and flickered under the moon's glare, where the gaping parking lot awaited.

"On the count of three," she said, "we run to the dock. We can hide behind the third pillar." It was the tallest pillar on the pier and the one closest to Stimpy's boat.

Adam nodded.

"One," she said. "Two." Before she got to three, a duck splashed in the water, quacking and calling a warning. She and Adam both jumped. They stared at each other. He covered his mouth and laughed into his hand. She started laughing too, a nervous kind of laugh that hurt her belly when she tried to contain the sound.

"Shhh," she said through jittery giggles.

When they had both settled down, they straightened up and looked around.

All was still.

"One, two, three." She took off across the lot. Adam was somewhere behind her. She didn't look back until she reached the pillar. A second later Adam slammed into her. They were both bent over, sucking wind. Adam wiped his face with the back of his arm.

Once they had caught their breath, he said, "Now what?"

"Now we set them free."

Caroline squatted next to a smaller pillar at the end of the pier. She pulled on the line that disappeared into the black water. The trap was heavy and lopsided, but she was able to tug on it an inch at a time, careful not to make a sound, until the trap surfaced.

"I'll hold it up," she said. "And you open the trap door."

"No way." Adam shook his head. "I'm not getting my fingers anywhere near those snappers."

He had a point. She wasn't thrilled about sticking her hand close to the trapdoor and the snappers' mouth, but what other choice did she have?

"Here." She handed him the line.

He struggled with the weight of the trap, and it slid underneath the water again.

"This isn't going to work." They had to move quickly if they were going to release all of them before the sun came up. She took a moment to think, then came up with an idea.

"I'll pull the traps out of the water and wrap the line around the pillar. All you have to do is make sure the line stays wrapped."

Adam nodded.

She raised the trap again and secured the line on the pillar before handing it off to Adam. "You got it?"

"I got it, but hurry," he said.

"Here goes nothing." She lay face down on the pier and stretched her arms over the side. The snappers shifted and jostled the cage, but she was able to unhook the latch and pull the door open. She stood up. "That wasn't too hard."

"They're not swimming out," Adam said, struggling with the line.

"Cripes." She'd have to tip the trap to get them to swim out, which meant sticking her fingers inside. She wiped her wet hands on her shorts. "Don't let go," she said, and lay down on her stomach again. She slipped her hands into the water and stuck her fingers inside the trap far enough to grasp the metal bars, lifting as best she could, tilting the cage to force the snappers out. She had to shake it several times to get them to move, but after a few seconds the two snappers swam free. She pulled the trap from the water and latched it closed. "Drop it in."

Adam unwound the line from the post, and the trap slowly sank to the bottom.

"That's one down."

They pulled each line, opened the traps, and shook the snappers free, one after the other in succession without stopping. They moved systematically, catching each other's eyes every so often, checking the gibbous moon.

On the last trap, tired and weary, Caroline's fingers slipped from the latch. The bigger snapper reared its head and opened its mouth in warning. She pulled her arms back. The sudden movement scared Adam, and he let go of the line. The trap scraped the side of the pier and splashed into the water. She lunged for it, catching the side, and shook it until it was empty.

Cougar started barking. The lights in Stimpy's cabin were turned on. There was no time to close the latch. She got off her stomach and grabbed onto Adam's arm. "Go, go, go," she said, pushing him forward.

They took off running down the dock and across the parking lot. They made it to the far side of the Pavilion and ducked underneath the steps. Caroline pressed her back against the wall. Adam did the same. Between heavy breaths and Cougar's barking, she listened for footsteps. She pinched her eyes closed. *Please don't let them catch us.* After what felt like several eternal minutes, Cougar finally stopped barking. She peeked around the corner toward the dock. The lights in Stimpy's cabin were off.

"That was close," she said. "We better get out of here." It didn't make sense for her to follow Adam home, since *The Pop-Inn* was in the other direction, but she offered to walk him to his cabin to make sure he got back safely.

"You don't have to walk me back," he said. "I can make it."

"Are you sure?"

"I'm sure."

"Okay, but be careful." She took a step out from under the stairs.

"Wait," he said. "Here." He pulled something from his pocket and handed it to her. "It's beef jerky for Cougar in case he starts barking again."

"You carry beef jerky in your pocket?"

"All the time," he said. "Doesn't everyone?"

She smiled. "Um, no, but thanks."

Adam crept along the fence line. She hustled across the road and slipped into the woods, weaving her way around to the path that led to the colony. Cougar yipped. She tossed him the beef jerky, and she made it to the cabin without further incident.

She looked at Willow and smiled. "I'm back," she said, and

crawled through her bedroom window and kicked off her dirty sneakers. She peeled out of her wet clothes and dropped them on the floor. She pulled on a nightshirt and slipped into bed. Her arms lay heavy at her sides, exhausted from all of the pulling, lifting, and shaking throughout the night. She closed her eyes, her conscience clear. She believed in her heart she had done the right thing.

CHAPTER TWENTY-TWO

Cold air blew through the open window, sending the curtains flapping into the room. Thunder rumbled. Jo lay still, listening to the storm. Her head pounded and her back ached. She rubbed the spot along her spine where she had been pinned against the tree. Her mouth tasted like an ashtray. A dried stickiness smattered her inner thighs, and she couldn't help but think that after all the ebbs and flows, the pushes and pulls, they always ended up right back where they had started.

Kevin stirred and rolled to his side. Dried blood stuck to his lip where she had bitten him. His hair fell in his eyes. She smoothed the bangs from his forehead, and for a second, a fraction of a second really, she closed her fingers around the strands and thought about ripping them from his scalp. His eyes moved behind his lids, but he didn't wake. She let his hair flutter through her fingers, and she gently kissed the cut on his bottom lip. "What have we done?" she whispered, and quietly got out of bed.

After two aspirin and a hot shower, she peeked into Caroline's room. Her daughter was curled into a ball, sound asleep. On the floor by the bed were dirty clothes and muddy sneakers. Something about it gave her pause, made her feel uneasy, but she had been feeling that way so often over the last few days, it was hard to tell whether it was her intuition or if she was just being paranoid.

She turned away.

Gram was awake, shuffling her feet in the back bedroom, talking in a hushed voice on the old rotary phone before hanging up with a click.

"Jo, is that you?" Gram called.

Jo didn't answer. Whatever Gram wanted could wait. She was sure it had something to do with cleaning closets, and just the thought of lugging old boxes around exhausted her. She had hardly slept last night, tossing, unable to shake the way the sheriff had looked at her, his questions, his accusations, the fractured bone.

Jo slipped out the screen door without making a sound. Thunder continued to roll, and the rain fell hard and fast, pelting her cheeks and shoulders. She didn't mind. It felt good to feel something real, tangible. And besides, summer storms never lasted long. Already the sun was peeking through the clouds on the other side of the mountain.

She walked across the dirt road, dodging the deeper puddles. She glanced in the direction of the *Sparrow*, the cabin Patricia rented. Patricia was standing behind the screen door, watching the storm, her arms wrapped around her waist. Jo waved, and Patricia called her over.

Lightning flashed.

"Please, come in out of the rain." Patricia held the door open. She smoothed her blond tangled hair away from her drawn face.

"Is there any news?" She clutched the collar of her blouse. Her clothes were wrinkled and worn, as though she had been wearing them for days.

Jo shook her head and stepped inside. "Not that I heard." She scanned the room. A stuffed cloth doll sat on one of the wicker rocking chairs in front of a child's tea set. Coloring books were scattered on the floor amidst spilled crayons and colored pencils. Drawings of ponies and kittens covered the coffee table.

Thunder continued to roar.

Jo picked up a drawing. "These are really good."

Patricia looked at the picture. A smile crossed her lips. "Sara's. She had an eye for detail. I teach art at the school. I guess she had a natural talent for it." She covered her mouth and turned away.

Jo put the picture down. "Why don't I make you some coffee?" She fumbled around the unfamiliar kitchen. She was aware that her wet shoes and clothes dripped onto the linoleum floor, but by the looks of the stained countertops and dirty dishes in the sink, the place hadn't been cleaned recently.

While Jo waited for the coffee to percolate, she washed the dishes and wiped the table and countertops. She wasn't sure what she was doing, why she was even here. But there was something about Patricia she found comforting. Maybe they were just two women who understood about regret and mistakes, two women who shared a similar burden in its own terrible way. She picked up a coffee cup.

Patricia settled into a chair at the kitchen table. She wore the expression of someone tired yet wired. The look in her eyes said she was barely hanging on. She turned to Jo as though she had remembered something important. "Tell me," she said. "Do you still talk to Billy?"

The question was so startling, the cup dropped from Jo's hand

and shattered on the floor. Thunder cracked and lightening lit up the room.

Patricia looked so innocent. Was she mocking her? Did she want to cause Jo pain? Before Jo could find her voice to respond, there was a loud knock at the front door.

"Hello?" Sheriff Borg called. He stepped inside and removed his sheriff's hat, his gray hair clipped short and neat.

Patricia sprung from her seat. "You found her?" she asked him.

"No, I'm sorry. Not yet."

Jo's heart pounded in her ears. She avoided Sheriff Borg's eyes and grabbed a tea towel. She dropped to her knees and wiped the floor, at the same time trying to make sense of what Patricia had said. Her hands shook as she picked up the pieces of the broken cup.

"Everything okay?" he asked, and raked his eyes over Jo's wet clothes, her chest, before scanning the mess on the floor.

"That last crack of thunder," she mumbled. "The cup slipped from my hands."

"You should be more careful," he said.

"I will."

He turned his hat around in his hands. "Have you given any thought to our conversation the other day? Is there anything you want to tell me?" he asked. "Maybe something you might've remembered?"

Jo shook her head, feeling his eyes on her as she continued picking up ceramic shards.

Patricia touched the sheriff's arm. "What about my girl?"

He turned his attention to her. "No one can be on the lake with the thunder and lightning." He hesitated as though he were making up his mind whether to continue. "We have another problem," he finally said. "One of the fishermen was up early before the storm to check the traps and found them empty. There were muddy footprints all over the docks: kids' footprints. They must've fooled with the traps and let the snappers out sometime last night."

"Why? Who would do such a thing?" Patricia asked.

"Kids pulling a stupid prank would be my guess."

All the blood rushed to Jo's head. *Caroline*, she thought. It would explain the wet clothes, the dirty sneakers in her bedroom. She pinched her eyes closed. *Why would Caroline do it?* Her daughter knew she wasn't supposed to touch a fisherman's traps. Did Caroline even know what they were using the snappers for?

"How do you know the turtles didn't just get out?" Patricia asked.

"Not possible unless they locked the trap doors behind them."

He continued. "It's a darn good thing the rain held off until now, or we never would have seen the footprints."

Patricia nodded.

"I wanted to stop by to let you know they'll have to trap more turtles," he said. "That is, if you still want them to. I can put an end to it if you say so, and we'll let the recovery team continue as they have been."

Patricia was quiet. The only sound was the splattering rain on the roof and the occasional clap of thunder. After awhile, without looking at him, she said, "I want them to do whatever it takes. I want my daughter found."

"Okay." He put his hat back on and turned toward the door. "I'll let the men know."

"Wait," Patricia said. "I'm coming with you." She chased after him, leaving Jo all alone on her knees in the kitchen.

As soon as the sheriff and Patricia were out of sight, Jo rushed back to *The Pop-Inn*, the pouring rain drenching her for the second time that morning. She pulled open the screen door, letting it slam behind her. Kevin sat at the kitchen table with a cup of coffee. He looked like hell.

"Forget your umbrella?" he asked, and smiled, but he must've seen something on her face, because he immediately furrowed his brow. "What's wrong?"

She didn't have time to explain. She darted into Caroline's bedroom. Her daughter wasn't in bed. She plucked the wet dirty clothes off the floor. She searched the room for the muddy sneakers. They were nowhere to be found.

"Where's Caroline?" she called to Kevin, and tossed the dirty clothes into the sink. There wasn't time to take them to the Laundromat. She turned on the faucet.

"She took off on her bike a little while ago," he said. His voice was deep and raspy from a night of drinking and smoking and singing. "I didn't think she should go out in the storm, but like mother like daughter." He leaned against the wall outside the bathroom door, sipping coffee. "Do you want to tell me what's going on?"

She didn't know where to begin; Patricia asking about Billy, the sheriff, or that Jo suspected Caroline had released the fishermen's snappers. Instead she said, "Do you know where she went?"

The screen door slammed.

She pushed past him. "Caroline," she called, but found Gram instead.

Kevin walked up behind her, and she suddenly felt trapped between the two. She pulled on her wet cotton shirt, which stuck to her breasts and constricted her chest, the collar tightening around her neck.

"Is someone in the bathroom?" Gram asked. "I hear water running."

Kevin shot out of the kitchen to turn off the water so the sink wouldn't overflow. Jo backed away from Gram. The distance was enough to open her throat and allow the air to return to her lungs. She pulled her damp hair from her face.

"Where's Caroline?" Gram dropped a bag onto the table.

"That seems to be the million-dollar question," Kevin said, returning to the kitchen. "What's in the bag?"

"Sneakers," Gram said.

"But how . . ." Jo started to ask, but Gram held her hand up to stop her. Someone must've tipped Gram off. Maybe that was why she had been on the phone earlier.

"I don't know anything for sure," Gram said.

For once, Jo and Gram were on the same side. She peeked into the bag at a pair of white sneakers. Caroline would have to get them a little dirty so they wouldn't look so new. "Where are her old ones?" she asked.

"I tossed them," Gram said.

"Will someone please tell me what's going on?" Kevin asked, and set his coffee mug down in the sink. He folded his arms and looked back and forth between them.

Johnny walked into the kitchen, scratching his head. His dark hair was almost to his shoulders, and the way it swooped to the side was a reflection of Jo's own hair, albeit a more masculine version yet with a hint of something feminine, too. Jo knew the girls his age thought it made him look *sensitive*.

"Why is everyone looking at me?" Johnny asked, and yawned.

"Have you seen your sister?" Gram asked.

"Why? What did she do?" He opened the refrigerator door and grabbed a gallon of milk. Then he pulled a box of cereal and large bowl from the cabinet, plucked a spoon from the drawer, and sat at the table.

"She didn't do anything," Jo said. At least, she hoped. "But we need to find her."

"Try her phone," Johnny said through a mouthful of cereal, milk dripping from his chin.

"I can't get a signal." She looked at Kevin. "Will you take Johnny and search the colony? I'll check to see if she's at the lake. Gram, you wait here in case she comes home."

Johnny dropped his spoon. "In the rain?"

"The storm is almost over," Kevin said and gave Jo a worried glance. "Are you ever going to tell me what's going on?"

"Later," she said. "Just go."

CHAPTER TWENTY-THREE

Kevin walked beside Johnny. The sun broke through the storm clouds. The rain slowed to a drizzle. There must have been a rainbow somewhere, but the trees in the colony were as big as giants and centuries old, blocking much of the view of the sky except for the occasional glimpses between branches.

Johnny stuffed his hands into his pockets. His hair covered his face. It was hard for Kevin to read his expression, but he could sense the boy's angst. The silence between them felt strained and uncomfortable. Kevin was sorry for it, knowing he was partly to blame. He had no idea how to cross the invisible divide that kept Johnny separate from him, or even if he wanted to.

"Maybe she's at the ballpark," Kevin said, knowing how much Caroline loved to play ball. Why she would be in the park in the rain he couldn't say. But the kids often hung out in the dugouts for the lack of anything better to do. It's what he might've done at her age.

He continued. "You know you're a pretty good ballplayer. Good enough to get a baseball scholarship if you wanted to go to college."

"Really?" Johnny said in his cocky voice. "We're going to talk about this now?"

"Do you have something else you'd rather talk about?"

Johnny sighed. "No."

Kevin lit a cigarette. Life would be easier if Johnny went to college and moved away. It was a selfish thought, but one he had often and believed to be true. He wondered if maybe it would give his marriage a fresh start, a new beginning, or as the kids say a "do-over."

He had rarely been alone with Johnny when he had been a toddler running around the backyard with his baseball bat, let alone the teenager he had become, the man he would be. Kevin had spent a lifetime on the road in his rig. It had been easier to stay away than deal with the tension at home, the guilt he felt whenever he looked at Jo and Johnny, the mother and son who were getting along fine without him. He admitted it was what he wanted. A part of him was afraid of Johnny. Hell, Kevin was just a kid himself when Johnny was born.

"This summer sucks," Johnny mumbled.

Kevin glanced at him. "They'll find the little girl and things will go back to normal. You'll see. Heil will make sure of it."

"Well, it sure is taking a long time." Johnny sounded annoyed and maybe he heard it in his own voice because he added, "I don't mean to sound cruel. I feel real bad about what happened. She was just a kid, you know? But why are they dragging it out? Why can't they find her?"

"It's a natural lake. It's deep." Kevin pulled in a long drag and exhaled slowly. "The lake community can't afford to bring in outsiders to help. Or they won't. It draws too much attention. The recovery team is the only one in the county. And there's a lot of lake to cover."

They stopped at the edge of the ballpark.

Johnny raised his arms and clasped his hands behind his head. "I guess." He stretched, twisting left and right, cracking his spine. "But it all sounds like bullshit to me," he said.

Kevin smelled something funny coming from Johnny's hair and skin. It wasn't cigarette smoke, but it was familiar. When Johnny lowered his arms, Kevin smelled it again a little stronger this time and recognized the scent of marijuana. He shouldn't be surprised and in fact, he wasn't. How could he fault the boy when he had smoked the stuff at the same age?

Eddie had rolled the first joint inside the dugout right there at the ballpark. Kevin had been strumming his guitar. He had taken the guitar with him almost everywhere he went that summer for the sole purpose of gaining Jo's attention. The others were sprawled on the benches, smoking cigarettes and eventually the poorly rolled joint.

"None for me," Kevin said when Eddie passed it to him. "It messes with my voice."

"Isn't that the point?" Billy asked, zeroing in on Kevin, giving him that undivided attention everyone in the group coveted.

"Maybe it is," Kevin said, thinking it must be nice to have everyone want your attention. He glanced at Jo. She was staring into the open field. He put the guitar down and took a hit. Billy directed his attention to Eddie, and the two became engrossed in some discussion over what Kevin could no longer remember. Sheila sat in Eddie's lap and joined the conversation.

At one point Jo had gotten up and walked away. Kevin watched her walk past the pitcher's mound and onto centerfield, where she lay down. Darkness enveloped her. He could barely make out her shape on the ground.

Maybe it was the weed or the beer, but Kevin felt brave enough to leave the dugout and join her. The others were distracted and no one mentioned his absence. He lay down next to her in the damp grass and stared up at the night sky. The brush of her arm against his forearm sent his pulse racing.

"Have you ever seen so many stars?" she asked in that stoned way of talking. "They're so far away and I don't know, otherworldly."

"Yes, one could say that about space."

She nudged his arm. "You know what I mean."

He didn't know what she meant, nor did he care. She could talk nonsense all night long as long as she talked with him, lay next to him.

But she remained silent after that. Billy and Eddie's discussion grew more animated, and their voices cut across the field. Occasionally, Sheila joined the debate. But to Kevin the others seemed as far away as the stars from where he lay next to Jo. It was just the two of them in the open field under the shimmering night sky. He could just make out the rise and fall of her chest, the slight part in her lips as she stared into the night.

"Do you ever dream about the future, Kev?" she asked. "About what you want to do with your life?"

"Sure, I guess. I mean, doesn't everybody?"

"I suppose." She turned to look at him. "What do you dream about?"

"I dream about this," he said. A shadow covered her face, and he couldn't see her eyes. "About lying next to you under the stars."

She swatted his arm. "Seriously, what do you dream about?"

"I am being serious," he said, and under the cover of dark, he found the courage to add, "I dream about you."

"Stop screwing around," she said, her tone suddenly sober. "I want something more than just this place. I want to travel and see the world. I want to be *of* the world, not just in it. I want to dance under the stars on faraway beaches. I want to taste exotic cuisine. I want . . . I want . . ." She broke off. "I want something more out of life. I want to be free." She wrapped her pinky finger around his.

His heart soared.

Billy's voice boomed from somewhere close behind them. "Hey, you two lovebirds," he said in an innocent, teasing way, as though the two couldn't possibly be anything more than friends.

Kevin's stomach suddenly burned with anger and something close to rage. Why was it so impossible for Billy to imagine Jo might actually want to be with him?

Jo unraveled her finger from Kevin's and reached for Billy. He pulled her up and into his arms, kissing her face and neck, his hands roaming up and down her body, gripping her in a tight embrace.

Kevin slowly got to his feet and made his way back to the dugout. He grabbed his guitar. Eddie and Sheila had moved to the far corner of the bench to be alone. Kevin looked back across the field. He could no longer separate Billy's body from Jo's.

He felt sick. He made it as far as the dirt road that led into the colony, dropped to his knees, and vomited.

He didn't fully grasp what Jo meant when she said she wanted to be free. Did she mean free of Billy? And if that were true, could he give her what she wanted? Would she even let him try? But she had held his hand, or his finger, as they gazed at the stars. She had reached out to him. What else could it have meant? He vowed he would do whatever it would take to make her happy. *Just give me a chance, Jo*, he whispered to himself. *I promise to do what I have to, to never let you go.*

"Hey." Johnny waved his hand in front of Kevin's face. "She's not in the dugouts," he said. "Maybe we should try the Pavilion.

Why is Mom looking for her anyway? I mean, what's the big deal?"

Kevin pulled on the cigarette, shaking off the memory. "I don't know, but I'm sure we'll find out."

They walked the Lake Road rather than taking the old path through the woods. The rain had finally stopped, but the path would be slippery and wet. The air was thick with humidity. Kevin's skin felt sticky, the booze from last night seeping from his pores.

When they reached the Pavilion and lake, Sheriff Borg's vehicle was in the parking lot along with several other cars. A crowd of teenagers gathered around a customized sports car. Kevin recognized Chris, Dee Dee's son, leaning in the driver's-side window, talking to whomever sat behind the wheel. A couple of teenage girls posed near the car, trying to look sophisticated, maybe even sexy. Kevin was embarrassed to catch himself looking at one of the girl's large breasts. She waved. He pointed to his chest as if to say, *Me?* Then he looked behind him and had to laugh at himself when Johnny waved back. She had to be Johnny's girl.

"So, uh," Johnny said. He couldn't meet Kevin's eyes. "I'm going to go. Tell Mom, if I see Caroline, I'll let her know she's looking for her." He started to walk away with a familiar swagger that made Kevin feel as though someone had kicked him in the gut.

"Johnny," he called.

Johnny turned, tossing the long hair out of his eyes.

"Do you love her?" Kevin asked, but only loud enough for Johnny to hear.

The personal question took them both by surprise. Johnny looked at his feet and then over his shoulder at his friends. He turned back toward Kevin. "Not really," he said.

"That's good," Kevin said, and crushed the cigarette he had been smoking underneath his sneaker. "You're better off."

CHAPTER TWENTY-FOUR

Jo sat at the far end of the bar, facing the door. She was drinking soda. It was too early for beer and, technically, the bar wasn't open. Eddie was kind enough to let her sit inside, out of the rain, although the storm had ended some time ago. He was in one of his moods and didn't offer much conversation, which was just as well. She didn't feel much like talking anyway.

She twisted her hair and let it fall in front of her shoulder. Her shirt was damp and her feet dirty from traipsing around the lake in flip-flops. She had searched everywhere after first stopping at Megan's cabin, where Megan made a point of telling Jo that she hadn't seen Caroline since they rode their bikes to the Country Store the day before. The Pavilion was open, but empty. She hoped Kevin had better luck. She checked her phone, considered calling her boss one more time, but she couldn't get a signal. She dropped it onto the bar. So that was that.

The crowd that had been on the docks started trickling in. Heil walked in with Stimpy and a couple of other fishermen, and she found herself amidst another community meeting. She sat on the edge of the stool and gripped the soda in front of her, wondering if Patricia would show up. She had to find a way to get

Patricia alone and ask how she knew Billy, and why she acted as though he was still alive.

The men were seated and the discussion started.

"Why is the sheriff asking questions about that boy Billy and those bones?" one of Stimpy's cronies asked. "Why's he bugging us? He said nothing's official, so why's he drudging up old news?"

Jo steadied herself, not making eye contact with any of the men. Although she could've sworn every one of them glanced in her direction at the mention of Billy's name.

"I'll talk to the sheriff," Heil said.

"It's bad enough that girl is still out there," someone bellowed. "He keeps talking about those bones, and he's going to scare people away."

"Hell, I don't think they're scared. I think they're bored," Jonathon jumped in. "I had two families pack up their vehicles and head home," he said. "No one wants to hang around the lake in the summer heat if they can't enjoy the water. Although it's tragic what happened, people are restless. They're good people, hardworking people, who spent their hard-earned money to come here. They want to spend their time on the lake fishing and swimming. It's what they expect, or they want their money back."

Some of the other cabin owners chimed in, complaining they, too, had worked hard to fill their rentals and couldn't afford refunds or cancelations.

"What about the Trout Festival in a few days? There are a couple hundred people or more expected to come. The kids expect to fish in the tournament. We can't disappoint the kids," the father of the Needlemeyer twins said.

"Okay, okay." Heil held up his hands to quiet them down. "We're not canceling the festival or the fishing tournament."

"Well, this mess has to be cleaned up by then. We can't have a tournament while there's a boat out there dragging the lake for that little girl's body," Jonathon said.

Heil stared at the men long and hard. "You're not going to lose anymore renters," he said to Jonathon. "And no one's canceling anything," he said to all of them.

"But I swear, I saw the families packing up the *Blue Hen*," a man from the back of the room said.

The crowd murmured. It was true. Other renters were talking about leaving. The gossip went round and round.

"Not one person has rented a boat in five damn days," Stimpy said.

Nate chimed in about not having any customers, about how he, too, couldn't afford to lose any more money.

"Let's face it: nobody is going to get near the water with those boats out there looking for that little girl," one of the men said.

Another said, "It's been too long. What's the likelihood of finding her now anyway?"

"You mean what's the likelihood there's anything left to find," someone said. The group nodded its assent. "They'll never find scraps. The lake is too damn big. She was small to begin with."

"You brought up a good point." Heil's voice boomed over the crowd. He pulled his shorts high on his expansive stomach. "Maybe we can talk the recovery team into limiting their search to early morning. There aren't many of them left now anyway."

"What about us?" Stimpy asked, motioning to his gang of fishermen.

"Same goes for you," Heil said. "Trap more snappers, but leave them in their cages. Let everybody swim and fish and enjoy themselves. We can pick up the search in the off-hours." He paused. "Although I agree, there's probably not much left of her to find."

Kevin stepped inside the bar as the rumble of the crowd subsided. Jo immediately went over to him. She grabbed his hand and led him down the stairs to the parking lot. She wanted to know if he had found Caroline, but she couldn't ask him here, not with Heil and the fishermen within earshot.

"Did you find her?" she asked once they were outside and alone.

"No." He stepped closer to her. He smelled wet like the rain mixed with cigarette smoke, but underneath it all, she smelled the soap on his skin, a scent unique to him. "Would you please tell me what's going on," he said.

"Caroline opened Stimpy's traps and let the snappers out."

"That doesn't sound like something she would do."

"I know. But I'm pretty sure she did."

"Come on, why would she do that?"

"I don't know. I don't understand her sometimes. Maybe she thought it was cruel to capture them." Caroline may have believed the ends didn't justify the means, and although Jo was frustrated with her daughter, she also couldn't help but feel proud of her too. In some ways Caroline was right. It *was* brutal both to the turtles, the ones who got tangled in the lines, and to the little girl now thought of as bait. It was a harsh reality. Sometimes life was cruel.

Kevin nodded.

She motioned to the bar, to where Heil and the group of men plotted inside. "They want to give up the search," she said. "And the sheriff"—she kept her voice low—"he was asking some of the men questions . . . you know, about Billy."

She waited for him to say something, anything, but he remained quiet. He always acted crazy whenever she brought up Billy. He wouldn't even look at her.

Then he said, "Why don't you go see if Caroline is back at the cabin with Gram? I'll find out what's going on inside." He took the stairs two at a time.

She looked across the parking lot, spotting Sheriff Borg and Patricia, and then turned her gaze to the lake and the lone watercraft with the last three men from the recovery team.

She raced up the hill to Lake Road and the cabin.

Jo pushed open the door to the screened-in porch. Inside she found Caroline and Gram sitting on the porch swing with a photo album opened in their laps. Gram exchanged a look with Jo and shook her head: a motion that Jo understood to mean that Gram didn't want her to confront her daughter. She wanted her to keep quiet. But since when did Jo listen to Gram?

"Caroline, where have you been?" She crossed her arms and looked down at the flip-flops on her daughter's feet.

"I went for a bike ride," Caroline said, and avoided looking at Jo in an attempt to hide her lying eyes.

Jo could always tell when Caroline was lying. She was terrible at hiding her emotions. Her face gave her away every time. All Jo had to do was look at her daughter to know what she was feeling on the inside. She suspected it had to do with her age and innocence. Thank goodness, her daughter at least had that.

"You wore flip-flops to ride your bike? Where are your sneakers?" she asked.

"I couldn't find them."

"Because they were covered in mud and Gram had to throw them away. Do you want to tell me how they got so dirty?"

"I don't know." Caroline stretched out the last word sounding like a whiny guilty child.

"Please look at me," Jo said. "And tell me you didn't sneak out of your room last night and mess with Stimpy's traps."

Caroline dipped her head and hid her face under the visor of her baseball cap. "I didn't," she said in the same whiny guilty voice.

"That's enough," Gram said. "She said she had nothing to do with releasing those snappers, and I believe her."

Over the top of Caroline's lowered head, Jo read Gram's lips. *Leave her alone.*

Jo looked away. So Gram was taking Caroline's side. Not once in all of Jo's life had Gram ever stuck up for her. Not when she had been a pregnant teenager, a time when she had needed her most. And not now, when Gram clearly understood that Caroline had broken a law. For an instant Jo felt envious of her own daughter, and at the same time she felt petty and childish, too.

"Who's this?" Caroline asked, and pointed to a photograph in the album.

Gram looked down through the reading glasses she had perched on the tip of her nose. "I'm not sure," she said.

They both ignored Jo at this point. It took everything Jo had not to yell that she was her mother, demand Caroline answer her questions, but she happened to glimpse at the colored photo and did a double-take. It was a picture of Billy at his cabin. He was holding up a lake trout. Jo had taken the picture. Dee Dee was in the shot, along with a little girl Jo couldn't place.

"Where did you get these?" she asked, but she already knew the answer. They were stored in the back closet all these years, the one Gram had finally decided to clean out.

Caroline kept her finger on the little girl in the photo. "She looks like Sara, the little girl who drowned." She looked up at Jo, a little frightened.

"Oh my god," Jo said. "That's not Sara, that's Pattie Dugan." *Patricia.* "Dee Dee used to babysit Pattie every summer. Pattie is Sara's mother."

"I'll be," Gram said. "I remember her parents, Bob and Jean.

They rented the *Sparrow* for many summers. Nice people. *Good* people."

Good people meant *lake people*, regulars who were accepted in the association and community. It meant Pattie had been one of them this entire time. Jo touched her neck and throat.

Gram continued. "But they stopped coming when Bob lost his job. I heard later they divorced," she said. "But that's all lake rumors. I don't know if any of that is true."

Jo had to sit down, and she plopped onto a wicker rocking chair across from Caroline and Gram and the photo. It wasn't the shock of seeing a picture of Billy that made her knees weak, although that was a part of it. It was the surprise to find out she had known who Patricia was all along. Patricia Starr was little Pattie Dugan.

Pattie must've been nine or ten years old in the photograph. It was no wonder Jo didn't recognize her now that she was an adult. It all seemed logical except the part about Billy.

Was it possible Patricia, *Pattie*, didn't know Billy had drowned that summer?

Jo tried to think if she had seen Pattie in the summers since then, but how could she be sure? Jo had only been able to stay with Gram for a couple of days at a time before taking off. She hadn't spent an entire summer at the lake since she was sixteen.

"Do you remember what summer they stopped coming?" she asked Gram.

"My goodness, I'd have to think about it. I'm not sure."

Jo didn't like the feeling that crept up her spine.

"This changes everything," she said. "It's Pattie's little girl out there. She's one of us. They must not know." She was referring to the lake association and even Sheriff Borg. "Heil will have to continue searching. He can't leave a regular out there."

The logic was twisted but true. A first-timer, an unknown

without any attachment to the lake community, someone who didn't contribute year after year to help line the pockets of Heil and the locals, wouldn't be treated the same. If the lake people had any rules—hell, if they had any conscience at all—it was their unwavering loyalty to their own kind. They may have reopened the beach when Billy had drowned, but they had never stopped searching or limiting their search like they planned to do with Sara. This was because Billy was one of them and Sara wasn't, but now it seemed as though she was.

"Mom," Caroline said.

Jo looked from Gram to her daughter. She had almost forgotten Caroline was there.

"Is that Billy?" Caroline asked.

CHAPTER TWENTY-FIVE

Gram slammed the photo album shut, startling Caroline.

"That's enough reminiscing for one afternoon," Gram said, and stood. "Is anyone hungry? I'll make sandwiches." She rushed to the kitchen, taking the photo album with her.

Caroline looked to her mother for an answer to her question, an explanation. Was the boy in the picture the same boy who drowned? Was it Billy, her mother's old boyfriend and her father's friend? But Caroline could tell from her mother's expression that she had already lost her. Her mother had retreated deep inside herself to those dark places Caroline recognized and wished she didn't. It was anyone's guess when her mother would surface. The only thing that surprised Caroline was that her mother hadn't raced out the door.

"Forget it," Caroline said. She'd find the answers to her questions on her own somehow, some way.

She returned to her bedroom where she found the new sneakers. She pulled on a pair of socks and then slipped the sneakers on. She'd get them a little dirty and no one would be the wiser. Gram had promised she'd keep her secret once she explained to Gram her reasons, the same reasons she used with Adam, although she didn't mention his part, not wanting to implicate him. She was willing to take full responsibility for the two of them if it came down to that. It was her idea, her plan, her doing.

When she had told Gram she couldn't stand the thought of what those snappers would do to Sara, Gram had more than understood—she had agreed and believed Caroline brave for taking a stand albeit an illegal one.

"Sometimes," Gram had said, "doing the right thing means you have to break some rules."

They agreed to keep it between themselves. It would be their secret and theirs alone. Gram wouldn't tell Caroline's mother what she had done, and this suited Caroline just fine. Her mother may suspect, but she would never know for sure, if Caroline could help it. Now Caroline and Gram had secrets too. *Take that*, Caroline whispered to herself about her mother.

Gram appeared in the doorway. "I've got everything out on the table."

"I'm not hungry," she said. "I think I'm going to find Megan instead."

"Well." Gram pressed her lips together in frustration at having set out food no one was going to eat. "Why don't the two of you come back here? There's more than enough sandwiches and you can play board games or cards, do something fun for awhile."

"I don't know, but I'll ask her." She didn't want to hurt Gram's feelings, but she didn't want to play games. She wondered if she would ever feel like doing anything fun again.

She stepped outside. The air was thick with humidity from the earlier storm. The day was hot. She rubbed the sides of her sneakers into the dirt where the grass would never grow. She kicked a couple of rocks to give the white tops a broken-in look, and hopped on her bicycle.

The seat was still wet from her ride in the rain that morning.

She had gotten up and went straight to the lake to discover her plan had worked. The men weren't on the water searching for two reasons: the storm and the fact that their turtles were gone. They were standing on Stimpy's porch. She could just make out their cross faces from where she sat on her bike in the parking lot.

When Sheriff Borg emerged from Stimpy's place, she took off, pushing her bike through the woods, which was no easy task. She wound her way behind the lakefront cabins as quietly as she could. She didn't stop until she reached Adam's cabin. She hid her bike behind a tree and tapped on his window much in the same way she had done the night before.

He wasn't happy to see her.

"I can't come out," he said. "My mom is mad. She wanted to know why the floor in my room was covered in mud."

"What did you tell her?"

"I told her I got up early to fish, but the storm chased me inside."

"Good thinking," Caroline said, and then she added, "Our plan worked."

"I know," Adam said. "It's all anyone's talking about."

"Okay"—she put her finger to her lips—"don't say a word to anyone. No one. And they won't catch us."

Of course, this was before she had learned about the muddy footprints they had left behind on the dock. She hadn't known then that Gram had replaced her sneakers with new ones, or she would've suggested Adam do the same. She wondered if she should risk another trip to his cabin to warn him and tell him to get rid of his old sneakers too. But then again, Adam had given his mother a solid explanation for the mud.

She pedaled across the yard, deciding to go to Megan's like she had told Gram. She entered the dirt road and almost hit a car coming toward her. She braked hard and swerved to the side.

"Careful, now," the sheriff said through the open window of the patrol car. He pulled up next to her. "Are your parents inside?" he asked.

She tried to swallow. "My grandmother's home."

"Good enough," he said. "Why don't you park that bike and walk me in?"

She did what she was told and got off her bike. She walked it into the yard on shaky legs. While she struggled with the kickstand, he stepped out of the car and put on his sheriff's hat.

"Gram," she called, and stepped through the side door that led to the kitchen. She was hoping to avoid her mother on the screened-in porch. With any luck, her mother had taken off.

The sheriff loomed behind her. He was twice her size and three times her weight. She thought she might cry.

Gram was standing at the kitchen sink washing a plate. When she saw the sheriff behind Caroline, she turned off the faucet and stuck her hand holding the wet towel onto her hip. It soaked the bottom of her shirt and the top of her favorite pants with the elastic waistband.

"What brings you by, Sheriff?" she asked. There was an edge to her voice Caroline heard her use only around people she didn't care for.

He removed his hat and turned it around in his hands as he spoke. "There's been some trouble down at the lake, and I was hoping you could tell me what you know about it."

Caroline stood still.

"Did you find that little girl, yet?" Gram asked.

"No, I'm afraid we haven't. Not yet," he said. "But that's sort of why I'm here. I got a complaint from some of the fishermen that a couple of kids messed with their traps."

Before Gram could answer, Caroline's mother walked into the kitchen. Her face drained of color, and the hollows in her cheeks looked deeper and darker than usual. If Caroline didn't know any better, she would think her mother was the guilty one.

I did it, Caroline thought. *Not you.* She didn't want to get into trouble, but why was everything always about her mother?

Her mother opened her mouth to say something to the sheriff at the same time Gram clutched her chest and leaned against the sink.

"Gram." Caroline reached for her.

Her mother rushed to Gram's side. "What is it?" she asked. "Your heart? Is it your heart?"

Gram kept her hand on her chest and slumped to the floor. Caroline's mother sunk to the floor with her. "Just hold on," her mother said, and looked at the sheriff. "Call an ambulance."

The sheriff shot out the door to radio it in.

Caroline knelt on the floor at Gram's side. "Gram, are you okay? Talk to me." She touched her shoulder. "Please, tell me you're okay."

Gram didn't speak. She pinched her eyes closed and kept her hand splayed over her heart.

"Don't crowd her," her mother said. "Give her air."

Caroline did as she was told and sat back on her heels, thinking she did this to Gram. She gave her a heart attack. "Please be okay," she begged.

Gram opened her mouth, trying to talk.

"Shhh," her mother said. "It's going to be okay."

The sheriff returned and announced the ambulance was on its way.

"You did this," her mother said to him, and glanced at Caroline as though she read her mind, letting her know she wasn't to blame.

The sheriff stood perfectly still, his face void of emotion. And Caroline hated him for not showing his concern for Gram, the one person Caroline loved more than anyone.

"Why can't you leave us alone?" her mother asked him, and turned back to Gram. "Hang on," she said. "Help is on the way. Hang on." Her eyes were teary.

Caroline's own tears dripped from her chin. She couldn't remember ever seeing her mother cry, and the sight of her tears and Gram on the kitchen floor terrified her.

Caroline heard the sirens long before the ambulance arrived. The sheriff had gone outside to greet them. Two men in uniforms entered the kitchen with a stretcher. The EMT examined Gram, listened to her heart, took her pulse, and asked her basic questions: her name, age, where she was born. He strapped a breathing device around her mouth and nose. "Oxygen," he said.

Caroline had been standing to the side, watching, shaking, wiping her eyes. The two men put Gram on the stretcher and lifted her.

"I'll be right back." Her mother rushed to Gram's bedroom to grab her purse and insurance card. While her mother was out of the room, Gram reached for Caroline's hand.

Caroline leaned in close and kissed Gram's cheek, her skin was thin and dry. "I love you," she whispered. "Please don't die."

"Stand back," one of the men instructed.

As she stepped away to let them carry Gram out, she saw a familiar twinkle in Gram's eye. The next thing she knew, Gram winked at her. Caroline looked around to see if anyone had seen what she had seen, if anyone had been paying attention. But the sheriff had left to get the door, and the two men carrying the stretcher were busy watching where they were walking.

Her mother rushed back into the kitchen with Gram's information.

"I'm ready. Let's go," her mother said.

As the shock wore off, Caroline realized Gram was faking it.

CHAPTER TWENTY-SIX

For the first time in Patricia's life, she lied.

She had told Jo and anyone who asked about her husband, Kyle, that he was a workaholic, that it was the reason he had left her alone at the lake even though Sara hadn't been found. It sounded cruel and it was, but the real reason wasn't anywhere close to being kind. For Patricia the real reason was much, much worse.

"Where are you?" Kyle asked on Patricia's first day there, hours before she had taken Sara to the beach, to the lake, hours before Sara had gone missing. Patricia had been unpacking the groceries in the *Sparrow* when the cabin's old rotary phone rang.

"You leave me this number, but don't tell me where you're going. What am I supposed to think?" he said.

"You're supposed to think I left you." She had planned the trip to the lake months ago, packing small items at a time, things they would need there but not at home: extra towels, old linens, books, and art supplies. Nothing Kyle would miss.

"Did you call a lawyer?" There was a hint of panic in his voice.

"No," she said, her own voice cool and even.

"Good," he said. "Good. We can handle it ourselves. There's no need to get a third party involved. I know all those blood-sucking lawyers anyway."

You know them because you're one of them, she thought but didn't say.

He continued without pause. "They will try to drag this out and squeeze all the money they can out of us. They'll bleed us dry, I tell you."

"Of course." He didn't care she left him. No, this phone call was about making sure one of his colleagues didn't get a dime of his money. If it wasn't so pitiful, she might've laughed.

"Okay, then we're in agreement? No lawyers?" He was in a rush. He must've had another call coming in or a meeting or a rendezvous.

"I guess." She didn't care one way or the other. For her it was never about the money. "Would you like to talk with your daughter?" *Please say yes, please show her you care even if you no longer care for me*. It was the only reason she had left him the phone number in the first place.

"I can't," he said. "I'm in a hurry."

"It will only take a second. She misses you."

"I have to go. No lawyers, Patricia. Do you hear me? I mean it." He hung up.

Sara trotted into the kitchen. "Was that Daddy?"

"Yes," she said, and kissed the top of Sara's head. "He wanted me to tell you how much he misses you and how sorry he is he couldn't talk to you. And"—she touched the tip of Sara's nose with her finger—"he wants you to have a whole lot of fun while you're here. Do you think you can do that?"

"Yes," Sara said. "Did you tell him I miss him, too?"

Patricia nodded and watched her daughter skip back into

the family room. She could've forgiven Kyle for the affair. Maybe. Eventually. But she could never forgive him for being a lousy father.

It was hard to believe that had been five days ago, five days that her daughter was missing. She had thought by returning to the lake, the one place from her childhood she had loved, she could escape her troubles back home—six hours west across the state of Pennsylvania in a small rural town where the gossip about her marriage, her once private life, was sure to have spread. She had thought by returning to the lake, she could finally be happy.

Patricia was sitting on the hood of a car with her feet propped on the front bumper in the parking lot outside of the Pavilion. She couldn't say whose car it was or what the make or model could be, but whoever owned it had parked it lakefront, close to the water's edge. It was where she had to be. And what difference did it make whose car it was anyway? What could they do to her that hadn't already been done?

Stars filled the night sky, the threat of another storm having evaporated hours ago. Music poured from the Pavilion's jukebox, glasses clinked, people talked and laughed. The lake spread out before her like an endless, bottomless, black pit.

She pulled Sara's cloth doll from the pocket of her jeans and hugged it close to her chest. Sara had slept with the doll, Dolly, since she was born. It was old and torn, and some of the stuffing had fallen out, but it was well loved. She could smell her daughter on the cotton fabric, the way she smelled from sleep, a mixture of sweetness and innocence.

Men's voices echoed across the lake and drew her attention. She gazed at the lone watercraft and what she believed was a fisherman. She dried her wet eyes with the doll the way Sara used to when she cried.

Dolly had dried a lot of Sara's tears that came with scraped knees and bumped elbows. She was always getting hurt. She was a fearless child. She had demanded riding her bike without training wheels at five years old. And just three weeks ago, in what felt like another lifetime, she had become fascinated with the neighbor's skateboard. "Look at me, Mommy," she had called, racing down the hill before Patricia could stop her. She had been going much too fast, barreling toward the neighbor's garbage cans.

"Watch out!" Patricia had shouted, and ran down the hill after her. Sara had crashed into the cans before she could reach her. She had scooped her up, inspecting her birdlike arms and skinny legs.

"I'm okay, Mommy," Sara had said, and swiped away her tears. "I want to try again."

The memory brought a smile to Patricia's lips. She imagined it was that same sense of adventure that had led Sara into the water. Maybe it was all the talk about the horse and the lake legend that had sparked Sara's curiosity. Sara loved horses, especially ponies. But Patricia would never know what led her daughter into the lake alone, and she blamed herself.

A light was turned on in one of the lakefront cabins across the way. She hadn't realized she had been staring, and started counting the cabins closest to the docks. Sure enough, the seventh cabin was *Hawkes'*, the one with the lighted rooms.

On their first day here, she had every intention of knocking on the Hawkes' door, the peach pie she never got around to baking in hand, and introducing Sara to a real family, a loving family. She had never forgotten Billy, of course, but she also had never forgotten his older sister, Dee Dee, who had babysat Patricia every summer when she had been a child. Patricia's parents had spent most of their nights at the Pavilion bar or the Lake House, dining, drinking, dancing. But to the Hawke family, the lake was home, not some place to whoop it up every night. And Patricia loved this about them. She had felt safest in their care.

She wished she had stayed in touch with them through the years. She was only ten years old when she last saw them. Her parents had come home fighting after a late night of drinking. Dee Dee had been babysitting. Her father had stormed into the Hawkes' cabin just before dawn.

"We're leaving," he had said, and grabbed Patricia's small overnight bag. Her mother had scooped her into her arms. She had stared over her mother's shoulder at Dee Dee standing in the middle of the family room, the money Patricia's father had tossed fluttering to the floor at Dee Dee's feet.

They had driven home that morning never to return. Patricia had never gotten to say good-bye.

Things with her parents had gone from bad to worse when her father had lost his job. It had been the last family vacation for the Dugans.

Tonight, sitting on the hood of some stranger's car staring at *Hawkes'* cabin, her daughter still out there somewhere, she wondered how her plans could've gone so terribly wrong.

CHAPTER TWENTY-SEVEN

Jo pulled the old Chevy into one of the two spots in the far corner of the yard reserved for parking. She cut the engine. They had been at the hospital for the better part of the day. The sun had set hours earlier. The rush of adrenalin she had felt speeding behind the ambulance, the fear for Gram's health, had all but faded. She was tired, but more than that, she was relieved.

Gram remained quiet the entire ride home. Caroline was silent in the backseat.

Kevin was sitting on the steps under the porch light waiting for their return. Jo had called from the hospital to tell him where they were, what had happened. He held a guitar in his lap, but he wasn't playing. The sight of him sitting there with a guitar aggravated her. A part of her blamed that damned guitar for all her troubles no matter how crazy it sounded.

He rushed to the passenger side door to help Gram out of the car. He wrapped his arm around Gram's waist. "You gave me quite a scare," he said.

"I'm fine, really," Gram assured him, and yet she let him help her. She was practically swooning with the attention.

He had always known how to suck up to her parents. Even Pop

had thought Kevin was Jo's savior, swooping in, marrying her when she had gotten pregnant, protecting her reputation, or rather, wasn't it the family's reputation Pop had been concerned about? She didn't know nor did she care. Kevin had the same effect on Gram, making a huge deal about Gram's cooking, jumping in to help with chores whenever he was around. He played the part of son-in-law so well, even Jo bought into it.

"So what did the doctor say?" he asked Gram once he had her seated at the kitchen table with a sandwich and glass of milk.

"They couldn't find anything wrong," Jo said, answering for Gram.

"You don't sound too happy about that," Gram said, but before Jo could respond, Gram continued. "The doctor thought it might've been a panic attack."

"That doesn't sound like you," Kevin said.

"No, it doesn't." Jo crossed her arms. She suspected Gram had pulled one over on them, but most of all on Sheriff Borg. Maybe Gram had thought she was protecting Caroline by drawing attention to herself and away from her granddaughter. Jo had to admit, it seemed to have worked. Caroline remained suspiciously quiet. She looked over at her daughter. She was wearing a baseball cap, her hair pulled back in a ponytail. The front of her baseball shirt was stained with dirt.

"I'm just glad you're okay," Caroline said, and kissed Gram's cheek before rushing into her bedroom.

Kevin picked up the guitar he had brought inside with him.

"Where did you get that?" Jo asked.

"I found it in the back of the closet when I was cleaning," Gram said. "It has to be his. No one else plays. Why don't you play something for us?"

"Oh, I don't know. It's a bit out of tune," he said.

Jo bit her bottom lip. Kevin and his damned guitar had wooed her, charmed Gram, and enticed women in general every single time. Sure, he was handsome, strong, and lean, but put a guitar in his hands, and he became so much more. What was it about a music man? Whenever he played the thing, his passion, his voice, moved her in ways she didn't want to think about. Hell, she wanted to throw her bra at him before he even plucked the first chord. Then again, she wasn't wearing one.

"I'm going to shower," she said.

Her mouth tasted funny, and the scent of antiseptic, a hospital smell, lingered on her skin. She tied her hair up and let the cool water wash away the muck of the day. In the kitchen Kevin played a couple of chords. She closed her eyes. He may have been able to bait her with his music, but she had to admit, she had been the one who seduced him.

She had lured him to the private beach on the other side of the lake and removed her bikini. She stood before him naked and exposed, only sixteen years old, wanting to explore this power she possessed but didn't quite understand. She had wanted him to see her, all her soft spots and sharp edges as only he could see her, this sensitive boy who she suddenly desired.

He had seemed frightened at first, unable to move, but drinking her in at the same time, almost drowning in the sight of her. How she had toyed with him, using her body, her sex, moving in close, so close she could feel his breath on her lips.

When she touched his chest, he gasped, his skin quivering beneath her fingertips. His whole body trembled when she pressed up against him. It was as though he was afraid to touch her for fear she'd disappear. When he finally did reach for her, his hunger was like nothing she had ever experienced, his appetite for every inch of her, insatiable.

When it was over and he lay next to her in the sand, weak and out of breath, he had wept. She felt beautiful and powerful embracing her sexuality like never before, a woman desired like no other. In the days that followed, they had become addicted to the sex, to each other, and neither could stop if they had wanted.

She became the fool between two lovers like in the old song from the seventies the jukebox played. She should've known nothing good could come from a craving so strong.

She punched off the water in the shower. A woman's voice came from the kitchen, asking about the ambulance and whether Gram was okay. It wasn't surprising. Half the colony came out to gawk and gossip. It was typical, and Gram could more than handle herself with a few nosy neighbors.

Jo thought about Sara and Patricia, Pattie, and her own bit of news. She'd have to tell Kevin what she had learned, but she wanted to talk to Heil first, to get the men back on the lake and searching.

She slipped into clean clothes and sneaked out the back porch, making sure the door didn't slam behind her.

Jo's hands were clammy by the time she had reached the Pavilion. The place was lit up, the jukebox blared, the sound of laughter rang through the air. She marched up the steps, grateful they were empty. On any given night, Johnny and his gang might have been hanging out drinking beer and smoking cigarettes and doing whatever else she didn't let herself think about.

Inside, the pool tables were crowded with kids. The Needlemeyer twins looked her way as she strode past. The snack stand was open. On the second-floor bar she heard the scraping of barstools and felt the vibrations of pounding, dancing feet.

She pushed Heil's office door open without knocking. He was sitting behind a cheap-looking desk next to a metal filing cabinet. Several mounts hung on the wall—lake trout, pike, big-mouthed bass. A couple of fishing poles were tucked in the corner of the room. His face registered surprise. His greasy head glowed under the bright light. He leaned back in the chair, exposing the expanse of his stomach, and slipped his hand underneath the waistband of his shorts, tapping his thumb on his bloated belly.

"What can I do for you?" he asked. "Although, after the way you barged in here, doesn't make me want to do much."

"Patricia is Pattie Dugan. She's one of us," she said, ignoring his snide remark and his hand in his shorts.

"Pattie Dugan. Now why does that name sound familiar?"

"Bob and Jean Dugan. They were lake regulars for years. Patricia is their daughter. She's Pattie Dugan."

He shrugged. "And what of it?"

"She's not some outsider. She's not a one-season wonder. And we have to do everything we can to help her."

He raised his hands as if to say, *Why?*

She stared at him, confused by his nonchalant attitude. It suddenly occurred to her that he knew all along who Patricia was. He knew and it hadn't mattered. "You knew all this time."

"Of course I knew. I make it my business to know everything about everybody who comes to my lake."

"It's not your lake."

"You see, that's where you're wrong."

She rubbed her brow. She didn't want to get into the same tiresome argument about lake ownership. She didn't see the point, not now. "You have to get the men back on the lake, searching. You have to find her daughter," Jo said. "She's one of *us.*"

"Do I?" Heil placed his hands square on the desk. He leaned forward. The chair creaked under his weight. He narrowed his eyes. "One of *us*? Is that who you think you are?" he asked. "Your family, your mother, especially, has given me nothing but trouble since she bought that cabin. So let's get something straight. You're not one of us. You never were."

Jo was taken back. "My family has nothing to do with this."

"Oh, I think they do," he said. "Have you talked with your daughter? If anyone is to blame for stopping the search, it's the kids who messed with those traps."

"She had nothing to do with that."

"Maybe. Maybe not," he said. "I can't prove it. I can't prove a lot of things that happen on my lake—not legally anyway—which brings me around to you." His eyes roamed her body.

She crossed her arms, covering her breasts. "What about me?"

"Don't play innocent with me. You may have fooled everyone else around here, but I know who you really are. I know what you're capable of."

"I don't have any idea what you're talking about."

He leaned across the desk. "I hear you like it rough."

"You're disgusting." She took a step back.

"Am I?" He came up out of his seat and leaned farther across the desk, his large stomach resting on top, his eyes narrowing to mere slits. "You don't think I didn't know what you were doing with those boys under *my* Pavilion steps? On *my* beach? Why don't you tell me what really happened to Billy Hawke?"

She stumbled backward. "This isn't about me or—Or Billy. This is about a little girl," she stuttered. "And her mother."

His face burned red. "You're damn right, it is. So why don't you just stay out of it?" He reached across the desk as though he was going to choke her.

She backpedaled out the door and ran through the Pavilion. People turned to stare. She ignored them and hustled down the stairs and into the parking lot. Heil was nothing but a pervert trying to scare her. That was all. He didn't know anything about her or Billy.

Heil was a dirty money-loving piece of shit.

Jo picked up a rock at the water's edge and launched it into the lake. *Plop.* She picked up two more and threw them as hard as she could. *Plop. Plop.* She tried not to think about Heil and his accusations. She stared at the floating pier. On certain nights in the light of the moon, under a star-filled sky, the pier became a beacon in the center of the lake.

When she had been younger, there had been countless times where she'd swim out to the pier and lie under the stars on a night much like tonight. Sometimes Billy had been with her. Sometimes Kevin had been there too. Other times, her favorite times of all, were the times when she had been alone, her thoughts drifting, floating on the water, at one with the universe. She missed that girl, the one with dreams, confident and strong—the one with hope for a future.

She folded her arms. The water kissed her toes. She continued staring out at the lake, wondering what had happened to that girl she used to be, where she had gone wrong, remembering the very last time she had swum to the pier, the very last time she had seen Billy.

They had been drinking, all of them, under the steps of the Pavilion. Eddie had pulled a long shift at the bar, carrying cases of beer, rolling out empty kegs, exchanging the barrels for full ones, busing tables. But it had been a special night for Kevin. He had been asked by Tony, one of the guys in the band, to play a few songs and warm up the crowd. It had taken some coaxing, mostly from Billy to get Kevin to do it.

"Don't be a wuss," Billy said. "You're really good. You should be playing to a crowd."

Kevin had looked at Jo. She believed he was asking what she thought he should do. Of course she wanted him to play, but she also wanted to be sitting in the bar listening, not outside under the steps hearing his voice as though it were secondhand smoke. No, if he was going to play on a stage in front of a crowd, in front of other girls, she had to be there, front and center, listening firsthand, smoking the cigarette herself.

"Why do you keep looking at my girl?" Billy asked, and ruffled Kevin's hair as though he was a child and Billy a man. Although Billy was messing around, the tension between the two was palpable. She felt sure Billy sensed there was something between her and Kevin the last few days, something much more than friendship.

"You should definitely play," Jo said to Kevin. She moved to stand next to Billy, touching Billy's arm and shoulder as she spoke. "It drives the girls wild when you do." She was teasing Kevin, or maybe she was goading him to see what he would do, who he would choose, her or some other girl in the bar. Or maybe she was trying to hurt him because she really didn't want him to play his guitar for anyone but her. She pressed her body against Billy, wanting to show her feelings for him, too. He was more than happy to wrap his arm around her and pull her close.

"Go on," she said to Kevin as though she didn't care what he did, and nibbled Billy's ear. She wasn't playing fair, but she couldn't help herself.

Kevin's eyes burned through her. "Yeah, I think I will play," he finally said to Tony.

"Well, all right. Let's go," Tony said, and Kevin followed him upstairs.

She stepped away from Billy and lit a cigarette.

"What is it with you lately?" he asked.

"Oh, Billy. It's nothing." She ran her free hand through his thick blond hair and kissed his cheek, tasting the earthiness of the lake water on his skin. She buried her nose in his neck wondering what she thought she was doing. She wasn't eating, barely sleeping, bouncing back and forth between the two. It was tearing her up inside, and yet she couldn't stop. Her feelings for both were strong, but for very different reasons. Billy was her first love and would always have a place inside her heart. But it was with Kevin that she shared her private thoughts and where her hidden desires flourished. What was she supposed to do? She no longer knew what could make her happy. All she knew was that she couldn't carry on this way much longer.

They continued their little party under the steps—Billy, Jo, and Sheila—while Kevin's guitar sang out through the night air. She longed to go upstairs and listen, but at sixteen and under the legal drinking age, she was sure to be thrown out.

By the time Kevin finished his set and Eddie's shift had ended, Sheila was bent over, throwing up most of the beer she had drank.

"I better get her home," Eddie said, and held Sheila's hair from her face as she bent down and wretched again.

After Eddie took Sheila home, an uneasy silence settled between Jo and the two boys. Kevin quietly leaned against the back wall in the shadows, nursing the same bottle of beer. Billy picked the label from his bottle.

She suddenly felt tired of the whole damn thing. Or maybe she imagined the tension brewing between them. The ground tilted beneath her feet. How much did she have to drink? There was no way of knowing. She stumbled out from under the steps, stretched her arms overhead, and spun around. Maybe she should make *them* choose. Maybe she should make them fight over her. Maybe it was the alcohol that made her do it.

"Catch me if you can, Billy," she called. "You too, Kevin," she said, and raced to the beach. She didn't think about what she would do when they both reached her. Instead, once her bare feet hit the sand, she stripped down to her red bikini, wanting nothing more than to swim under the light of the moon and stars.

She rushed into the cool water and dove under. She was a good swimmer, a strong swimmer. Gram had made her take swimming lessons ever since she was little. She had learned the basic strokes, how not to panic when she was in trouble, like the time her legs got tangled in lily pads and threatened to pull her under.

It was safe to say she was comfortable in the lake as long as she didn't dive too deep. Even the strongest swimmers, the lake regulars, lost their way in what lay below, in the dark, murky depths of the bottom.

She swam to the floating pier with clean even strokes, despite the alcohol that made her clumsy on land. She climbed the ladder and pulled herself up, thinking it was up to the boys now. Let them fight it out and make the decision for her. She stretched out on the pier—one leg bent, the other straight. She flipped her long wet hair from her shoulders and leaned back on her elbows, posing in a way, and waited. And waited. What were they doing?

She could see them on the beach, talking or arguing. It was as if they were deciding whether to join her. She was irritated. Fine, if that was the way they were going to play it, then neither could have her. She lay flat and looked at the stars. For a brief moment she tasted something sweet on the tip of her tongue. She licked her lips. In that second she felt totally, utterly, completely free. Her breath moved easily through her lungs. Her chest expanded, her heart swelled. She was free.

Until she turned her head to the sound of splashing water and watched her freedom slip away as Billy and Kevin raced toward the pier to claim her.

Tonight, under the same moon and stars, the lapping water against the shore told a different story. She smoothed her wavy hair away from her face. The humidity made it frizz and crowd her cheeks. She should leave this place. She shouldn't have stayed this long. What was keeping her here? So what if they had found some old bones?

She turned back around toward the parking lot with every intention of heading straight to the cabin and then home to New Jersey. She'd return to work in the morning and beg Rose to cut her a break. She had only missed a couple of days. She was sure she could make it up to her.

But then she noticed a woman sitting on the hood of a car. Although her face was hidden in the shadows, Jo recognized her. She recognized the slumped shoulders, the bowed head. In that moment Jo knew she wasn't going anywhere. She would stay until Sara was found. She would stay because she owed it to Billy to see this through.

"Do you mind if I join you?" she asked, and climbed onto the hood without waiting for a reply.

CHAPTER TWENTY-EIGHT

Caroline was hiding in her bedroom. Her hands were clasped behind her head, and she was staring at the ceiling. On occasion, in-between the chattering of Gram and the woman next door, the one with the two young boys, the sound of a plucked chord from her father's guitar drifted into the room. Caroline wondered if the neighbor woman had brought her boys to the beach that day. She had heard people had been swimming and enjoying themselves even though Sara had not been found. Some of the newcomers even rented fishing boats.

It didn't seem right. She wondered if it was her fault. If she hadn't let the snappers go, the lake might've been off-limits while the fishermen searched. For the first time she felt a pinch of guilt and questioned whether she had done the right thing. Gram thought she did, although that was before Heil reopened the beach, the lake, and convinced people things were back to normal and life moved on.

She thought of Gram, how she protected Caroline's secret and chased Sheriff Borg away by faking a heart attack. Caroline smiled with the knowledge that she now had two secrets she kept from her mother. Why should she tell her mother the truth about the turtles or Gram when her mother had never shared anything close to the truth with her?

She rolled onto her side. Her stomach growled. She wanted to get up and find something to eat, but she wasn't in the mood for adults and their stupid small talk. She wished the neighbor woman would leave. She wanted to talk to her father about Billy. She believed her father would at least answer her questions. Wouldn't he?

There was a light rapping at her window. She jumped up, thinking it was Adam. Maybe he had news from the lake. She pushed the window all the way up where it had been opened only a crack. She found Megan on the other side.

"Where have you been all day?" Megan asked. "Can you come out?"

She could, but she didn't want to. "I don't think so."

"Well, I'll come in. Should I use the door so your parents know I'm here?"

"Don't bother." Caroline pulled the screen out.

Megan climbed through the window and grabbed Caroline's hands. "I have news." Her face was shiny and flushed. Her neck looked burnt and her scalp red. She had been out in the sun too long, *tanning*. Caroline felt a pang of envy. She was sporting a farmer's tan. She hadn't been in her bathing suit in four days.

"Did they find Sara?" she asked.

Megan furrowed her brow. "What? No, not that kind of news. This is better." She squeezed Caroline's hands and shook her arms wildly. "I have a boyfriend."

Now it was Caroline's turn to furrow her brow. This was the better news? Really? "Who is it?"

"Jeff." Megan smiled and batted her eyes, the lids covered in the same blue paint. "We sat on the pier together at the beach today."

"Wait, you went swimming?"

"Not exactly," Megan said, and shrugged. "It's a little weird going in the water knowing, you know, what's in there."

"A little weird? God, Megan, it's way worse than that."

"I know, I know." She pretended to inspect her pink fingernails. "But my folks say there's a good chance they'll never find the little girl now anyway. And what are we supposed to do? Melt in the hot sun all summer long?"

Caroline didn't have an answer.

"Anyway, what do you think of Jeff and me? Don't we make an awesome couple? His eyes are, like, the deepest brown. Oh, and wait until you hear the best part." She clutched Caroline's arm. "He held my hand. I swear, he did it for, like, a couple minutes. And you know what comes next, don't you? He's going to kiss me."

"Do you want him to kiss you?" Caroline pulled a face.

"Caroline! Of course I do."

"But you don't even know him."

"I know he's cute." Megan picked up Caroline's pillow and turned it over. "Have you ever practiced kissing?"

"No." She yanked her pillow from Megan's hands. "And you're not going to practice on my pillow. I sleep on that. Gross."

Megan rolled her eyes. "Don't be such a baby."

"I'm not being a baby." She hugged the pillow close to her chest.

They sat quietly, the silence becoming uncomfortable. Caroline tried to think of something they could talk about, something other than boys or Sara. What did they do other summers when things weren't strange and difficult?

"Want to play cards?" Caroline asked. They used to play cards, eat popcorn, and watch old movies with Gram. Maybe by doing the things they used to do, they'd stop talking about boys and kissing, she'd get her old friend back, and things would return to semi-normal.

"I don't think so. Do you want me to paint your nails? I brought some polish with me." Megan pulled a small bottle of pink nail polish from her shorts pocket.

Caroline shook her head.

"Do you have any magazines? *Teen Vogue*?" Megan asked.

She shook her head.

They were quiet again until Megan stood and said, "Well, I guess I'll get going." Before she crawled out the window, she turned to look at Caroline. "I'm meeting Jeff at the Pavilion tomorrow. You can hang out with us if you want to. Or not. It's totally up to you."

She found herself saying, "Yeah, okay." Or rather, *whatever*.

Once Megan had gone, Caroline no longer heard voices in the kitchen. She found her father sitting alone at the table. The guitar was in his lap. He was smoking another cigarette. His brown wavy hair looked messy, as though he had raked it with his fingers more than once.

"Where's Gram?" she asked.

"She went to lie down." He turned a guitar pick over in his hand.

She opened the refrigerator and stared at its contents, not finding much of anything other than old sandwiches. Normally, the shelves would've been stocked with leftovers from dinner: meatloaf, baked beans, potato salad, rice pudding.

It was the first time she became aware that maybe Gram had been affected by the events at the lake, more so than she had let on. Otherwise, Gram wouldn't have let their supplies run so low. Caroline decided she would offer to go to the Country Store for

Gram tomorrow. It was a perfect excuse to search more news-papers for a headline she might've missed.

She grabbed an apple and sat across from her father. She eyed him up. He seemed faraway, but if she was going to talk with him, it was now or never while she had him alone.

"Hey, Dad." She bit into the crisp apple and said while she chewed, "I didn't know you were friends with Billy." She meant to shock him, or at least surprise him with the little knowledge she had about the mysterious boy from his past.

But his face remained neutral. He didn't answer for a long time. Instead he continued turning over the pick in his fingers. Then he took a drag from his cigarette before snuffing it out in the ashtray.

For a second Caroline didn't think he had heard her. She was about to repeat the question when he looked up. His face took on an expression she had never seen before.

"Who said we were friends?" he asked in a voice she didn't recognize.

CHAPTER TWENTY-NINE

Jo pulled a pack of cigarettes from her pocket. "Do you want one?" she asked Patricia, and fished around for a lighter.

"No, thank you. I don't smoke." Patricia's blond hair fell loose around her face in waves. She clutched a cloth doll in her hands.

Jo imagined the doll had belonged to Sara, the same doll that had been on the rocking chair in front of the tea set. For a moment her thoughts drifted to Caroline and how it would feel if her own daughter was missing. Would Jo be clutching Caroline's softball mitt, struggling to hold it together like Sara's mother? But Jo didn't think she could. She'd fall apart if it was her daughter, if it was either one of her kids.

She lit the cigarette, letting the nicotine soothe her. A melodic rhythm poured from the jukebox into the night air, although Jo couldn't name the tune. Kevin would know. All he had to do was hear the first few notes and he could name the song and the band that played it. He had a gift.

She took a long drag and exhaled. "I remember you," she said in a voice barely above a whisper. She was embarrassed she hadn't known who Patricia was this entire time. In some ways she felt as self-absorbed as she had been as a teenager. "I'm sorry I didn't realize who you were earlier."

"Oh, that's okay." Patricia wiped her eye with the doll. "I was what, ten years old the last time you saw me?"

"I guess. Heil remembers you."

"Heil's an asshole," Patricia said.

Jo looked at her, somewhat surprised, and then smiled. "He is an asshole. But seriously, I should've known who you were. I mean it." She hesitated. What did she mean? She was sorry she didn't recognize Patricia as one of them? Why did it make a difference whether she was or wasn't a lake regular? A little girl had drowned. That should be enough for all them to care and do everything possible to find her. But somehow it wasn't. Somehow, Patricia knowing Billy, being here at the lake all those summers, it made a difference to Jo. She felt connected to Patricia in ways she couldn't explain, not logically, but she felt she owed her something.

"You're not the only one, you know," Patricia said. "Other than Heil, I'm not sure anyone else remembers I used to come here with my parents."

It was true. Gram hadn't known who Patricia was, and she had been friends with both Bob and Jean. She was certain Kevin didn't know. If anyone else had been privy to Patricia's connection to the lake, the news would've spread through the colony and the search may have gone differently. Or maybe not, based on her previous conversation with Heil.

"Why didn't you tell anyone?" Jo asked.

Patricia shrugged. "I was going to tell everyone, but I never got the chance. And then, it no longer seemed important," she said.

Jo touched Patricia's arm in a comforting way. "I'm sorry."

"It doesn't matter. Nothing matters now." She wiped her eye

with the doll again. "I got as far as the beach on our first day here and that was it. I never even got to introduce Sara to anyone, not even the Hawkes."

Jo waited for Patricia to continue, but she didn't. She disappeared somewhere deep inside herself, staring off at some point in the distance. Jo flicked the cigarette butt to the ground. She watched the ember fade and burn out. Whatever Patricia hoped to gain by returning to the lake, it had ended in a nightmare. But it still didn't explain her comment about Billy.

"Do you remember when I stopped by your cabin?" Jo spoke in a soft, soothing way, hoping to lure Patricia back into the conversation. "You mentioned Billy."

Patricia turned to look at her. In the dark, Jo could scarcely make out her eyes.

"Yes," Patricia said. "Billy." Her voice lifted. "How is he? And Dee Dee?"

Jo's mind raced to catch up with what Patricia was asking. My God, she was right. After all these years, she didn't know what had happened to Billy. How could she tell her he had drowned? How could she tell her they may have found his missing bones while searching for her daughter? She wouldn't tell her, not about the bones. It didn't change anything where Patricia was concerned. In fact, it seemed cruel.

Her throat felt dry. "Dee Dee is okay. The same." *Bitter.* She swallowed hard. "But Patricia," she said as gently as she could for both their sakes. It had been so long since she said the words out loud. "Billy is dead."

"What do you mean, dead?" She held the doll to her chest and searched Jo's face in the dark. "I don't understand." She grabbed Jo's forearm. "He's really dead?"

"Yes."

Patricia continued trying to see something in Jo's face. Jo could only imagine what she was searching for—grief, guilt, truth. Eventually she released the grip on Jo's arm. She turned away. She was quiet for some time. "It's just so shocking." She curled in on herself, hugging the doll. "How?"

"He drowned," she said, surprised how much it still hurt, how raw the pain still felt.

Patricia shook her head. "No, that can't be. Not Billy. He knew the lake better than anyone. He couldn't just drown."

"You're right," Jo said, and turned her head away. "He couldn't." Not unless he'd had help.

CHAPTER THIRTY

Caroline rubbed her eyes and sat up in bed. Her mother was talking to someone in the kitchen. She picked up the old alarm clock from her nightstand. A sliver of moonlight gave off enough light to see that it was three a.m., the dead hour. She had heard the term watching one of Gram's television detective shows. She thought it was a cool phrase. However, having been awakened in the middle of the night during the dead hour wasn't as cool as it sounded in daylight.

Someone in the kitchen burped, which meant it had to have come from Johnny. When wasn't he disgusting?

Her mother continued talking in a hushed voice, and something about her tone pulled Caroline from the bed. It was obvious whatever they were saying they didn't want anyone else to hear. She dismissed the idea they were whispering because it was the middle of the night and they didn't want to wake anyone. Johnny wouldn't have cared. He only thought of himself.

She could say the same for her mother, but that kind of thinking always made her feel bad. She couldn't discount the times her mother had tried to be the kind of mom Caroline had wanted— one who baked treats for special occasions, cheered from the stands at sporting events, applied Band-Aids to booboos, prepared home-cooked meals.

Her mother wasn't good at being a regular mom.

But maybe Caroline should give her a break. After all, Caroline was fed—mostly fast food—but still, she never went hungry. Her mother had sent store-bought cookies into school for Caroline's birthdays, and twice her mother drove past the ballpark looking for one of Caroline's softball games, only to discover she went to the wrong field.

She peeked through the crack of her bedroom door. The overhead light in the kitchen allowed for a narrow view of the table, the pantry, a basket hanging on the wall. Gram had several baskets, all hung in the kitchen for decoration, but also for use. Gram thought nothing of grabbing one of them off the wall and filling it with chips or pretzels or popcorn.

Her mother and Johnny were sitting at the far end and out of sight, their voices muffled. She slipped into the hall to listen, stopping to hide in the shadows.

"I'm glad Gram's okay," Johnny said. "I would've been here had I known."

Her mother said something Caroline couldn't make out.

"We took the girls to the drive-in. What else were we supposed to do? It's too damn depressing hanging around here."

Caroline heard the strike of a match. Her mother or Johnny or both were smoking.

"Whose car did you use?" her mother asked.

"Chris's mom's."

"Damn it, Johnny. I wish you wouldn't have. Why didn't you ask to use one of our cars?"

"What difference does it make whose car we used?"

"It just does. I don't want you taking anything from them."

"What does that mean? I wasn't taking anything from them. What do you have against Chris? What has he ever done to you?"

"I don't have anything against Chris. It's not him."

"Then who is it?"

Her mother didn't respond.

"Tell me, Mom, because I know it's something, and whatever it is, I can handle it."

There was a long stretch of silence.

"It's Chris's mom, isn't it? What happened between you two?" Johnny asked. "Why don't you like each other?"

Caroline craned her neck, eager to hear her mother's reply. There was another long silence. Caroline's mind raced. It must have something to do with Billy. Wasn't Chris's mom, Dee Dee, Billy's sister?

Movement across the hall caught her attention. There was a dark shadow behind her parents' bedroom door. Her mother said something, but she missed what it was, too distracted by the dark figure.

"Dad," she whispered.

He darted away without saying a word, taking his shadow with him. Then Caroline heard Johnny say, "Whatever, I'm going to bed."

Caroline scurried back to her bedroom and climbed underneath the covers. She wondered what her mother had said to Johnny. It couldn't have been much, or he wouldn't have retreated so quickly. But what was strange and what bothered her more than missing a big part of their conversation, was why her father would be spying on her mother and Johnny too?

She burrowed under the sheets. Maybe her father felt as she had—closed off from her mother, pushed away. Johnny was the only one who had a solid relationship with her. When was the last time her mother had sat in the kitchen and talked with her? Had she ever? Not that Caroline remembered.

A batch of tears threatened to spill, and she swiped her eyes repeatedly until the skin underneath was dry and raw. She wouldn't cry over the things her mother did or didn't do. She was too old for that. She just wished she didn't feel so alone and mixed up inside. What she wanted more than anything was for her mother to hold her, comfort her, and tell her everything was going to be okay, that what she was feeling was normal. It would pass. The summer would continue, and there wouldn't be any secrets to hide. And whatever happened with Billy was not a big deal, nothing for her to worry about, she should leave it lie, forget about it, and enjoy herself while she was here.

But Caroline knew she couldn't do that. Her parents were both involved in something and she had to know what it was and why. Besides, how could she pretend this summer was like all the others when a little girl had drowned? Wasn't Sara the reason her parents stayed at the lake? Wasn't another drowning the reason her parents' past felt so close to the surface, to the here and now? Otherwise, her mother would've split after a day or two, and her father would've hit the road hauling whatever it was that kept him away from home sometimes for weeks. Caroline would've been dropped off to stay with Gram like every other summer, forgotten about by her parents, tormented by her brother.

She was restless most of the night. Her mind wouldn't settle down. Thoughts of both Billy and Sara washed over her, pulling her under, sinking her into the deep, dark abyss to the bottom of the lake.

The next thing she knew she was standing outside her bedroom window in her nightgown. The summer air was unseasonably cool. She shivered underneath the swaying branches of Willow. She didn't remember crawling out the window, but she must have. Otherwise, how could she have gotten outside?

One of the branches brushed against her arm as though vying for her attention. *What is it?* She asked the tree, saying the words inside her head. *Do you want me to climb up?* She took a step closer, when a little girl poked her head out from behind the trunk.

Caroline rubbed her eyes. She was dreaming. Of course she was. She felt the warmth of the bed and the sheets wrapped around her legs. But somehow when she opened her eyes, she was still outside under the tree. *Sara*, she called.

Sara appeared wearing the same yellow-and-pink polka dot bathing suit. Her braids dripped water onto her shoulders and down the front of her chest. Her skin was pale, almost translucent.

What are you doing here? Everyone's looking for you, she said in a dreamlike voice, although she could feel herself talking inside her chest. Could she be talking in her sleep?

I want my mommy, Sara said.

I know you do, she said in an understanding voice, because wasn't that what Caroline wanted too? *I'll take you to her.* She reached for her, but Sara recoiled.

Don't let them find me, Sara said.

I won't. I promise. But you need to come with me now. I'll take you home, she said. *I'll take you to your mother.* It was then Caroline noticed holes, hundreds of them, up and down Sara's arms and legs. It was as though bits and pieces of her body had been rubbed out, chunks of her skin removed. Caroline covered her mouth to keep from screaming.

Find me, Caroline, Sara said in a whispering voice. *Find me.*

Caroline sat straight up in bed, her hands over her mouth. She was shaking so hard, her knees knocked. She breathed in and out, trying to slow her speeding heart. She was dreaming again. It was only another bad dream. The room was warm and humid. The curtains sagged in the stagnant night air. The window screen lay on the floor beneath the window. She thought she had put it back after Megan had left. She was pretty sure she had.

The chill she had felt in the dream crept up her spine and settled in her bones. *It wasn't real*, she told herself, and sprung from the bed. She stuck the screen back in the window and pulled the curtains closed. It wasn't real. Then why did it feel that way?

CHAPTER THIRTY-ONE

Patricia returned to the *Sparrow*, thinking about the recovery team. They had promised they'd be back to searching before the sun came up. She didn't doubt them, although she was losing hope at a rapid pace. The lake was big, several miles long, and who knew how deep? There was no telling where the storms, *or whatever else*, the voice in the back of her mind screamed, could've dragged her little girl. She didn't want to think about her daughter lying on the murky bottom. The image of the half-eaten eel the men had dumped onto the beach cut across her mind, and she quickly forced it away. Far, far away. She was barely holding it together. If she went there, to the dark place of reality, she'd never be able to pull herself out. And now wasn't the time to fall apart, not while her daughter was still out there, waiting to be found.

She wrapped her arms around Dolly and paced the living room. She stopped moving when the rotary phone rang. She grabbed the receiver.

"Hello?" Her breathing quickened, thinking it might be news about Sara. But all she heard was static and Kyle's faint voice calling her name. The connection was poor, and after a few seconds of white noise, she hung up and continued walking.

Most of Sara's toys were strewn about the place much like Patricia's toys used to be when she had stayed in this very cabin with her parents. Now that she had been in the place a few days, she noticed other things, things she remembered from her childhood. Like how the wicker rocking chairs creaked underneath a person's weight, how the pipes groaned when the water was running, how the old claw-foot bathtub still looked a little creepy.

Evidence of mold stained the corners of the ceiling in most of the rooms despite the fact that the brochure had stated the cabin was recently painted. She supposed it couldn't be helped. The colony had a way of holding onto moisture whether it was dampness or humidity. Nothing ever felt totally dry—not the air, the towels, the clothes, your skin.

And the smell, the ones she remembered from childhood that had hit her at full force when she had first stepped through the door. They were a mixture of the same damp earthy lake air and smoke from the fireplace. The sight and scent had filled her with such a state of happiness; she didn't think anything bad could happen while she was here.

She looped around the couch and chairs. When she grew tired of the pattern, she circled the kitchen table, walking, pacing—the movement soothing. Sometimes her mind raced with thoughts of Sara, her heart too heavy for her chest to hold and she'd stop, bend over, and release the most terrifying sound she had ever heard, one laden with grief.

She continued on, stepping in and out of one of the three bedrooms. She couldn't bring herself to walk into Sara's bedroom, where her daughter should be sleeping. And the master bedroom, if you could call it that since the space could just about fit the queen-size bed and chest of drawers, where Kyle had slept on their second night when she had telephoned about Sara, reeked of failure and loneliness. The thought of both empty beds was too much to bear.

She took to biting her nails, moving haphazardly through the rest of the cabin. She lost track of time. At one point she poured a glass of water and swallowed it down in large gulps. Within minutes, the water sloshing around her belly, she bent over the kitchen sink and threw up. She couldn't remember the last time she had had something to eat or drink. Her body ached with exhaustion. She walked on.

Gradually, slowly, her thoughts turned to Jo and the news about Billy. No, no. She wasn't ready to think about it yet. She couldn't bear to think he was gone from this world. Not Billy, too.

But she did think about him, the boy he was the last time she saw him. He was wearing a white T-shirt and jeans even though it had been a particularly hot day. In fact, it had been a hot summer. The days were long and the humidity relentless. But somehow not even the heat could touch cool Billy. Or maybe because he spent so much time on the lake, the coolness of the water never truly left him. It was as though he had been a very part of what made the lake special.

True, she had been young, but not so young that she didn't recognize the way her stomach flip-flopped and her heart skipped whenever he was near. "Are you feeling okay?" Dee Dee would ask. "I feel funny," she would whisper, only to have Dee Dee whisper back, "That's why they call it lovesickness."

She had followed Billy everywhere. He had never given any indication he had minded. In fact, thinking back, he had encouraged her.

"What do you think, Pattie-cakes?" He had looked into her eyes. There had been something about his gaze that had invited you in. A girl, young or old, could have lost herself in those eyes, so deep and full of mystery. "Should we take the boat for a spin?"

She had tried to answer, mixing up her words and stuttering. In the end, she had resorted to nodding. He had picked her up, his biceps bulging, sunglasses perched on the top of his head. He had placed her in his boat and off they went, speeding across the water after dinner well before the partying started, before Jo had turned up to take him away.

Patricia stopped pacing when a car pulled into the yard and parked. Her first thought was that it might be the sheriff. She yanked the curtains aside and looked out the window, recognizing Kyle's BMW. He knocked on the door. She didn't know what else to do but let him in, caught off guard, surprised to see him. It must've been why he tried calling earlier, to let her know he was coming.

"Is there any news?" he asked, straightening his tie, the crease in his pants still evident even after a six-hour drive.

The sight of him in his crisp suit, fresh and pulled together, more than bothered her. She touched the tangles in her hair, glanced at her wrinkled clothes. "Nothing yet," she said.

"How are you holding up?" He crossed the room and sat in one of the wicker chairs.

"I'm okay. Can I get you anything? Coffee? You must be tired after the long drive," she said, wondering why she felt compelled to play the role of wife, to pretend nothing was wrong.

"No," he said, and rubbed his brow. "I'm good."

She sat on the couch across from him and waited. He obviously wanted something from her, but she couldn't force herself to care enough to ask, to show him any empathy. Instead she picked up a couple of Sara's pictures from the table and started shuffling them around, making the collage she had promised her daughter she would make on their first day here.

"Can you put those down?" he asked.

She carefully set the pictures back on the table and folded her hands in her lap.

"How long is it going to take to find her?" he asked.

"I don't know."

"But they must've told you something, given you some idea."

She shook her head. "They're doing what they can."

"Is it possible they'll never find her? I mean, is it possible it could take weeks, months, even years? How long are we expected to wait?"

"I'll wait as long as it takes," she said.

"But I can't. Don't you understand?" He stood, smoothing back his hair. He walked around the chair. "I just can't take off days and days to sit around and wait."

No, of course not, you always were weak. It took a tremendous amount of strength to sit and wait and hold it together. "What do you want, Kyle? Do you want me to tell you it's okay that you left? That you went back to work knowing your daughter was still out there? That you didn't care enough about her to stick around until they found her, her body?" She raised her voice.

"No. Yes." He walked around the chair again. "I don't know. Maybe."

"You want me to ease your guilt?" She stood, her anger building, understanding that was exactly what he wanted.

"No," he said, and stopped. "I want her found as much as you do." His voice cracked.

There was pain in his eyes when he looked at her. He was hurting, and for a second she wanted to reach for him, to have him put his arms around her, to grieve with her. It was their child and nothing could change that. But before she had a chance to go to him, to comfort him, to comfort her, he opened his mouth.

"Just promise me, when all this is over, we'll handle it between us. That you won't get anyone else involved." He held his hands up, pleading with her.

"What are you talking about?"

"We can do this on our own. I can draw up the papers. I promise, I'll be fair."

"Papers?" My God, he was talking about their divorce. Her body stiffened. How could he bring up their divorce at a time like this? Her teeth rattled with rage. "Get out," she said.

"What?" He cocked his head. "Where do you want me to go?"

"Get out!" she shouted.

"Calm down. There's no need to shout," he said, trying to placate her. "Somebody will hear you."

"I don't care. Just get out." She pushed him in the chest. "Now." She screamed.

"Be reasonable. I drove all this way."

"Get out." She continued pushing him, slapping him in the arms, shrieking. "Get out. Get out. Get out." She hollered until she pushed him outside. The screen door banged shut between them. He stood on the other side, staring in at her.

"We're not done talking about this," he said.

She slammed the wood door in his face.

She returned to the living room and dropped into the wicker rocking chair. How could she have loved him? He was an awful human being. She cried into Dolly's soft stuffing, but still she wouldn't allow herself to unravel. Not now. She wouldn't give Kyle the satisfaction.

What she needed was to talk with someone, someone who would listen, someone who would understand what she was going through. She could no longer do this by herself.

CHAPTER THIRTY-TWO

Dee Dee drove straight to the sheriff's office after receiving a message he wanted to see her. She was still in scrubs having worked a double shift. She had covered for one of the nurses who had called in sick. The extra shift had felt like it would never end. Her feet hurt in spite of the comfortable sneakers. Her skin was sticky and smelled like a mixture of stale air and antiseptic. But she wasn't about to stop home for a shower. She pressed the accelerator. She couldn't get to the sheriff's office fast enough. She broke every speed limit, skidded into the parking lot, and burst through the door, surprised to find Heil stuffed into one of the metal chairs in front of the sheriff's desk.

Heil stood as soon as she entered. "I'll leave you two alone," he said, and moved toward the door, but not without making eye contact with the sheriff first. "Dee Dee." His fat stomach brushed against her arm on his way out.

"Frank," she said. Neither one hid their apparent dislike for one another.

"Please, sit," the sheriff said when they were alone.

"What was he doing here?"

"He wanted to know if he should be calling his lawyer," the sheriff said.

"What did you tell him?"

"I've got a couple of witness statements saying they saw Billy drinking under the steps of the Pavilion bar. I told Heil to do what he thinks is in his best interest."

"Does this mean you're reopening the case?"

"Yes," he said. "I got the final report this morning. The DNA is a match. The bones are Billy's."

Relief overwhelmed her and rendered her speechless. She hadn't realized just how badly she needed it to be official until now, how much she had relied on the DNA results for validation. The bones were Billy's, and one of them was fractured.

The sheriff continued. "After reading the original file and the new report from the medical examiner, something about his injuries doesn't add up. Your brother fractured his skull here." He touched the left side of his head above his temple. "But he fractured his right arm. You would think if he fell on the pier like we assumed, a flat surface with no obstructions, his injuries would be on the same side of his body, say his left arm and left side of the head. But that's not the case. So the question is, how did he fracture his skull on one side and fracture his arm on the other?"

It didn't make sense. But she was still too stunned, exhilarated, to respond. After all this time the very thing she had been hoping for was finally happening. She gripped the car keys so tight, the jagged edge dug into her palm.

"Now, I suppose it's possible he fell twice, first hurting his arm and then hitting his head before falling into the water. But even that troubles me. The toxicology report confirmed there were traces of alcohol in his bloodstream. It's hard to know the exact amount, since five days passed between the time of death and when his body was recovered. Minus the lower half of his right arm, of course, until now. But there's not one statement in the file claiming your brother was drunk. Drinking, yes, but not falling down drunk. So what else could've happened that made him fall twice?"

She was nodding. Yes, she agreed with all of it. He didn't have to sell it to her. She had known all along it didn't make sense. Nothing about Billy's drowning had ever made sense.

"There's one other thing." He was scowling.

Oh, here it comes, she thought. Nothing good ever came without a price. "What is it?"

"You know it's a sensitive issue, especially when we're still trying to find that little girl. People around here are reluctant to talk about drownings, past or present."

"What are you saying?"

"It was one thing to poke around and ask a few questions, but now I'm going to be asking in an official capacity. And I have no doubt Heil is going to tell everyone to keep their mouths shut. Remember, he's worried about his own liability in this."

"I don't care about Heil or that the damn alcohol came from his bar."

"That may be. But he cares. And people aren't going to want to speak out against him."

She shook her head. The sheriff was missing the point. He needed to focus on Billy's friends. He needed to interrogate *Jo*. "You're still going to try, right?"

"Yes," he said.

"Even Jo? Because I know she knows something about that night that she's not saying." She wanted to be present when he questioned her, but knew he'd never allow it.

"I'll talk with her." He paused. "I need you to be patient a little while longer. Like I said, it's a sensitive matter, and I don't want people to clam up before I even get started. You need to be patient and let me do my job."

She didn't respond, and continued squeezing the keys in her fist.

"I'm serious," the sheriff said. "Let me handle this." He waited for her to say something. When she continued giving him the silent treatment, he said, "You know I never would've closed the case if we would've found his arm with the body. If we would've had all the evidence back then, things would've gone differently."

When she still refused to acknowledge what he was saying to her, he asked, "Did you hear me?"

"Oh, I heard you," she said, and turned her head away.

CHAPTER THIRTY-THREE

Caroline woke to a wet stickiness between her legs. She tossed the covers off. The sheets were stained with blood. Oh my God, oh my God, oh my God. What happened to her last night? Her underwear was soaked. She pulled at her nightgown and found the back of it spotted red. It took a few more panicked seconds for her to understand.

She jumped from the bed and felt a warm gush between her legs. She cupped her hand over her private parts as if she had to pee. She peeked into the hallway, looking, listening for any sounds. The bathroom door was wide open. She made a break for it, not knowing what else to do. She stripped off her pajamas and cleaned herself with a washcloth. She knew she needed supplies. She had read all about menstruation from the stupid pamphlets the nurse had handed out during the school year. But it wasn't until she had read Judy Blume's *Are You There God? It's Me, Margaret* did she fully understand what was coming. It wasn't like her mother had ever sat her down and had "the talk" with her. She wondered if there were parents who actually did stuff like that with their kids.

She doubted it.

What she knew about sex she had also learned from reading books. The information the other girls her age had imparted was mostly misinformation, like how you couldn't get pregnant the first time, how anal sex wasn't really sex. Books set Caroline straight. They saved her from the embarrassment of having to ask her mother to explain.

Although she had to give her mother props for standing up to the school board when they had threatened to remove some of the more graphic health books from the school library. Caroline's mother had stepped out of her dark place and into the world, rallying a group of women's rights activists into the largest protest the school had ever seen. With the support of the librarians and most of the other mothers behind her, the books stayed on the shelves. She was proud of her mother and embarrassed, too. The subject of sex had made Caroline feel all weird inside. It was a subject her mother cared about deeply.

She sometimes heard strange sounds coming from her parents' bedroom, the moans, the creaking bed, the thumps and crashes. Once, she banged on the door, shouting for them to stop, thinking they were killing each other. They never answered her cry, but the rest of the night had been eerily quiet. She shuddered. Don't think about it. No child ever wanted to think about their parents having sex, let alone the loud boisterous kind her parents had.

She searched in the cabinet above the toilet for supplies. Nothing. Her mother had never stayed at the cabin for more than a day or two, except for this summer. None of her feminine products were stored here. She guessed Gram went through her phase already, *meno*-something. What was she going to do? No way could she tell her mother. But what other choice did she have?

She thought about buying supplies at the Country Store. What if someone saw her? She'd die of embarrassment. Maybe she should tell Megan and she could help, but it felt too personal, a private matter she didn't want anyone to know about. She plopped on the toilet and covered her face. *Stop being a baby*, she told herself.

"Caroline," Gram said in a soft voice, and knocked on the bathroom door.

"Yeah," she said, wiping her eyes. "Just a sec." She grabbed a towel and wrapped it around her. How was she going to get out of the bathroom without anyone knowing what happened? Her pajamas were stained, and she was still bleeding. "Gram," she said. "Are you still out there?"

"Are you okay?" Gram asked.

"I need some help." She opened the door a crack and waved Gram inside. She didn't know which one of them was more embarrassed when she showed Gram the pajamas and underwear.

"Oh," Gram said. "Is this the first time?"

Caroline nodded.

"Do you want me to wake your mother?"

"No." She shook her head.

Gram touched her arm in a sympathetic way. "Stay here. I'll bring back some clean clothes. We'll go the store. I planned to go today anyway. You can come along and get what you need."

Gram returned with clean clothes. "Use these for now." She handed Caroline a stack of cloth rags she was supposed to put between her legs. She must've made a face, because Gram said, "It's what women had to do before. It won't kill you to use them for a little while." She left Caroline alone in the bathroom, mumbling on her way out something about Caroline's mother and not being better prepared, not stocking up for what was obviously coming.

Caroline stuffed a cloth rag in her underwear and pulled on her shorts. She felt as though she was wearing a diaper. She didn't want any part of this. She finished getting dressed and met Gram in the kitchen.

"I stripped your bed," Gram said. "I'll go to the Laundromat later. Now, let's get to the store. I have a long list."

At the Country Store, Mrs. Nester made a point of ignoring Caroline, maybe because Gram was with her, and maybe because she regretted giving Caroline the old newspapers. Gram went about getting the food and paper products on her list. Caroline lingered in the candy aisle, working up the nerve to go down the aisle where the feminine products were located. She took a deep breath and turned the corner, pretending to be lost, looking for something, anything other than what she was there for. She plucked the first box of pads she saw off the shelf and tucked it under her arm.

With her head down, she darted away to find Gram and hide the small box in the grocery cart. She made it to the end of the aisle and bumped into someone. When she looked up, she was staring into Chris's two-toned eye. He smiled. She fumbled the box and quickly hid it behind her back.

"Sorry," she said, and scurried around him. She found Gram in the next aisle over, and she stuffed the box in the cart. Gram was too busy with her shopping list to notice the flustered look Caroline imagined was on her face.

Gram pushed the cart farther down the aisle. Caroline felt someone's eyes on her back and turned to find Chris at the other end, watching her.

"You're up to something," he said, and folded his arms. The grin on his face made her feel as though he was the one hiding something.

"No, I'm not."

He motioned for her to come closer. She looked over her shoulder for Gram, but she must've moved to a different aisle. Caroline took a tentative step in his direction. Her uncertainty seemed to amuse him.

"Come here," he said. "I'm not going to hurt you."

Right, said the wolf to Little Red Riding Hood, she thought, but walked up to him anyway. "What do you want?" she blurted, wishing she knew how to act cool.

"Why'd you do it?" he asked.

"Do what?"

"Why'd you release the snappers?" Something in his eyes told her that he liked the idea she might've done something bad.

"It wasn't me." She was a terrible liar.

"Yeah, it was."

She crossed her arms and then uncrossed them. She pulled at her fingers. "Fine." God, she was weak, but she wanted to believe she could trust him. She felt the need to explain. "It's not right what they're doing. I think it's cruel and gruesome."

"They're just using the natural resources the lake provides." He shrugged. "And it's probably the only way they're going to find her now."

She looked at her feet. "I suppose," she said, wondering if he would answer a question for her if she could work up the courage to ask.

He leaned in close. "What is it?"

Standing so close to him made her palms clammy. She cleared her throat. "Why doesn't your mom like mine?"

"You don't know?" he asked as though everyone knew the reason. "It has something to do with my uncle Billy and what happened to him. He died before I was born, but my mom and him were real close." He shrugged. "She doesn't go into it, but I guess your mom was Billy's girlfriend at the time. She thinks your mom knows more about what happened to him that night than she's saying."

"So my mother was there when he drowned?"

Again he shrugged. "Listen, don't put too much into anything my mom says. She can be real paranoid." He tapped the visor of her baseball cap. "And don't worry. Your snapper secret's safe with me." He winked before walking away with the same cool swagger as her brother.

Watching him go, Caroline was reminded of something she had learned in biology class. It was a lesson on genetics, how there were dominant and recessive genes, how certain traits were passed from parent to child, how certain characteristics could be detected throughout family members.

But what did her teacher call the way a person walks? Gait? Could two people from different families have a similar gait? She wasn't sure, but it didn't seem plausible. Maybe if two people spent every second together, they could pick up each other's habits. But it didn't make sense for Chris and Johnny. They were best friends a month or two out of the year. And yet they walked the same way, and yes, now that she thought about it, their smiles were similar too, with one cheek rising slightly higher than the other. Why hadn't she noticed it before?

"There you are, Caroline," Gram said. "Are you ready?"

"Yeah," she said absently, and followed Gram to the checkout counter. Her thoughts scattered, unsettling the very balance of everything she believed she knew about Johnny and her family.

In the bathroom Caroline read the directions on the box of feminine products, which were simple enough. When the pad was in place, she left the bathroom and helped Gram unpack the rest of the groceries. She didn't bother trying to be quiet. She knew by the opened bedroom door that her parents were up and gone. Johnny was snoring in the back bedroom and, knowing him, he wouldn't wake until sometime after lunch.

Gram moved with purpose, trying to get the frozen items into the freezer. The day promised to be another scorcher. She turned on the oscillating fan. "Let's get some air circulating," she said. Her face looked flushed.

"I can do this," Caroline said. "Maybe you should sit down." It was the first she thought about the little trip to the hospital. Maybe Gram hadn't been faking after all.

Gram laughed. "There's nothing wrong with me," she said. "I thought you knew that."

"I do," she said.

Gram patted Caroline's shoulder.

They finished putting the rest of the groceries away. Gram mentioned heading to the Laundromat to take care of the other business, the sheets and soiled clothes.

"Why don't you head on down to the lake? I bet they have the forms posted for the fishing tournament. That is, if you're still considering entering."

"They're still having it?"

Gram put her hand on her hip and pursed her lips. "They wouldn't cancel that thing for nobody. It's all about greed. They think money rules the world." She picked up the laundry basket. "Fools, that's what they are, a bunch of ignorant, greedy fools."

"I'm not sure I would've fished anyway, you know. It's kid stuff." After the morning event, it no longer felt like she should compete. The tournament was meant for kids twelve years old and younger. Maybe it was time she stepped aside to give the younger kids a chance to hook the largest lake trout. This would be the first summer since she could remember where she'd have to stand back and watch. In some ways, she felt her body betrayed her.

Gram looked at her. "Suit yourself." She supposed Gram understood why.

Caroline rode her bike to the Pavilion. The place was a flurry of activity despite the underwater recovery team's watercraft in the middle of the lake. The parking lot was sectioned off by wooden horses. Several people were vying for spots to set up their stands for the Trout Festival. Near the dock where the fishing competition would take place, men were assembling the poles for the larger tents. The sign-up sheets were posted on the Pavilion wall.

Caroline climbed the stairs and checked the names on the sheets. The Needlemeyer twins had signed up, along with Adam and the two young boys in the cabin next to *The Pop-Inn*. She recognized some of the other names, but they were all much younger. "Well, that settles it," she said to herself, and stepped inside.

The jukebox was between songs. The bells and whistles from the pinball machines were sounding off. Customers stood in line at the snack stand, and the doors to the beach were flung open. She spied Megan leaning against the railing that led down to the beach, laughing at whatever Jeff, *her boyfriend*, was saying.

There was an air of excitement about the place, the vacationers getting swept away by the undercurrent of doing something maybe they shouldn't be doing in the midst of an ongoing search. But wasn't that part of the lure, to do the thing you shouldn't? Outside in the open lot, more and more tents were constructed. Brightly colored signs were posted with promises of tasty desserts and handmade crafts. The tragedy that had started the summer was dissipating. Life at the lake was returning to normal.

Caroline found she was unable to get swept away so easily, thinking about her dream and Sara. She turned her back on the crowd at the snack stand, the kids at the pinball machines, on Megan and Jeff. She wondered if she'd find *M+J* carved into the Pavilion steps or painted on a rock in the woods, which brought her to thinking about her mother and Billy and, ultimately, her brother, Johnny.

She wondered if Chris's mom, Dee Dee, had the answers to the secrets her family was unwilling to share. Maybe it was time she asked her.

CHAPTER THIRTY-FOUR

Kevin pretended to be asleep when Jo got out of bed and left the cabin. She would often take long walks in the morning whenever he was home for any length of time. He took these early morning walking excursions as a personal affront. He couldn't help it. It was as though being with him, sharing a bed for more than one night, suffocated her.

Good, he thought. *Go.* He was glad to be alone. It gave him time to think. He had an uneasy feeling, or maybe it was more than that, something pushing him closer to the edge, ever since the sheriff had started asking questions. Even Caroline had asked him about Billy. He had been vague with his answers, sticking to the facts she had already confessed to knowing after reading an old *Lake Reporter*. Why Mrs. Nester had given his daughter those old newspapers baffled him. What was she looking to get out of it? And what in the hell were Jo and Johnny whispering about the night before?

He kicked the sheets off and ran his hand down his face. He felt as though he were on a collision course with the past, and everything he had worked so hard for was slipping away. He had done it all for the love of Jo. And he'd do it again if he had to. He wasn't going to lie here and take it.

The cabin was empty except for Johnny snoring in the back bedroom. Damn kid could sleep the day away. Kevin decided to head down to the lake for the latest news. He wasn't two steps out the door when he spotted the young woman Patricia stumbling down the dirt road. Her hair was tied in messy braids underneath a big crazy sun hat. Her blouse and flowing skirt looked slept in. Her sandals slapped the bottoms of her feet as she wove her way down the hill. If Kevin didn't know better, he'd think she was drunk.

She didn't notice him. How could she with her back to him and her head down? He had heard who she was from a couple of the fishermen the last time he was in the bar. Patricia was little Pattie Dugan, daughter of Bob and Jean, the couple who had come to the lake every summer for years and then one year had packed up and left, never to return. He had stopped listening to the gossip after that. It didn't matter why the Dugans had stopped coming. He was more interested in what made Patricia, Pattie, come back.

He started following her, lagging far enough behind so she wouldn't hear him—or if she did, she wouldn't be alarmed. It was the road everyone in the colony took to the lake unless they took the path that cut through the woods, but which most adults avoided for practical reasons, bugs, poison ivy, or Cougar, Stimpy's noisy, pathetic dog.

The sun was high in the sky, promising another hot day. He reached into his pocket for the pack of smokes. He paused briefly to light up. The Pavilion was open for business, and it was bustling. The parking lot was full of lake locals and their tents. Everyone was preparing for the Trout Festival. Heil was a man who got his way more often than not. He was a man who got things done, and nothing was going to stop this festival from taking place. It was one of the biggest money-makers of the season. People from all around the Poconos area, from all different vacation sites, flocked to the lake for a day of fishing, food, and crafts. The locals made a killing.

Kevin watched Patricia shuffle through the chaos. Most people got out of her way and looked a little guilty upon seeing her. The underwater recovery team was in the middle of lake doing their job. A few fishing boats were also out on the lake, but they respectfully kept their distance from the watercraft, although if they had any respect, they wouldn't be out there at all.

Patricia stopped and gazed out at the lake. She started walking again, heading straight for the docks. Kevin followed, stopping briefly to say hello to Mr. and Mrs. Roberts, Megan's parents, who were carrying their beach chairs, obviously going to the swimming area to enjoy the day, *drowning, be damned*. Stimpy had his men working near the docks. Nate waved as Kevin passed. There were too many distractions, and Patricia was almost clear to the other side of the lake by the time Kevin broke free from the crowd. He passed Eddie's cabin and found Sheila sitting outside on the front porch with a cup of coffee and the *Lake Reporter*. He dropped his cigarette and stepped on it.

"Join me," Sheila said.

He glanced in the direction in which Patricia had been walking along the docks. Then he sat next to Sheila, deciding it was better to chat for a few minutes than make up some lie about where he was going and what he was doing.

"Eddie's inside sleeping it off. And to think I'm usually the one who can't handle the alcohol." She laughed.

They reminisced about their partying days, and for a moment it felt like old times, how easily they had reverted to their teenage selves just by being together under the hot summer sun by the lake.

But after a few minutes of idle chitchat, the underwater recovery team's watercraft pulled alongside the floating pier and silenced them. Kevin became keenly aware of a distance that spread between them—the space that never seemed to have closed after Billy had died. In ways, his death bound them to each other, and at the same time tore them apart. The little girl's drowning, the recovery team on the lake—both were reminders you could never go back.

Sheila drank from her coffee cup, keeping her eyes over the rim and on the watercraft. Kevin sensed she wanted something from him. He wiped his palms on his shorts.

"You know," she said, "Sheriff Borg stopped by to see me. He told me they confirmed the bones are Billy's."

He didn't say anything, only nodded. So the DNA results were in.

"He asked if I knew how Billy might've hurt his arm."

"What did you tell him?"

"I told him I didn't know."

Sheila had never asked him any questions about his version of what had happened the night Billy had drowned. She believed the story he had given to Sheriff Borg back then. Although he suspected she had known he and Jo had been sneaking around behind Billy's back. He wondered if she also assumed like the sheriff had that there had been a fight between them that night. If she did, he wasn't going to admit to anything. Not now. Not ever.

"I don't know anything about it either," he said, and stood. "I hope Eddie feels better." He stuffed his hands in his pockets and headed toward the dock in the direction of *Hawkes'* cabin, where Patricia had stopped and was now standing outside the front door.

Kevin lingered on the pier by the fishing boats, waiting for Patricia's next move but pretending to look over the boats as though he were thinking about renting one for the afternoon. There was a time when he had enjoyed fishing, or rather he had acted like he did. Everything he did at the lake, every summer, had been centered on Billy. Billy loved to fish. To be fair, so did Eddie. Two of his best friends enjoyed the sport, so Kevin figured he should too.

But he didn't.

It wasn't that he got motion sickness from rocking on the water or that he wasn't good at casting a line. He just didn't see the point in spending hours on a boat to catch a fish, only to turn around and toss it back again. He'd have rather played his guitar, written his own songs, and hung out on the beach with Jo while she had tanned in her red bikini.

There had been countless times when he had watched her stretch her body on the towel, her flat stomach practically concave, leaving a gap in her bikini bottoms. He had imagined sliding his hand inside that gap, running his palm over her silky hair, slipping his fingers between her legs. And once, he'd had to pick up his guitar and put it in his lap to hide the erection in his shorts.

But like so many of his fantasies back then, even that one had been interrupted. A shadow had cut across her torso. Billy had dropped down on top of her and started doing pushups. His back was slick with sweat. His muscles bulged. Jo had laughed and pushed him away, pretending to be angry he had blocked the sun.

"Let's head out on the boat," Billy said to Kevin. "And leave the girls to their tanning."

Kevin had forgotten Sheila was lying on the beach towel on the other side of Jo. He placed his fingers on the guitar strings, thinking about a song to play and the shrinking erection in his shorts. "I think I'll stick around here for awhile."

"What for? Come on," Billy said. "Let's go fishing." He grabbed Kevin's arm to pull him up.

Kevin shook his arm free. "Nah, that's okay. I don't feel like it."

"Don't be such a girl," Billy said.

A familiar rush of anger shot through Kevin, reaching as far as his toes. Billy had a way of making him look like a sissy, like less of a man in Jo's eyes. Sometimes he hated him. "No thanks," he said.

"You're killing me." Billy placed his hand over his heart. "Please. Eddie's got the boat ready. I have the gear packed. All you have to do is show up."

Kevin played a couple of chords. "I don't think so," he said.

Jo leaned on her elbows, watching them.

"You're breaking my heart," Billy said in such a sincere way, the girls took pity on him.

"Aw, that's so sweet," Sheila said.

"He wants to hang out with his best friend," Jo said to Kevin. "Look at him. He's begging you. How can you say no?"

Kevin looked at Billy. In his eyes he could see that Billy's sincerity was real. Damn him. How did he do it? How did he make Kevin feel like the bad guy every single time?

"Fine." He put the guitar down next to Jo, stealing one last look at her in the bikini, his erection long gone. He followed Billy to the docks, where Eddie and the boat awaited them. Eddie was shirtless and wearing cut-off jean shorts. A cigarette was pinched between his lips. He wiped his hands on a towel. "She's ready to go. All I need is someone to run up to the cabin and grab the tackle box."

"Great." Billy turned to Kevin and poked him in the chest.

"That means you. Oh hey, while you're there, grab some sandwiches and some cold ones."

"I thought all I had to do was show up?" Kevin didn't wait for Billy to reply. Instead he turned and marched back the way he came, arms pumping at his sides. He overheard Eddie ask Billy, "What's wrong with him?"

Eddie's cabin was only a few feet away. It wasn't like he had to walk miles. But still. Still. He stomped inside and yanked open the refrigerator door. He pulled out cold cuts and a couple of beers. Fuck it, if Eddie's dad noticed he was missing a few cans. He threw the sandwiches together and tossed everything into a small cooler. On his way out the door, he grabbed Eddie's tackle box and an extra fishing pole. Maybe he was overreacting, but Billy had a way of making him do things he didn't want to do. Billy made him feel every bit the chump.

He returned to the boat, stashed the gear, and untied the lines from the dock. When they were well on their way to the far end of the lake and miles from the beach, for a moment, a fraction of a second, he thought about pushing Billy overboard and drowning him.

CHAPTER THIRTY-FIVE

Caroline walked out of the Pavilion and into the lot where the tents were being constructed. She took two or three steps before she noticed Adam and his mother approaching. His mother had her hand gripped tightly around Adam's arm, dragging him through the crowd of men and women blocking their path.

Caroline stopped and waited for whatever was coming. By the look on Adam's face, it wasn't good.

"I suppose this was your harebrained idea," his mother said.

Caroline glared at Adam. He kept his eyes on his dried muddy sneakers. "She figured it out. What was I supposed to do?" he mumbled.

His mother continued. "Sneaking out and releasing those snappers."

"Yes, ma'am. It was all my idea," Caroline said, and Adam's head snapped up. He stared at her.

"Do your parents know about this?" his mother asked.

"Yes, ma'am."

The sheriff's vehicle rolled to a stop a few feet from where they were standing.

"Well," his mother said, "here comes Sheriff Borg now. Do you want to tell him or shall I?"

"I'd rather if neither one of us said anything," Caroline said.

"I'm sure you would, but I'm not the only one who's going to pay a fine because you two knuckleheads did something stupid."

The sheriff stepped from his car. After placing his hat on his head, he walked toward them. He tipped his hat at Adam's mother and said to Caroline, "How's your grandmother doing?"

"She's better." Caroline avoided his eyes.

"Glad to hear it," he said, and glanced out at the lake before settling his gaze on the three of them.

Caroline didn't say anything more, waiting for Adam's mother to turn them in. But she said nothing. The sheriff tipped his hat again and headed in the direction of the docks, where Stimpy and his men were finishing setting up the large tent that would become the control center for the tournament.

Caroline and Adam exchanged awkward glances.

"Well," his mother said, "maybe he's forgotten all about it with everything else going on." She motioned to the festival and then the recovery team on the lake. "I suspect it's because they're still searching." She waved her finger at them. "You won't be so lucky if there's a next time. Do you hear?"

"Yes, ma'am," Caroline said.

Adam's mother grabbed his arm again. "And one more thing," she said to Caroline. "I'd appreciate it if you two would stop all this wild talk about that horse's bit and that stupid lake legend."

Adam's face was flushed. "It's not her fault, Mom," he said.

Caroline wondered what Adam had said to her. She didn't understand why his mother was so worked up. Unless . . . "Ma'am, do you believe in the legend?"

His mother hesitated. "I suppose when I was a kid, I did. And I understand why you kids find it fascinating. Finding that metal bit is like discovering buried treasure. I understand that, too. But the whole thing is giving *him* nightmares."

"Mom," Adam protested.

His mother continued. "I think it's best if you two just stopped talking about it altogether. In fact, maybe it's best if you two just stayed away from each other for awhile," she said to Caroline.

The look in Adam's eyes said he was sorry. His mother held onto his arm and marched him into the Pavilion.

Caroline walked with her head down, kicking up pebbles and dust as she made her way across the lot. She didn't know Adam was having nightmares. She was having them too, but a different kind. She was sorry she had gotten him in trouble with his mother. She didn't know what to do to make it right.

By the time she had reached the docks, she decided to stick to her original plan to talk with Chris's mom. She had nothing to lose. The summer had been ruined, or so it seemed, anyway. And now all she wanted was the truth.

"And the truth will set you free," she said, wondering where she had heard the expression before. It may have come from Pop. He was always offering up quotes as little life lessons, a habit that drove her mother crazy. Caroline had never minded. Her mother saw them as judgmental, a personal attack on the decisions her mother had made, the ones that revolved around teenage pregnancy. And now Caroline was sure Johnny was at the center of whatever tortured her mother. But why?

Out of guilt, she avoided the pier where the fishermen's boats were docked and their traps were set, trekking her way through the woods behind the lakefront cabins. She zigzagged around trees, ducked under branches, and counted, the seventh cabin being *Hawkes'* cabin. Another one of Pop's expressions crossed her mind: *Be careful what you wish for.* She ignored the warning and kept moving.

The shade of the trees did little to block the heat from the sun. She tried to ignore the warm flow between her legs, making her body temperature run hotter than normal. When she reached her destination, she pressed her back against one of the old oak trees. What if Chris was home? She couldn't face him again, not twice in one day. How would she explain what she was doing here? Would he think she didn't believe the things he had said about his mom? Would he think she was stalking him? God, he was so cute.

She hid behind the tree in the back of the cabin, when she heard the screen door open and voices coming from the front porch. Two women were talking. Their conversation was stilted at first and then turned into a hushed silence. Caroline imagined them hugging when one of them sobbed. The screen door banged shut, muffling their voices now that they were inside.

She slid down the trunk and sat at the base of the tree. She'd have to wait it out. She picked up a twig and poked some leaves on the ground. Then she made circles in the dirt. She spelled her name and then wiped it away. When she looked up from the ground, she noticed the old fire pit and the rock with the painted initials *J+B*.

She threw the twig at the rock. She hated Billy for reasons she didn't fully understand and she couldn't properly explain. It wasn't nice hating someone who was dead, but she did hate him. She thought about the old *Lake Reporter*: *Sixteen-year-old local boy William J. Hawke disappeared.* Her father said he wasn't friends with him, but the article in the paper said otherwise. She wondered if maybe her father didn't like Billy either, since he was once her mother's old boyfriend. It was possible. Maybe that was why she had such strong feelings about not liking him too.

"William J.," she said to herself. A disturbing thought crossed her mind. Could the *J* stand for "John?" William John Hawke. And if it did, could Johnny be named after Billy? Was that the big secret? She did the math, figuring the date Billy died and the month Johnny was born. And then there were the similarities between Johnny and Chris, their smile, their swagger.

Her stomach took a slow roll.

The possibility that Johnny was Billy's son and not her father's left her breathless. She sprung to her feet, gasping for air. How could her mother lie to her and her father? Or did her father know Johnny wasn't his? Then again, maybe she was wrong. Maybe she was working herself up for no reason. But she felt so much rage inside her.

She picked up a large branch and struck the rock with her mother's and Billy's initials over and over until the branch snapped. She searched the ground, grabbing rocks and throwing them at random into the woods. She picked up more stones. One of them sliced her palm with its sharp edge. The cut was small, but deep enough for blood to drip down the side of her arm.

I hate you, she said about her mother. With all her might, she lifted the rock with the stupid initials and flipped it over so she didn't ever have to look at it again. *I hate you.*

She pulled the baseball cap off her head, covered her face with it, and cried.

Everything felt like a lie. Her family was a lie.

CHAPTER THIRTY-SIX

Dee Dee opened the screen door to find a strange woman on her front porch. The woman's clothes were rumpled, her sandaled feet dirty. The wide-rimmed sun hat cast shadows across her face, and yet there was something familiar about her.

"Can I help you?" She leaned against the doorjamb, holding the door open with her bare foot. She crossed her arms. She had been home for a total of ten minutes, her body exhausted after pulling a double shift. And after sitting in the sheriff's office the last hour, her emotions were just as worn, cast, and dragged like grappling hooks, sharp with anger but also filled with hope now that the bones were in fact Billy's and the case was officially reopened. She didn't have the energy to humor this woman who was holding a small stuffed doll in one hand and extending the other for her to shake. She looked at the woman's hand, the nails bitten down to the cuticles. She kept her arms folded.

"It's me." The woman clearly was on edge, and her voice had a desperate pleading quality.

"I'm sorry. Do I know you?" The second the question came out, she recognized her as the woman whose little girl had drowned.

"Yes, you do," the woman said, and launched herself at Dee Dee, wrapping her thin arms around Dee Dee's neck. She laid her head on Dee Dee's shoulder, letting the sun hat fall to the porch floor, and sobbed. Her breath smelled like coffee. Her hair was greasy. She was filthy, and she was on the verge of coming undone.

Dee Dee wasn't the type to offer comfort. Years of nursing had a way of desensitizing her. She considered herself tough, thick-skinned, detached. But she wasn't unkind. It was just that life on the lake had hardened her. But she understood the woman's anguish whether she wanted to admit it or not. The woman had lost her child, and Dee Dee knew all about loss.

"There, there," she said, and patted the woman's back. The woman collapsed farther into her arms, and it was all she could do to hold the two of them up. The woman continued to burrow in close, wanting the kind of affection a child seeks from a parent.

"Okay, okay," Dee Dee said. It was then she recognized the scent of the lake on the woman's skin, an odd mix of earthiness and sunshine and whatever was rotten on the bottom. It was the identifying factor of anyone who had spent any time here, anyone who the lake had claimed as its own.

"Come inside." She led the woman into the kitchen, where she helped her into a chair. She set a cold glass of lake water she had pumped from the well onto the table. "Drink," she said.

The woman gulped the water down. When she finished, she wiped her eyes with the doll. "It's me, Pattie," she said, and choked back a sob. "Pattie Dugan. You used to babysit me."

Dee Dee's hand flew to her chest, surprised at hearing the name of the little girl she had babysat all those summers ago.

"It's Patricia now. Patricia Starr. My daughter, Sara . . ." She shook her head, unable to continue.

Dee Dee ran her fingers through her hair, trying to get ahold of the situation. It took a second or two for the shock to wear off, but once it did, something that had gripped her chest all these years loosened. She gazed into the woman's blue eyes and saw the child she used to be. The guard she kept in front of her heart had lowered just enough for her to reach out to Pattie, Patricia, and hug her tight. It was the most affection she had shown anyone in quite some time.

"I always wondered what happened to you," she said. She had babysat Pattie every summer since she was three years old. It was as though she were seeing her long-lost daughter for the first time after an unwanted, painful separation.

Dee Dee had so many unanswered questions, she wasn't sure where to start. She pulled back and collected herself. She had waited a long time, a lifetime, for Pattie to return, and now she wanted answers. She put a pot of coffee on and sat across from her.

"Start from the beginning," she said. Patricia told her about her parents, their divorce, and later, her awful marriage to Kyle, his affair, how she was alone, how she had no place to go, how she ended up back at the lake after all these years.

"It never left me," Patricia said. "This place. The lake. It lived inside of me and became a part of me if that makes any sense. I thought by coming here, I would be saved from everything wrong in my life. I believed me and Sara would finally be happy if I could just get us back to the one place I always felt safe."

Dee Dee understood better than anyone what the lake could do to you, how it could take ahold of you like a lover, drowning you with its beauty, how the mountains could blind you until you could no longer see that there was a whole other world out there, waiting for you, but by then it was too late, and you were too far gone to notice. No, it wasn't safe at all.

"Why did you wait so long to come to me?" she asked.

"I had planned on coming our first night here. I was going to bake a pie. But Sara . . ." She broke off. "I swear, I only turned my back for a second," she said. "I didn't know what to do. Everything happened so quickly."

Dee Dee reached for Patricia's hand. "It's not your fault. A second is all it takes for accidents to happen around here." She sat quietly for awhile, letting Patricia cry.

When Patricia was able to collect herself, she lifted her head and started talking about Sara. She told Dee Dee about her pregnancy, how Sara had been an easy baby and an even sweeter child. She told her stories about Sara's determination to tie her own shoes, how she loved bedtime stories and drawing pictures. She talked about Sara's wild imagination and Sugar, the imaginary Doberman that lived in their attic. "One time during a snowstorm—you know the kind of storm you get around here in the mountains with a foot of snow—well, Sara insisted Sugar got out. She had me driving all over the neighborhood in the middle of the storm looking for her imaginary dog. And I did it. I did it for her. I'd do anything for her."

She continued telling Dee Dee story after story about her daughter, their adventures, until Dee Dee felt as though she knew everything there was to know about the child. Hours later, when Patricia was talked out, clearly drained, Dee Dee suggested she lie down.

When she was sure Patricia was asleep, Dee Dee lit a cigarette and stepped onto the front porch. She stared out at the water. And for the first time in a long time, she let herself cry.

CHAPTER THIRTY-SEVEN

Caroline stormed into *The Pop-Inn*. Her heart was pounding, and she was out of breath. Her shirt was soaked with sweat, and she was pretty sure so was the pad between her legs. The thought made her queasy. She wasn't ready for her period, not now, not with everything else making her life so miserable.

The screened-in porch was empty. She tore through the family room and found both Gram and her mother at the kitchen table. They looked up when Caroline barged in.

"What happened to you?" her mother asked.

Gram shot her mother a dirty look and rushed to Caroline's side. "Your hand is bleeding," Gram said. "And why are you so sweaty? What happened?" She removed the baseball cap and felt Caroline's forehead with the back of her hand.

Caroline turned her head away. "I'm fine," she said.

"No, you're not. You're overheated and you're bleeding." Gram pulled her by the arm and stuck her hand underneath the faucet at the kitchen sink. Once the dirt was washed away, she inspected the cut on her palm. "It doesn't look too bad. You won't need stitches."

Gram poured a glass of lake water from the jug and handed it to her, which she gratefully accepted. She stared at her mother over the rim and gulped the water down in defiance, remembering her mother's agitation the last time she filled the jug from the well. When the glass was empty, she wiped her mouth with the back of her arm and said, "Mom, I have something to ask you."

Her mother eyed her. "What's going on?"

"You should sit down," Gram said to Caroline.

"No, I want to stand." She turned toward her mother.

"But you're burning up," Gram said.

She ignored Gram and stared at her mother. "Is Johnny named after Billy?"

Gram was the one who sat down. Her mother's face paled, the dark shadows in the hollows of her cheeks growing darker, blacker, like the look in her eyes.

"Sit down, Caroline," her mother said.

The tone of her mother's voice normally would've made Caroline do whatever it was she was asking, but not this time. She crossed her arms. "Answer my question. Is Johnny named after Billy? His *real* father."

Gram gasped.

"He is, isn't he?" she asked her mother. She turned to Gram. "And you knew this entire time," she said. "You were supposed to be on my side."

"Oh, Caroline," Gram said. "It's not about taking sides."

"It's more complicated than that," her mother said.

A small part of her couldn't believe her mother wasn't jumping all over her, shouting, *Of course not! Johnny is your father's son.* But she wasn't doing that, and something inside of Caroline shattered. She heard Pop's saying again: *Be careful what you wish for.*

"Please, sit down," her mother said. "Let's talk about this calmly."

"I can't believe you." Caroline stomped her foot like she used to do when she was three, throwing a tantrum whenever she didn't get her way. "Gram?" she asked. "Is he or isn't he my brother?"

"Of course he's your brother," Gram said, and glanced at Caroline's mother.

Her head felt fuzzy and the room was spinning. She blinked several times to make it stop. She refused to pass out, not until she had heard the truth from her mother. She concentrated on standing upright. "So what, is he like my half-brother then?"

Gram stood and touched Caroline's arms. "Honey, you don't look so good. Come sit down."

She threw Gram's hands off of her. "No." She had never lashed out at Gram—ever. She didn't talk back to her or roll her eyes at her or push her away. But she wasn't herself. She didn't know who she was, uncomfortable in her own skin, her changing body.

Her mother slid from the bench seat of the picnic table, taking her time in a cool casual way, remaining in control no matter the circumstances.

It pissed Caroline off even more. Black spots raced across her vision. The angrier she got, the faster they darted past. "Answer me, Mom!" she shouted. "Why won't you just answer the question?"

"I will when you calm down." Her mother stepped toward her, reaching for her.

Caroline held her arms out, warning her not to come any closer. For a second the request struck her as funny. All the times she wanted her mother's arms around her, comforting her, loving her. Right now she couldn't stand the thought of her mother touching her.

"Is he or isn't he Billy's son?"

"Billy had a son?" Johnny asked.

Caroline whipped around to find Johnny standing in the doorway. She hadn't known he was home. He must've still been sleeping. His hair was sticking up in the back and his long bangs were matted to his forehead. He was wearing boxer shorts. His chest was bare where two days ago there had been hair. He must've shaved his chest hair. It made his pectorals look more defined and his shoulders broader. He scratched his butt and reached for the refrigerator door, pulling it open.

Her mother hadn't taken her eyes off Caroline. Gram stared at her mother. No one said anything. Johnny pulled out a jug of lake water and drank from the container without bothering to get a glass. When he finished, he looked at the three of them. "What?"

"Do you know who Billy is?" Caroline asked him.

"Of course. He's Chris's uncle who drowned when Mom and Dad were teenagers."

Caroline was stunned. Everyone in her family knew who Billy was and what had happened and no one thought to tell her. Why were they keeping it a secret from her? Why didn't Johnny ever tell her? Then again, she couldn't expect Johnny to tell her anything. It's not like he confided in her. She had assumed it was the four-year age difference, a brother/sister thing. But the circumstances had changed, and he knew only half of the story. She knew something he didn't, and the power tasted good on her tongue.

"Tell him the rest," Caroline said to her mother. "Go on. Tell him the truth."

"Tell me what?" His chest rose and fell. "What's going on?"

"Nothing," her mother said. "Caroline is upset with me."

"What else is new?" Johnny winked at Caroline, teasing her.

She glared at her mother, challenging her to tell him, or she would. When her mother didn't say anything, the anger burned so hot, she thought she might combust.

"Billy is your real dad. You're named after him," she said to Johnny, wanting to hurt him for the constant teasing, hating him and loving him too. But mostly, she wanted to hurt her mother for lying to her. "You're not my brother," she spit. "And I hate you!"

Johnny put the jug of lake water down and turned to his mother. "What is she talking about?" he asked, his voice quavering.

"Why would you say such a thing?" Gram asked Caroline, but her words sounded false, and it was then that Caroline knew for sure that Gram had been in on it from the beginning. Somehow Gram's betrayal was worse than her mother's lies.

CHAPTER THIRTY-EIGHT

Dee Dee was sitting in the kitchen when Patricia woke and appeared from the back bedroom. She walked into the living room, running her hand over the back of the couch, touching the wicker rocking chair, smoothing out the old throw Dee Dee's mom had knitted. She stopped in front of the mantel over the fireplace and picked up a wedding photo of Dee Dee's parents. "What happened to your folks?" she asked.

"Dead," Dee Dee said, sounding matter-of-fact. Her father's health had gone downhill fast after Billy's death. His heart hadn't been able to take it. Her mother had followed him a few months later. Although a piece of all of them had died with Billy, her parents had taken it a step further and gone with him.

"I'm sorry," Patricia said, and returned the wedding picture to the mantel. "I would've come back had I known. They were so good to me." She walked into the kitchen and put her hand on Dee Dee's shoulder. "You were all so good to me."

To Dee Dee's surprise, she didn't push Patricia's hand away. Instead she let her shoulders relax, finding the intimacy soothing. It had been such a long time since she had allowed someone to touch her in a caring, gentle way. Her ex, Neil, had deserted her only a few months before Chris had been born, and she hadn't been close to anyone since, other than her son. She couldn't think when the last time someone had wanted to touch her was, let alone spend time with her.

"You look so much like your brother. Did you know that?" Patricia asked, and sat across from her.

"I know." She *did* look like her brother. Although where Billy was handsome—broad shoulders, lean, muscular build, strong chin—the attributes weren't as flattering on a woman. Her masculine features made her look hard, and most men found her height, her strong arms and legs, intimidating.

"I'm sorry," Patricia said of Billy. "I'm sorry about a lot of things." Fresh tears left dirt tracks down her cheeks.

"Come on," she said, and pulled Patricia up and led her to the bathroom. "Take a shower and clean up. We'll talk when you get out." She grabbed a clean towel and handed it to her.

Dee Dee waited in the kitchen, listening to the water run. She had already laid out a clean pair of shorts and a white T-shirt and set them on the bathroom sink. She lit a cigarette and thought about popping open a can of beer, but the shower stopped and she didn't want to drink in front of Patricia. It was stupid, but in some ways, she felt as though she were babysitting her all over again, and a babysitter shouldn't drink on the job.

Patricia returned to the kitchen wearing the clean clothes that were much too big for her. She rubbed her thin pale arms.

"Sit," Dee Dee said. "Let me get you something to eat." She pulled leftover egg salad from the refrigerator. If she had had food that was heavier, fattier, she would've made it instead. But she made do with what she had. It was what she did best.

When Patricia finished eating, she began braiding her hair. She kept her eyes away from Dee Dee's when she said, "Tell me what happened to Billy."

Dee Dee rubbed her brow. It had been so long since anyone asked to talk about Billy, years since anyone cared to listen, or at least to her version of the story. She told Patricia what she knew. He had been hanging out with friends under the steps of the Pavilion and later on the beach, apparently drinking. It had been late at night under a full moon. After his friends had gone home, Billy must've gone swimming alone. No one had seen him after that night. He was reported missing the next day. Five days later they found his body near the floating pier in the middle of the lake. She didn't bring up the recent discovery of his missing bones found by the recovery team while they were searching for Patricia's daughter. The fact that they had found sixteen-year-old bones and not her little girl's body was far from comforting.

Patricia listened quietly, her brow furrowed. "It doesn't make sense. He was good in the water. He knew the lake better than anyone."

Dee Dee snorted. "It never made sense to me, either. Kevin said he was the last one to see Billy. That he had left him alone on the beach, thinking he was going home too. But I think Kevin is covering up for somebody. I think Jo was on the beach with Billy and *she* was the last one to see him alive. I think she has something to do with him drowning."

Patricia shook her head. "I don't think Jo would've hurt Billy. She loved him."

"Maybe she did, maybe she didn't. I don't know and I don't care. But what I do know is that she's hiding something. She knows more about that night than she's saying."

"Was there an investigation?"

"They ruled it an accidental drowning even though he cracked his skull. And after lying on the bottom of the lake for five days, his body was torn apart by the snappers. They couldn't find any evidence to prove otherwise." Until they found the bones from his forearm, but again, it wasn't the right time to share this information.

Patricia suddenly looked horrified.

Dee Dee realized the insensitivity of her comment, forgetting Patricia's daughter hadn't been found, and it was coming up on six days. "Pattie," she said, and stopped. It was the harsh truth, and she wouldn't apologize for it. Patricia needed to hear it, not only about Billy, but what to expect if there was anything left of her daughter to find. But she couldn't bring herself to tell her that, and neither of them spoke for some time.

Patricia was the first to break the silence. "When did he drown?" she asked.

"You don't know?"

"I only heard about it yesterday."

"Jesus," Dee Dee said, thinking after all this time. "July 1997," she said.

She looked surprised. "But I was here that summer. How could I not have known about it?"

"It happened the same night your parents dragged you out of here. I was babysitting, and they stormed into the cabin, fighting. You left that morning, and I never heard from you again."

"I remember," she said. "It was awful. My parents fought so often that summer." She covered her mouth and appeared to be thinking. After a few moments of silence she said, "And he drowned that same night?"

"Yes," Dee Dee said.

Patricia disappeared inside her own thoughts once again. She shook her head. "No," she said. "That's not right. They weren't on the beach."

"What are you talking about?" Dee Dee clasped Patricia's hand.

Patricia held on tight. "They're lying."

She looked into Patricia's eyes. "What are you saying? Who is lying?"

"They are," she said. "They weren't on the beach. They were on the pier."

"Who was on the pier?"

"I saw them."

"Who?" Dee Dee asked. "Who did you see?"

"You know how you can see the pier when the moon is bright?" Patricia said.

"Yes." It was true. You could see the floating pier clearly under the light of a full moon. "Who did you see on the pier that night?"

"Billy. He wasn't on the beach."

Dee Dee grabbed Patricia's arms, wanting to shake her to get the answers out of her quicker. "Was anyone with him?"

Patricia flinched. "You're hurting me."

"Sorry," she said, and patted Patricia's arms where her hands had been. More gently, she asked, "Was anyone else on the pier with him?"

"Jo."

"I knew it," she said. "I knew she was lying." She stood, knocking the chair over. "That bitch." She turned toward the counter, not sure what to do with the new information. Jo wasn't on the beach after all. She was on the pier with Billy, right where his body had been found. "And you're certain it was Jo?" She had to ask one more time. It's not like Patricia was of sound state of mind, going through her own personal hell.

"Yes, I'm sure. I was by the lake catching lightning bugs. You remember. You gave me a jar and punched holes in the lid."

"Yes." Dee Dee nodded. She remembered. Patricia should've been asleep, but it was such a clear beautiful night, she had let her stay up way past her bedtime playing outside, catching bugs.

And it was almost dawn by the time Patricia's parents had burst into the cabin to collect her.

"Kevin was there too," Patricia said.

Dee Dee whipped around. "What did you say?"

"Kevin. He was there too."

"That can't be. He said he was on the beach."

"No, he was on the pier with them."

She bent close to Patricia's face, searching her eyes. "Are you sure?"

"Oh yes, I'm positive."

CHAPTER THIRTY-NINE

Caroline ran from the kitchen and into her room. She slammed her door and threw herself onto the bed. She pulled the quilt Gram had made over her head. She hadn't meant what she said to Johnny. She didn't hate him. It was just the opposite. She loved him and wanted him to continue being her brother. She wanted to take back her words. He was as much a victim of their mother's lies as Caroline was.

Johnny's voice bellowed from the kitchen. Caroline threw the covers off to listen. "Is it true?" he asked.

Her mother must've nodded because the next thing he said was, "Jesus Christ. And you didn't think to tell me until now?"

She pulled the quilt over her head again. So it was true. She hadn't realized a small part of her was still hoping she was wrong. Knowing the truth didn't make her feel any better. It made her feel worse.

Her bedroom door creaked open.

"Go away," she said, not even knowing who it was. She didn't care. She didn't want to talk to anyone.

The door closed and someone sat on the edge of her bed. She

smelled coffee and talcum powder, the two smells she identified with Gram.

"Caroline," Gram said. "I know you're hurting. It's a lot to take in."

"You think?" she shot back.

"Your mother should've told both you and Johnny a long time ago."

"Yes, she should have." She pulled the quilt down, uncovering her head, but she couldn't look at Gram. Instead she looked over Gram's shoulder at a spot on the wall. "Why didn't you tell me the truth?"

"It wasn't my place."

"But I thought you didn't like Mom. How could you let her lie to me?"

"You think I don't like your mother?"

"Well, yeah. You two are always fighting. You're never nice to each other."

"Oh, Caroline. I love your mother. I may not like the choices she's made, but I love her."

"You could've fooled me."

Gram sighed. "A mother-daughter relationship is a complicated thing. We each have our own way of doing things, our own ideas of how things should be, and sometimes we don't agree on what that thing is. We clash. We may fight. But we love each other anyway. It's just how it is between your mother and me." She touched Caroline's cheek. "It doesn't mean it has to be that way with you and your mom. You can make it be the way you want."

"Tell that to her." She wiped her eyes, refusing to let the tears fall.

"I think you should tell her. Talk to her."

Caroline picked at a thread that had started to come loose from one of the stitches on the quilt. She was too angry to talk to her mother. She didn't even want to look at her.

"I don't hate Johnny," she said instead. "I didn't mean what I said."

"I know you don't. I'm sure he knows it, too." Gram paused as though she was considering whether to say anything more. Then she asked, "How did you find out?"

"It's not rocket science. I did the math." She stared at the ceiling. "Plus, I found out Billy's full name. William J. And then I saw a couple pictures of Billy. And then there's Chris. In ways, Johnny looks like them, their family. I didn't know for sure. I was only guessing, but it seems I guessed right."

Gram pressed her lips together and nodded.

"Does Dad know?" she asked, already knowing the answer, but finding she needed confirmation so she wouldn't question herself later about who knew what and who had lied.

"Yes," Gram said. "He knows."

Caroline rolled over and put her back to Gram. She wished she could start over and return to the first day of summer, when her family had made sense in their screwed-up way. She wanted to go back to that day on the beach when Sara had drowned so that she could pull her off the pier rather than what she did, which was to leave her alone. Sara's death was the catalyst that pushed her into asking questions about drownings, about Billy and her mother. Now that she knew the truth, she didn't know what to do with it, with all the anger she felt inside.

Gram put her hand on Caroline's hip. "Are you going to be okay?"

"Sure, I'll be okay," she said, but she didn't sound convincing even to her own ears.

———

After Gram left her room, Caroline sneaked into the bathroom. Her mother and Johnny were arguing in the kitchen. They started shouting. Caroline didn't think she had ever heard her mother raise her voice at Johnny. A rush of adrenalin shot through her as the screen door banged shut. She saw Johnny storm past the window. She ran out to catch him.

"Johnny, wait," she said, hustling down the steps and onto the dirt road. He kept walking, turning down the hill toward the lake. "I don't hate you," she called after him. "I'm sorry."

"Fuck off, Caroline," he yelled, and disappeared around the corner.

Caroline turned and saw her mother standing at the edge of the yard. Their eyes locked for a brief moment before her mother turned her back and walked away.

Caroline glanced at Willow and scurried underneath the swooping limbs. She climbed into the crook of the thick branches, pulled her knees to her chest, balancing her chin on top. The cut on her palm throbbed.

She had really screwed things up. She hadn't meant to hurt Johnny. She wasn't sure what her intentions were anymore. She was only certain of one thing. She wasn't going to win her mother's love, not after what she had done.

Maybe Gram was right, and it was up to Caroline to determine what her relationship with her mother would be. She admitted, beneath the pain and anger, she felt a kind of power, believing it was her choice to make.

The only problem was she no longer knew what she wanted from her.

CHAPTER FORTY

Jo kept walking. She hadn't meant to turn away from Caroline, but she didn't know what to say to her. She made a promise to herself to find her daughter later and talk with her once she'd had a chance to figure out how to explain to her the decisions she had made so long ago. But right now the only thing she could think to do was to keep moving.

The more distance she put between herself and the cabin, where she had left Gram wringing her hands in the kitchen and after Johnny had stormed out on her, the more relief she felt. There was freedom in having the burden of a secret lifted. Johnny finally knew the truth about Billy being his father. He was angry, but he'd get over it. He'd finally understand who he was, why so many of his interests and mannerisms were the opposite of Kevin's. And maybe he'd finally understand why Kevin wasn't as accessible as a father should be to his son, especially in his younger years when he had needed Kevin most. There had always been an invisible divide between them that neither knew how to cross. The secret had become bigger than both of them, expanding into every aspect of their relationship until one day the distance was too large to bridge. It was what happened to lies over time.

Yet there was one lie, a bigger secret, she kept.

She picked up her pace, a thread of fear pulling at her thoughts. She imagined Johnny was going straight to Chris, his best friend and newfound cousin, but also to Chris's mom. Jo believed Dee Dee always suspected Johnny was Billy's, but Jo had promised Kevin she wouldn't tell her the truth. He was adamant people believed Johnny was his son for reasons Jo could no longer remember. It had something to do with protecting her, hiding the truth about what really happened the night Billy drowned.

She had to get to Kevin first before he heard part of their secret was out. She wasn't sure how he would react. They had to get their stories straight. She wound her way to the lake, taking the long way so she wouldn't bump into Johnny. He needed space. She understood that.

The sun was starting to set by the time she had reached Lake Road and the Pavilion. The water sparkled in the diminishing light. The beach crowd was thinning as families made their way home. The parking lot was emptying of the men who had worked to pitch the tents all afternoon. The festival was moving forward as planned, and by the looks of things, it would be ready for the crowds tomorrow.

The sound of metal clanging drew her attention to the docks. Stimpy and two of his men were pulling the cages from the water, the traps once again filled with snappers. They were removing the larger of the turtles and tossing the smaller ones back. Her gazed shifted to the tents and the stand with a newly painted sign reading SNAPPER SOUP. She had a sinking feeling in her gut. Stimpy was abandoning the search for Sara. She ground her teeth. This was Heil's doing.

The recovery team was on the lake on the other side of the

floating pier, but there wasn't much movement on the boat. She wondered if perhaps they were giving up too. The three-man team had to be exhausted.

The entire scene, the feel of it, the stands and tents, the signs posted promising homemade pies and funnel cake, the red flags flying around the docks for the fishing competition, all of it reminded her of the night they had pulled Billy from the lake. She half expected the recovery team to signal her, letting her know they were bringing up a body.

She walked toward the beach, the strength of the memory pulling her forward. For the moment she forgot about the urgency to find Kevin. SWIM AT YOUR OWN RISK, written in big black ink glared at her. She opened the gate of the chain-link fence and stepped onto the sand. It was something about the way the recovery team lingered next to the floating pier, the way the light from the setting sun flickered across the waves that pulled her onto the beach and to the water's edge.

It was an accident, she caught herself saying. She hadn't meant for it to happen.

In her mind, she was back on the pier, lying down looking up at the stars. Drops of lake water covered her skin. She shivered in the chilly night air. Billy and Kevin were racing toward her, arms and legs kicking in a frenzy to reach the pier first. The splashing water and the hum of crickets on the shoreline were the only sounds she heard. The bar on the second floor of the Pavilion had closed. The three of them were alone on the water.

Billy climbed the ladder first, beating his chest in triumph. He reached down and pulled her up, wrapping his arms around her waist. "To the victor go the spoils." His lips tugged her ear.

She tossed her head back, exposing her neck and thrusting out her chest, encouraging him to take it a step farther, thinking this was how it was supposed to be. Billy was the first to have her then, and it was no surprise he was the first to have her now. He nibbled her neck and collarbone, kissing the swell of her breasts spilling out the top of her bikini. Her body responded with pleasure, but all the while she was thinking about Kevin, strangely disappointed he didn't make it to her first. But he was on his way, she reminded herself. He was still swimming toward her. Her heart beat a little faster.

Kevin made it to the pier and climbed the ladder. She could hear his heavy breathing from the long swim, could feel his eyes on her, watching her. She closed her eyes and moaned, enjoying the attention, the longing, the physical pull from both boys. Oh, how she loved the power, the way every fiber in her body pulsed, alive and electric.

"Tell him about us," Kevin said.

"Oh, Kevin," she teased, thinking he was enjoying this as much as she was, watching her, playing his part in her game.

Billy pulled back. "Tell me what?" he asked her.

"Nothing, silly," she said, and pulled Billy to her again. He continued kissing her shoulder.

"Tell him or I will," Kevin said, his voice deepening, pleading with her.

"Hey, Kevin," Billy said between kisses. "Why don't you swim back to the beach? We're busy here."

"Tell him!" Kevin hollered.

Billy dropped his arms from Jo's hips and stepped back. "What's your problem?"

Kevin kept his eyes on Jo. "Tell him or I will." His nostrils flared.

Maybe she had taken things too far. He wasn't messing around, playing her game, but she figured she could smooth things over by showing him a little affection. She stepped toward him and put her hand on his cheek, whispering, "It's okay."

Kevin grabbed her and kissed her hard. She didn't expect it, and for a second she didn't try to fight him off. His mouth smashed into hers. He was hurting her. She put her hands on his chest to push him away, but he wouldn't let her go.

Billy hesitated. Confusion crossed his face. "What the hell do you think you're doing?" He pulled Kevin off her. "What's gotten into you, man?" He shoved Kevin in the chest, not too hard, but hard enough to let him know he wasn't joking around.

Jo wiped her wet mouth and neck from both boys' kisses. The two of them fighting over her wasn't the thrill she thought it would be. In fact, it wasn't even close. She was overcome by an awful, horrible feeling, not wanting either one of them to be hurt. "Leave him alone," she said to Billy, and touched his shoulder to get his attention. "It's not his fault."

"You're defending him?" Billy turned on her. "What the hell is going on?"

"She's with me now," Kevin said.

"What do you mean, she's with you now?" Billy asked.

"She's with me. Tell him, Jo." Kevin straightened up, and by the look on his face he was enjoying sticking it to Billy.

It pissed Jo off. "Shut up, Kevin," she said.

"What is he talking about?" Billy asked her.

She couldn't look at him, and she turned away.

"What's going on? Wh-what are you saying?" He stuttered. "My best friend and my girl?" He shook his head. "No way."

"It's true," Kevin said. "I'm sorry, but it's true. I love her."

Billy got up in his face. Kevin tried to step away from him, but Billy moved right back in his space. His chest was puffed out and his shoulders squared.

"Are you screwing my girl? Is that what you're telling me?" he asked, bumping him with his chest, pushing him back toward the edge of the pier.

"Stop it, Billy." Jo had never seen this side of Billy before, and it frightened her.

"You are, aren't you? You son of a bitch." He cocked his arm and swung, but Kevin was quick and moved away. Billy's fist only grazed Kevin's jaw. Billy went to throw another punch, but Jo rushed in and grabbed his arm.

"Stop it!" she shouted. "Just stop it."

Billy turned and shoved her. She flew backward and landed hard on her right hip.

"Oh, shit, Jo, I'm sorry," he said, and immediately went to help her up.

Kevin lowered his shoulder and rushed Billy, hitting him in the stomach like a linebacker. Billy's right forearm took the brunt of the fall, hitting the pier with a crack. The two of them started wrestling, their arms tangled around each other's waists. Billy landed blow after blow to Kevin's kidneys. Kevin tried to roll away, holding his side. Billy jumped up and kicked him. Kevin curled into a ball. Billy went to kick him again, but before his foot made contact, Jo pushed him square in the chest, sending him over the edge of the pier, his body striking the water with a splash.

"Are you hurt?" She knelt by Kevin's side and placed her hand on his shoulder. His skin was slick and warm under her fingertips.

After a few long seconds he caught his breath. He lifted his head. "I'm okay."

"I'm sorry," she said. Her nose was running. "I didn't think he'd hit you. Are you sure you're okay?"

"Yeah." He sat up, cradling his stomach where he had been punched and kicked.

She put both hands on his cheeks and kissed his forehead. "I'm so, so sorry." She sat back on her heels and looked around for

Billy, wanting to tell him off, and yet needing to explain she hadn't meant for any of this to happen. She loved them both.

But Billy hadn't surfaced.

He wasn't climbing the ladder. He wasn't on the pier. She looked toward the beach to see if he was swimming toward the shore. The lake was still and silent.

"Where's Billy?" she asked, and looked over the edge where he had fallen into the water. Panic gripped her chest. "Billy!" she called, and frantically looked around, spinning in circles, searching.

He wasn't anywhere.

Please, please, please, she silently begged. *Please let this be a game.*

"Billy!" she shrieked, her voice echoing across the lake.

CHAPTER FORTY-ONE

After Patricia's shocking news, Dee Dee paced the kitchen, pulling at her lip, deep in thought for the rest of the afternoon. The sun was setting. Long shadows cut across the old wooden floor. Dust floated in the remaining slivers of light.

Patricia had fallen asleep again in Dee Dee's old bedroom. Dee Dee had moved into the master bedroom not long after her folks had passed. She had taken over the cabin, the upkeep, and the bills. Although the position at the hospital didn't pay much, she didn't need much to make ends meet. When money was tight, the lake provided her with food and water, the cabin with shelter. And then there was Chris, the lone heir to the Hawke name. He was a good boy for the most part, growing into a fine young man. Who could ask for more?

But she did want more. If she couldn't have her family back, then she at least wanted the truth so she could finally have some kind of closure.

The old scar pulsed with the beat of her heart. She opened a can of beer, the last in a six-pack, and lit a cigarette. She had the fractured bone, and now she had a witness. She thought about what Patricia had said, wondering how much she should believe.

Patricia was clearly a woman on the edge, suffering from a traumatic loss.

Dee Dee pulled in a long drag and exhaled slowly. She could talk with Heil, make sure he was doing everything possible to find Patricia's little girl. But knowing Heil, he wouldn't listen. Drownings weren't good for business. Heil was a heartless man.

She continued another lap around the kitchen table, mulling over her options. If Heil called off the search, she would step up and demand the fishermen continue. She didn't have much faith in the recovery team. Too much time had passed for their scanners and whatever other equipment they were using to find such a small body in the expansive lake.

But what should she do about Patricia's version of the night Billy had drowned? Patricia might have misunderstood what she saw at ten years old. It was possible. She was a kid.

But she couldn't discard the fact that her version also made a lot of sense. There was a full moon that night. The floating pier would have been visible to anyone looking out at the water. And if anyone were on the pier under a moon that bright, they would have been recognizable.

Many times Dee Dee had peeked out the curtains and caught teenagers messing around on that very same pier. It was as though a spotlight had been turned on and the teenagers were caught in the act of being teens. She had done it herself when she was younger.

So it was possible Patricia was telling the truth. Besides, she had never known Patricia to lie. As a child, she had been honest. She wouldn't even lie about the number of cookies she had eaten when asked. Where most kids would confess to eating two or three, Patricia would look Dee Dee in the eye and say, "I had fourteen."

And then there's the fact that Billy's body was found near the pier, the exact spot Patricia had seen Jo with him. *Kevin had been there too*, the voice inside her head whispered, but she silenced it by pushing it away. She didn't want to believe anyone was to blame for what had happened to Billy other than Jo.

Billy and Kevin had been best friends every summer since they were boys. And later they had both become victims, targets of a manipulative teenage girl who flaunted her sexuality, tossing it around as though she were free for the taking, teasing them until neither boy could think straight.

Jo was beautiful, sexy, and careless with what she had been blessed with. She knew how to use her body and good looks to her advantage. She didn't care who she hurt as long as she got what she wanted. She was out of control. Dee Dee had wanted to shake her, to warn her to be careful with how she used the weapons she had been given. But she didn't dare touch her because of Billy. He was smitten with her. And Dee Dee didn't have the heart to say a bad thing about her for fear of hurting him. So she bit her tongue, hoping he'd outgrow what had started as puppy love, and praying he would lose interest, or Jo would.

Neither had happened, and there wasn't a day that went by that Dee Dee didn't curse herself for not opening her mouth and exposing Jo for what she really was, a selfish tramp. Although in the end, she wasn't sure it would've mattered.

Patricia walked into the kitchen, dragging her feet. Her blond hair fell in tangles around her face. She looked like a child in the waning light, standing in an oversize T-shirt and underwear. If it wasn't for the healthy bumps underneath the shirt or her wide hips, she could've passed for her ten-year-old self.

"How long have I been sleeping?" she asked.

"A few hours." Dee Dee dropped the empty beer can in the trash. She had smoked half a pack of cigarettes. She fingered the lighter, contemplating firing up another one.

Patricia shuffled to the table and sat down. She pushed her messy bed hair behind her ears. "Thank you," she said. "For letting me stay here and for giving me your bed. I haven't been able to sleep at the *Sparrow*. All Sara's stuff is there and . . . I just don't know what I'm supposed to do now."

Dee Dee poured a glass of lake water and handed it to her. "There hasn't been any news." She was certain she would've heard news about Sara had there been any.

Patricia nodded. She sat quietly for a long time. The clock on the fireplace mantel ticked off the seconds one by one. A couple of ducks honked on the lake. The squirrels rustled in the trees behind the cabin.

"Listen," Dee Dee said, and sat across from her. "I want to talk with Sheriff Borg about what you told me about Billy. I know now might not be the best time to bring this up, but I think it's important. Sara's drowning was an accident. You're not to blame for an accident. But Billy's drowning might not have been. We owe it to him to find out the truth."

Patricia didn't say anything right away. Her face was drawn. She stared at nothing. Dee Dee worried her hands in her lap, waiting, wondering if Patricia would hold up in an interrogation by Sheriff Borg even if she could convince her to talk with him.

She cleared her throat, scratchy from the dozen cigarettes she had smoked throughout the day. "What do you think?" she asked. "Do you think you're up to talking to the sheriff?"

Patricia nodded. Someone knocked at the door.

Dee Dee turned. "Who could that be?"

Patricia's hand shot out and grabbed Dee Dee's wrist. "Sara," she whispered.

She patted Patricia's hand. "It's going to be okay." She went to the screen door and pushed it open to find Jo standing on her front porch.

CHAPTER FORTY-TWO

"Well, well, well," Dee Dee said. "Look what the cat dragged in."

"We need to talk," Jo said.

"You bet we do." Dee Dee stood aside to let her in. The door bang closed behind them.

Jo was somewhat surprised to find Patricia in Dee Dee's kitchen. "I'm sorry to barge in," she said to her. Patricia gave her a weak smile. Jo turned toward Dee Dee. "Is there somewhere we can talk in private?"

Dee Dee leaned against the countertop and crossed her arms, taking her usual defensive position. "Oh no, I think Patricia should be here for this."

Jo hesitated. "Fine," she said. "This really can't wait."

"No, it can't." Dee Dee pulled a chair from the kitchen table. "Sit," she said.

Jo did what she was told and sat, leaning forward and resting her forearms on the table. Her leg bounced up and down. By the look on Dee Dee's face, she thought perhaps Johnny had already been here. She had wanted to be the first to break the news to her about Billy being Johnny's father. On some crazy level, she supposed she had hoped Dee Dee would help her make the situation easier for Johnny. But seeing Dee Dee's stiff jaw and the anger in her eyes, she knew she had made a mistake. Dee Dee wouldn't behave rationally about anything.

"So," Dee Dee said, "Patricia told me some very interesting news today."

"Patricia?" she asked, confused. How would Patricia know about Johnny? "What news?"

"She has proof you're a lying bitch."

Patricia flinched.

Jo rested her head in her hands. "Can't we have a civil conversation?"

"Patricia saw you on the pier with Billy the night he drowned." Dee Dee pushed off the counter, taking on a fighter's stance.

"I don't understand," Jo said. "I don't know what you're talking about. I came here to talk about Johnny."

"Forget Johnny. Patricia was here at the cabin that night. I was babysitting her. And you know we have a clear view of the floating pier from here." She pointed her index finger in Jo's face. "She saw you with Billy. He wasn't alone on the beach like Kevin said. Kevin's been covering up for you this entire time."

Jo glanced at Patricia cowering in the chair, clutching Sara's dolly. She looked like a scared child. "What did you tell her?" Jo asked her. Her tone was harsher than she had intended. But what could she have seen? She *had* been a child when it had happened.

"I . . . ," Patricia began, but Dee Dee cut her off.

"Leave her alone," Dee Dee said. "She's been through enough."

Jo ignored Dee Dee and reached across the table toward Patricia. In a more soothing tone she asked, "What do you think you saw?"

"Hey." Dee Dee poked Jo in the shoulder. "You talk to me."

"Whoa." Jo raised her hands. "Back off."

Patricia still didn't say anything.

"What did you do to my brother? What are you hiding?" Dee Dee asked.

Jo pushed back in the chair and stood. Her legs wobbled and her arms shook. "I don't have to listen to this." She took a tentative step, but before she could get any farther, Dee Dee moved in front of her, pushing her, getting up in her face.

"What did you do to him?"

"Nothing," Jo said, and tried to step around her, but Dee Dee's body was big and strong, like Billy's. Yes, just like Billy's, and she was certain this was how Kevin had felt when Billy had thrust his chest at him, intimidating him with his physical strength. "Get away from me," she said in a voice much too weak to have any impact.

"Did you kill him?" Dee Dee grabbed Jo's shoulders.

"No," Jo said, panicking. "No."

"You're lying." Dee Dee wrapped her hands around Jo's neck. "Tell me the truth or I swear, I'll kill you myself."

She clawed at Dee Dee's fingers, gasping for air. Black spots marred her vision. Her head felt light. Patricia sat there, staring at them as though she was in shock, never having seen this side of Dee Dee before. Jo reached for her. "Pattie," she croaked. When it was clear Patricia wouldn't be of any help, Jo returned to scratching at Dee Dee's hands, trying to pry them open. "Let go," she managed to say.

Dee Dee loosened her grip ever so slightly. Her cold dead eyes glared at her. "Not until you tell me what happened."

"Okay," she said, and coughed.

Dee Dee dropped her hands and stepped back. Jo bent over, gasping, trying to catch her breath.

"I'm waiting," Dee Dee said.

When the air moved through her lungs and she could talk, she blurted, "It was an accident."

Dee Dee blinked several times. "You're going to tell Sheriff Borg my brother didn't just slip and fall. You're going to explain exactly what happened to him. And you're going to pay for what you've done."

"No," Jo said, shaking her head. Her body trembled. She needed Kevin here to explain how it had happened, how it was nothing but a terrible horrible accident. Where was he? She had looked for him everywhere: the Pavilion, the bar, Eddie's. It wasn't like him to disappear. Vanishing was her talent. Not his.

"If you won't talk, then I will. With everything Patricia told me, you won't stand a chance, not against the two of us," Dee Dee said.

Jo shook her head. "I don't think you want to do that."

"Oh, you see, that's where you're wrong. I've been waiting a long time for this day to come." She pushed Jo's chest, sending her backward until she had her pressed against the edge of the countertop. Dee Dee placed both hands on either side of her. She smelled of body odor and adrenalin.

Jo was no match for Dee Dee's strength. "You're not going to hurt me," she said, pleading to the kinder, softer side of Dee Dee's temperament. It was there, buried beneath her tough exterior, but she knew it was there. Dee Dee hadn't always been a brute. The little kids had adored her in the past, and parents at the lake used to fight over her for babysitting. Once upon a time Dee Dee had laughed and joked. She hadn't always been the bitter woman she had turned into. Jo needed to use this to her advantage to save herself. And she had one weapon to do it. Maybe it was the real reason for keeping the secret about her son, Billy's son. "You really don't want Johnny to lose his mother, too, do you?"

At first Dee Dee's brow furrowed, and then her eyes widened. "What are you saying?"

"I'm saying Johnny is Billy's son."

Dee Dee pulled back. Her face softened. The corners of her mouth turned up. She nodded. "I always wondered." In the next instant, she brought her arm back and slapped Jo hard across the face.

Jo grunted. The table and chairs went out of focus. Her ear was ringing. She covered her stinging cheek where the skin burned hot.

"That was for not telling me I had a nephew," Dee Dee said. "And that Chris had a cousin."

Jo's mouth hung open, shocked at the forcefulness of the hit. She tried shaking it off by standing up a little straighter.

"Does Johnny know?" Dee Dee asked.

She dropped her hand from her cheek, opened and closed her mouth, testing her jaw before she spoke. "He found out to-day."

"How?"

"It doesn't matter, does it?"

"Where is he now?" Dee Dee asked.

"I don't know. He needed some space, but if I had to guess, he's with Chris."

Dee Dee slapped her again, sending her to the floor. The pain radiated across her cheek and temple. Spots floated in front of her eyes. She thought she might black out.

"That was for Johnny," Dee Dee said.

"Please stop," Patricia said, and reached for Dee Dee.

"Yes," Jo managed to say. "Please stop." She didn't think she could take another blow, although she was sure she had another one coming. She inched her away across the floor and put her back against the bottom cabinet for support. If she stood up, she might pass out.

"It wasn't Jo's fault," Patricia said, her eyes steady on Dee Dee. "I saw her dive off the pier."

"Yeah, after she pushed my brother into the lake," Dee Dee said.

"Yes," Patricia said. "That's true." She put her hand on Dee Dee's shoulder. "But Billy climbed onto the pier after she left. He was with Kevin. I thought they were messing around, playing rough like boys do. It was Kevin who pushed Billy into the water."

CHAPTER FORTY-THREE

Caroline stayed tucked in the arms of the willow tree, the swooping branches draped around her, protecting her from the outside world. She wasn't sure how long she stayed hidden under Willow, but long enough for her butt to ache and her legs to fall asleep. She stretched them out, careful to hold onto the branch above her, and she shook her feet until they tingled. Once the sensation traveled to her thighs and she could feel her legs again, she climbed down to the ground. She brushed the dirt from her hands onto her shorts and tightened her ponytail, which was sticking out from underneath her baseball cap.

Outside the ring of drooping branches, she heard the sound of footsteps. The door to the screened-in porch creaked open and slammed closed. Her father's deep voice came from inside calling, "Hello? Is anyone home?" She wondered if he had heard their family secret was out and she was to blame. She bet he would be mad with her like everyone else was. She wasn't ready to face him or anyone in her stupid lying family.

She darted from her protective cocoon and ran up the dirt road toward the ballpark. She wasn't even halfway there, not really sure where she was going, but she was breathing hard and wishing she had grabbed her bike. She slowed her pace when her lungs burned, only stopping when she reached the *Meadowlark*, Megan's cabin, and found herself knocking on the door.

"It's open!" Mrs. Roberts called from somewhere inside.

Mr. Roberts was in the family room reading a book next to an oscillating fan. Mrs. Roberts emerged from the kitchen, wiping her hands on a tea towel. "We haven't seen you around much, Caroline. I hope you and Megan didn't have a fight."

"No, ma'am," she said. "Nothing like that."

"Well, I'm glad. Megan's in her bedroom. Go on back."

Caroline crept down the narrow hall and peeked inside Megan's room. Megan was sitting on the bed, surrounded by magazines, nail polish, and makeup. Her head was down. Her blond hair fell into her face and her scalp was pink from the sun.

"Hey," Caroline said, and slipped inside, quietly closing the door behind her.

"Where've you been?" Megan grabbed Caroline's hands. She pulled her onto the bed on top of the magazines and nail polish and plastic lipstick tubes. "I've got news," she said.

Caroline nodded. Her lips trembled and her nose started to run. She didn't want to cry and look like a baby. But she wanted to tell someone what she had done. She needed to talk to someone who wasn't in her family.

"Jeff kissed me," Megan said. "A proper kiss."

Caroline nodded again and wiped underneath her nose.

Megan blabbed about Jeff's tongue in her mouth. "He tasted kind of funny," she said. "Like spit." She shrugged. "I thought he would've at least brushed his teeth or used mouthwash if he knew he was going to kiss me, but whatever. What do you think? Don't you think he should've been more prepared? I mean, I made sure my breath was fresh. What?" She gave Caroline the once-over, as though she was seeing her for the first time. "What's wrong?"

"Can you keep a secret?" Caroline asked, and looked at the bedroom door to make sure it was closed all the way.

"Of course. Tell me," Megan said.

"Well, to start," she said. "I got my period."

Megan nudged her and smiled. "That's great. Oh my God, are you crying? You didn't do anything wrong. It's normal." She crinkled her nose. "But you know, now you can officially get pregnant."

Caroline rolled her eyes. "That's never going to happen." She wasn't like her mother. She'd never end up a pregnant teen. "You have to swear not to tell anyone I got it. Promise me."

"Who would I tell?"

"Promise."

"Okay, okay, I promise. Is that it?"

"No." Caroline started from the beginning, telling Megan about the times she had overheard bits and pieces of Billy's name mentioned by Gram and her mother through the years and especially now after Sara had drowned. She told her how she discovered Billy had drowned when her parents were teenagers. She read about it that day at the Country Store when she had searched the old *Lake Reporters*.

"I remember. Boring," Megan said. "What about it?"

Caroline told her how she had put two and two together, that Johnny was named after Billy and that he was really Billy's son, not Caroline's father's.

"Holy shit," Megan blurted.

"Shhh," Caroline said. "Keep it down."

"And you told Johnny?"

"Sort of."

"Wow, that's totally messed up." Megan shook her head. "So, now what are you going to do?"

"I don't know."

There was a knock at the door.

Caroline grabbed Megan's arm. "Promise you won't say anything. Not until my family figures this out."

Megan held up her hand. "I get it. You don't have to worry."

"Megan," Mrs. Roberts said. "Jeff's out front looking for you."

Megan flung the door open.

Her mother started. "It's late. I'm not sure you should be going out tonight."

"Please, Mom. It's summertime. And Caroline is out. She'll come with me." Megan looked over her shoulder at Caroline, pleading with her to say yes.

Mrs. Robert's crossed her arms. "And what do you plan on doing?"

"I don't know. We'll think of something. Isn't that right, Caroline?"

"That's what I'm afraid of," Mrs. Roberts said.

"Please, Mom. I promise we won't get into any trouble."

"Well," Mrs. Roberts said, "as long as you two stay together."

"We will," Megan said, and pulled Caroline with her.

Mrs. Roberts followed them to the door. She touched Caroline's shoulder. "Everything all right, dear?"

"Yeah," she said. "Everything's just super."

Caroline dragged her feet a few paces behind Megan and Jeff, not wanting to tag along on their date or whatever it was they were doing. She'd split as soon as they were far enough away from Megan's cabin and out of sight. She was trying to think of where she could go, since home wasn't an option. But when they reached the ballpark, the Needlemeyer twins and Adam were waiting for them.

Ted held a flashlight over a sheet of paper that explained the rules and regulations for the big fishing tournament tomorrow.

Megan stepped back from the group and mumbled, "More boy stuff."

"I'm totally doing this," Jeff said about the tournament. "First prize is a hundred bucks. Who wouldn't try for that?"

The boys nodded, an air of excitement surrounded them.

Adam tugged on Caroline's arm. "Are you fishing tomorrow?" he asked.

"Nah," she said, having made up her mind while talking with Gram. "Not this year. Besides, I'll be too busy rooting for you."

"Well, I know just the spot to catch the biggest trout anyone has ever pulled out of the lake," he said.

"You do not," Ted said.

"Yeah, I do."

"Then show us."

"I'm not showing you," Adam said. "You're the competition."

"You won't show us because you're lying. You don't have a fishing hole."

"I do too," Adam whined.

"Leave him alone," Caroline said, although the boys ribbing had started lifting her mood. The familiar role of mediator was comforting, a sign something hadn't changed. She gazed across the open field. Every few seconds the lightning bugs flashed their presence.

"Show us your fishing hole, and we'll show you ours. That way we're even," Ned said.

"Yeah, help the new guy out," Jeff chimed in.

Adam looked at Caroline, and she nodded. Catching the

biggest trout was more luck than anything else. Besides, she didn't want to go home.

It was that easy. They were off on some kind of quest to find Adam's honey hole. Caroline trailed behind Adam, the Needlemeyer twins behind her. Jeff grabbed Megan's hand and pulled her along, taking up the rear. They made their way through the path in the woods that would take them to the lake.

They walked single file, sticks and leaves crunching under their sneakers. Poison ivy spread through the woods to their left. Cougar barked on their right. Adam stopped abruptly, and Caroline nearly walked into the back of him. He reached into his pocket and pulled out a handful of beef jerky. "Always prepared," he said, and exchanged a knowing look with her.

Cougar yanked on his chain the closer they got, stretching every link as far as it would go until he was choking. The stake he was chained to bent at a diagonal as though at any moment it would fly out of the ground. The funny thing was, Caroline wasn't worried about the dog breaking free. He didn't sound vicious or mean. His barks sounded more like a cry for attention.

Adam walked up to Cougar but stayed far enough back as not to make contact. The dog yelped, cried, and pulled at the chain in excitement. Adam tossed a chunk of beef jerky over the dog's head so he wouldn't continue choking himself. Cougar whipped around and gnawed on the jerky. Adam threw two more pieces.

"One was enough," Ted said. "Save some for us."

Adam stuffed the rest of the jerky into his pockets.

The sight of the hungry, attention-starved dog made Caroline feel bad. While he continued to chomp on the beef jerky, she walked up to him and unhooked the chain from his thick leather collar.

"What are you doing?" Megan squealed.

Cougar rubbed against Caroline's legs, chewing and rubbing,

circling her. She reached down and scratched behind his ear. Adam joined her. And soon the twins, Jeff, and even Megan surrounded the dog, petting him, letting him lick them all over.

"Let's take him with us," Adam said.

The six of them, seven if you included the dog, proceeded down the path, single file, with Cougar running circles around their legs, darting on and off the trail, tongue hanging out and tail wagging. They stopped when they reached the parking lot, which was now filled with tents for the Trout Festival. People were still working under battery-powered spotlights, setting up displays, preparing for the events the next day. The dark of the night seeped in between the cracks of light. The Pavilion was open, and music blared from the live band performing in the bar upstairs.

Caroline couldn't help but think, after everything that had happened, summer had come after all.

She turned to Adam. "Which way?"

"It's on the south side." He pointed. "Past that old private beach nobody uses. Closer to where the lake feeds the stream."

"That's nothing but a muddy hole," Ted said. Ned agreed.

"No, it's not all mud. There's a spot where the water is deep. All the big fish are there. I swear." Adam's head bobbed. Cougar poked his nose inside Adam's pockets, searching for the jerky.

"We'll have to take the long way around so no one sees us," Caroline said. A gang of young kids walking around at ten o'clock at night was sure to draw attention. "We can go the way we went to the pump that day," she said to Adam.

The twins balked. Megan picked at her cuticle, obviously bored. Jeff shrugged.

"You don't have to come with us," Caroline said to the others, and started walking.

Adam and Cougar followed. After more bellyaching, the twins and Jeff and Megan chased after them. It took almost an hour to get to the private beach, walking through the woods behind the lakefront cabins with nothing but slivers of moonlight cutting through the branches of trees to guide them. Cougar panted, but his barking had stopped. Once, he drifted toward the lake to get a drink of water, but otherwise he walked alongside Adam the entire way. He was a good dog and meant to be with kids.

The cabin that sat at the back of the private beach was deserted. It had been dark and empty every summer for as long as Caroline could remember. Although she had heard the family who owned the property preferred to stay away from the lake during the peak summer months, coming only in autumn when the air was cool and the trees were dressed in their finest colors.

Caroline didn't see the point. Why would you need a beach if it was too cold to sit on it and too frigid to swim? And it wasn't like they weren't in the most secluded spot on the lake, a place to hang out where other vacationers couldn't bother them.

Johnny and his friends had used the private beach for their end-of-summer party, figuring if they got caught, it wouldn't matter since they'd be going home the next day.

Thinking about Johnny hurt, and she pushed the thoughts away. She turned toward Adam. "You better lead from here."

"This way." The moonlight caught the back of his ears, making it look as though he had two big orbs on the sides of his head.

She followed close behind. The twins pushed and shoved each other, cackling about how this was nothing but a waste of time. Jeff and Megan dropped back from the pack.

"You go on ahead," Megan called. "We'll catch up with you."

Ned made kissing, sucking noises. Ted mumbled, "Gross." They continued on, leaving Jeff and Megan on the beach. Caroline didn't want to think about what Megan was doing. The idea of kissing a boy still made her feel icky.

"Here," Adam said.

They had been walking a good ten minutes. Mud caked to their sneakers, and it was hard to find a safe place to step. The brush was thick and trees lined the water's edge. Not many people came down this far where the lake narrowed and eventually emptied into a stream that really wasn't much of a stream at all, but a trickle of water that ran through the woods another half mile until it dried up altogether. Some believed with the rate of erosion, global warming, and dry summers, the lake would one day cease to exist. But Gram had told her it wasn't possible. The lake was a natural lake made from a glacier and fed by underwater springs from deep inside the earth's core.

She believed Gram's version and realized she still trusted her. She had to trust in someone. And she didn't doubt Gram would've told her about Billy and Johnny if she could have. She found comfort in the thought.

The twins and Adam approached an area where it did look as though the water was blacker, deeper.

"There's big fish in there," Adam said. "I know it. I've seen them swimming around."

"Yeah, but who's going to come all this way to prove you pulled a trout out down here? You need a parent with you for it to count," Ned said to Adam.

While the boys argued over the rules and whose parent would be willing to walk all this way, Cougar had wandered farther down near the stream. He yipped and whined. Caroline went to see what was wrong. She had to weave around trees and wind her way around moss-covered rocks. A thorn bush pricked her thigh, and her sneakers sunk in the deepening mud.

"What did you find?" she asked the dog. "Bring it here so I can see it."

Cougar yelped and whimpered.

Her first thought was that he must be hurt, but then she saw something lying on the ground near his paws. She took a couple of steps closer. In the mud, not far from where she stood, was Sara's body. Her braids splayed in the puddles surrounding her head, and her eyes, cold and lifeless, stared into the night sky. Her bathing suit was tattered and torn. The skin on her arms and legs was shredded. Only the ghostly glow of her face hadn't been touched, as if the snappers had known to leave something for her mother.

"Guys." Her voice cracked. "Guys," she said a little louder. Cougar continued to paw at the muddy water near the body, whimpering and whining as if he knew he had found what everyone was looking for.

"Guys!" she yelled, and stumbled backward. She turned and ran back the way she came, slipping on the rocks, tearing through the thorny brush. Cougar followed on her heels. "Guys," she said out of breath when she had finally reached them.

Adam looked as though he had been crying. The twins must've been really giving it to him. She bent over, putting her hands on her knees. She thought she might be sick. The boys stared at her, sensing whatever was wrong was important.

"Cougar," she said. "He found Sara's . . ." She couldn't finish. She couldn't say the word *body*.

They didn't ask what she meant. They didn't have to. Every kid knew Sara's name. Every kid knew she hadn't been found. They may have been pretending she hadn't drowned the last few days, but they didn't forget even if their parents had moved on. Kids wouldn't forget about another kid dying.

"Are you sure? Where?" Ned asked.

Caroline pointed downstream. "It's her," she said, swallowing the warm saliva in the back of her throat.

"How did she get all the way down here?" Ted asked. "It doesn't seem possible."

"It's totally possible," Adam said, his wet eyes darting from Caroline to the twins. "The water current carries a lot of cool stuff here." He scrunched up his face. "You know what I mean." He continued, "Once, I found an old license plate and a Coke bottle. And don't forget about the snappers. They love the mud. Maybe they drag stuff here and, you know, eat it. I know they like to burrow in mud so only their eyes and nostrils stick out. Then they wiggle their tongues like tiny worms to attract small fish. When the fish gets close"—he smacked his hands together—"they grab it and chomp it to pieces."

"I thought they only ate dead stuff," Ted said.

"No. They eat small fish and plants, too. But I think they prefer the dead stuff. . . ." Adam's voice trailed off.

Maybe they realized the impact of what Adam was saying because after this, they were quiet. Even Cougar didn't make a sound. In the silence Adam and the twins stared at one another, each muttering to the other, "Did you hear that?"

"Hear what?" All Caroline heard was the sound of her own breathing.

Adam put his finger to his lips.

She strained to listen.

"There it is again," Adam said.

"I don't hear anything," she said.

Adam looked at her. "It's a full moon," he said, and pointed to the sky, his hand shaking. "You can hear the horse during a full moon."

"I bet it's because you found Sara," Ted said to her. "I mean, she drowned the same day Adam found that bit."

"It was probably the wind," Ned said.

"You didn't hear anything?" Adam asked her.

"No," Caroline said. "I didn't." She knew Adam was disappointed in her. But what could she say? Too much had happened.

She no longer believed in the things she once had at the start of summer, the kinds of things that only kids believed in like lake legends. She wasn't the same girl who had once accepted the world as it was without question. For her the world had forever changed.

Megan and Jeff came crashing through the brush. "What?" Megan asked, and looked at them. "What's going on?" It was obvious Megan and Jeff didn't hear anything either.

"Cougar found Sara," Caroline said, because finding the little girl was the most important thing. "I know where she is."

"You do?" Megan asked. "Where?"

"Maybe it's not even her," Ned said. "We're all a little spooked right now."

Caroline shook her head. "It's her." There was no mistake. The image of Sara's body flashed in her mind's eye, the face of an angel resting peacefully on a tattered body.

"Let's make sure," Ted said to the others. "Adam, you stay here with Cougar. We don't want that dog to get a hold of her. If it's really her," he added.

"Cougar wouldn't do that," Caroline said at the same time the dog lowered his head as though he were ashamed. "You didn't do anything wrong," she said to Cougar.

"I'm coming with you, guys," Adam said.

"No." Caroline reached for Adam's hand. "Stay here with me. You don't want to see." She didn't want to treat Adam like a baby, but she knew it wasn't something he should look at. He was too young. It was bad enough the others were going to look.

No kid, no matter how old, should ever have to see another kid's dead body.

CHAPTER FORTY-FOUR

Kevin stood on the balcony of the Pavilion, which overlooked the lake. It was a clear night. The sky was littered with stars, and the moonlight bounced off the still water. The air was warm, but not uncomfortably so. He kept his back to the bar and the crowd inside. The live band belted out a cover song, the electric guitar singing louder than the girl's voice into the mic. He had stepped outside in need of fresh air, which was ironic, since the first thing he did was light a cigarette.

He took a deep drag, welcoming the smoke into his lungs. He had waited on the docks for Patricia to leave *Hawkes'* cabin for as long as he could without drawing attention to himself, but she never came out. He wasn't sure why he had bothered, but something about her troubled him, and it had nothing to do with her little girl drowning. He had spent much of the afternoon and evening alone, stopping briefly at *The Pop-Inn*, but no one was there.

Eventually he wandered into the bar and spent the last several hours hanging out with Eddie and Sheila. The two were still hopelessly in love. Or perhaps he was thinking like the silly romantic Jo had always accused him of being.

The smoke snaked from his mouth in slow, deliberate swirls.

His stomach churned from too much beer and lack of food. He hadn't eaten in hours. His temple throbbed. He was dehydrated. He licked his dry cracked lip.

But no matter how bad his stomach clenched in need of food or how bad his body needed water, his feet were rooted to the spot. He couldn't tear his eyes off the two boys in the middle of the lake on the floating pier. It was as though he were staring into the past, looking out at two ghosts.

He recognized Johnny and Chris and realized just how distinguishable he and Billy must have looked under the same moon. His mind had gone back to that night so many times before, but now, looking in from the outside, it was a miracle no one had witnessed what he had done.

Billy had climbed the ladder right after Jo had swum to shore. They stood and watched her run across the beach, staggering and falling in her attempt to flee. She grabbed her clothes and disappeared behind the Pavilion. She had listened to Kevin when he had told her to run home and tell no one. She was terrified, thinking she had pushed Billy into the lake and that he had drowned.

But Billy was back on the pier, cradling his right forearm where he had hurt it. The water dripped from his shorts, making tiny splattering sounds on the wood. He tossed his head to the side to get the wet hair out of his face and smiled a cock-sure smile. He had intended to scare them. To him, it was a game.

But it wasn't a game to Kevin. Billy had played him for a fool one too many times. And now Billy had done the same to Jo. He had frightened her to death. And Kevin couldn't take it any longer. He had had enough. He'd show Billy once and for all he shouldn't mess with him, he didn't deserve Jo.

He took a deep, sobering breath. His mouth tasted like metal.

He clenched and unclenched his hands. He felt as though he were someone else, that someone full of rage and frustration had invaded his body.

Slowly, he turned toward Billy.

"She'll never choose you over me," Billy said so confidently and smugly.

Something much more than rage shot through Kevin: a thick, hot fury. Before he could stop himself, he struck Billy hard in the chest, much harder than he thought possible, surprising Billy and knocking the wind out of him, sending him back over the edge of the pier. There was a loud crack, but this time it wasn't Billy's arm striking the pier; it was his head hitting one of the wood planks before his body slapped the water with a *thwump*.

Kevin's blood rushed in his ears. Sweat seeped from his pores and adrenalin pulsed through his veins. He got him good this time. He did. He wouldn't be pushed around anymore. He wouldn't. But my God, what was he thinking?

Billy was going to kill him when he climbed back onto the pier.

Kevin had to pull himself together. His breath was ragged. He lifted his chin and hiked his shoulders back, prepared to fight again. He stood with his fists up, waiting for Billy to surface. He wasn't sure how long he was standing that way, waiting—long enough for his arms to get tired.

"Come on," he said. "You're not fooling me. Not this time."

He strained to look over the edge where Billy had gone into the water, not wanting to get too close in case he was waiting to pull him into the lake. There was no way he could win a fight with him in the water. Billy was too strong a swimmer. But from where he stood, Kevin could see the waves lapping in slow rhythm against the side of the pier, the water showing little to no disturbance in its cadence, no sign of someone swimming, splashing.

"Where are you?" he asked.

After several long minutes, how many minutes he had no way of knowing, Billy still hadn't shown himself. The lake remained calm, silent.

"Billy," Kevin said, and looked over the edge again.

Nothing.

"Billy," he called, panic settling in. He raced around the pier, searching the water, much like Jo had done. "Where are you?" he asked, but even as the words left his lips, he understood what had happened. The air had rushed from Billy's lungs. Kevin had knocked the wind out of him. Billy had hit his head before falling into the water. He wasn't coming back up.

Ever.

Kevin dropped to his knees, his head in his hands. His best friend's body sunk to the darkness below, joining whatever else was dead at the bottom of the lake.

And this time, this time it was all Kevin's fault.

Kevin's body shook from the memory. His arms hung at his sides, limp and weak, remembering the physical exertion, the emotional trauma of the night he had gotten rid of Billy forever.

From the balcony he watched Johnny dive into the lake after Chris, both boys swimming for shore. *Lucky for them*, Kevin thought, and crushed the cigarette butt with his foot. He wiped his cheek. His hand came away wet. He hadn't realized he had been crying.

He turned to head into the bar for another drink but stopped when he saw a lone figure stumbling up the docks toward the parking lot. Something about the person's movements was familiar. When the figure stepped under one of the tent's spotlights, he recognized the hollow of her cheeks, the swell of her breasts and hips. He knew something was wrong.

CHAPTER FORTY-FIVE

The light under the tent temporarily blinded Jo. She stopped walking, waiting for the spots to clear. Her face was still sore where Dee Dee had smacked her not once, but twice. She touched her cheek tenderly. After Patricia had explained everything she had witnessed the night Billy had drowned, Dee Dee had tossed Jo a frozen bag of peas as a kind of peace offering for slugging her. They talked for the next several hours, a game of Remember When, with all their memories centered on Billy.

Jo wouldn't go as far as to say she and Dee Dee were friends. She wasn't sure they would ever define their relationship in those terms, but they had reached an understanding, one of tolerance for each other for Johnny's sake. It was a start. Or maybe it was the end of something. Dee Dee was unpredictable. But whatever happened from this night on, Jo no longer felt threatened by her.

Once her vision had cleared, she kept to the perimeter of the parking lot near the edge of the woods and away from the festival. Most of the stands and tables under the tents were empty, waiting for the merchandise to be displayed in the morning. The last of the temporary lights turned off as the few remaining workers headed home for the night.

She was closing in on the path that would lead to the ballpark and colony when Kevin stepped out from a shadow and blocked her way. She stiffened at the sight of him, unprepared to confront him so soon after learning what he had done. His hair was sticking up as though he had been running his fingers through it for hours. His eyes were wet and glassy. He smelled as though he had been drinking.

"What happened?" he asked, and motioned toward her cheek. She turned her head away.

"What's wrong?" He reached for her.

"Don't touch me." She glanced over his shoulder at the woods, looking for a way to escape, spying the entrance to the path.

"What did I do?" he asked.

She stared at him in disbelief. "What did you do?" Something inside of her came undone and thrashed in the air around them. "You let me think I was responsible for Billy drowning because I pushed him into the lake. But all this time, it wasn't me." She shook her head. "It was you."

"What are you talking about? You're not making any sense."

Her words stumbled out in a rush. "You were the last one with him. Not me. *You* pushed him into the lake. He hit his head when *you* pushed him."

"No," he said, and grabbed her arms. "You're wrong."

She struggled to pull herself free. "Patricia saw you. She saw the whole thing that night. He was alive after I left, and she can prove it."

He gripped her biceps tight and looked as though he was trying to work out what she was telling him.

"She saw *you* push him. Not me." She yanked her arms free. "She saw you push him." She cried. "And what about his arm, Kev? What did you do to his arm?"

"I think he hurt it when we were fighting on the pier," he said.

But she wasn't looking for an answer. All she wanted was to get as far away from him as she could. She couldn't stand to be near him for one second more. All these years he let her believe she was the one to blame for Billy's death. But it was him. It was his fault.

She took off running. She entered the woods a few feet from the path, tripping through the bush until she found the narrow trail.

He wasn't far behind. His feet stomped the ground, heavy and uncertain. She could outrun him if he were drunk, and she lengthened her stride, losing her flip-flops along the way. They were too hard to run in anyway.

"Jo, wait," he called. "I can explain."

She kept running. Why wasn't Cougar barking, alerting everyone there was someone in the woods? She wanted someone, anyone, to know she was there, she wasn't to blame.

She reached Lake Road and darted across. She stumbled into the ballpark. She was a few steps away from the dirt road that led into the colony, a few steps away from the cabins when Kevin caught up to her. His feet tangled with hers, tripping her from behind. Her body hit the ground with a thud.

He moved on top of her. She tried to roll him off, twisting and turning, wrestling her way out from under him. He grabbed her shoulders and flipped her onto her back, pinning her hips with his weight. Sweat dripped from his nose and chin.

"Let me explain," he said, panting.

She bucked. "Get off!" she yelled.

He held her down. "Not until you listen to me."

She wriggled.

"Please," he said. "Just let me explain."

"No." She brought her leg up and kneed him as hard as she could. He cried out and rolled off her, cupping his hands between his legs.

She sprung to her feet. He remained coiled in the grass, his face contorted in pain. She should leave him here, run back to *The Pop-Inn*. But she didn't. She couldn't. Instead she stood over him, unable to move away. After all their years together, growing up together, a part of her understood she would always love him no matter what he had done. She couldn't switch her feelings off as though she were turning off a light. It wasn't that easy.

After a few minutes he unfolded his body, still lying on his side. Neither of them spoke for several more seconds.

"You deserved that," she said.

"I know."

"I was never yours to take. I will never be yours. But if it makes you feel any better, I was never Billy's, either." She wouldn't, couldn't, be owned by either of them, not then and not now.

He didn't say anything, and rolled onto his back, staring at the night sky.

"How could you let me think what happened that night was my fault? How could you not tell me the truth?"

"I'm sorry." He was crying, sobbing. "You have to understand. You wouldn't have married me if I did."

"How do you know what I would've done?" she asked. "You never gave me a chance." She paused, sure of only one thing. "I won't tell anyone what you did. I already have one child who lost a father. I don't want to have two." Her own tears started falling, and she wiped them from her cheeks. "But I don't know what Dee Dee and Patricia will do."

He turned his head away as though it hurt to look at her. "Everything I did. All of it," he said. "I swear, I did it for you."

"No, Kevin, you didn't. You did it for you."

Jo pulled open the screen door to *The Pop-Inn* and stepped inside. Every inch of her body hurt from the inside out. It even hurt to think. All she wanted was to fall into bed. She wasn't more than two steps across the porch when Caroline rushed in behind her. Caroline's sneakers were covered in mud and her arms and legs were marred with scratches. Her face was pale and she was breathing hard.

Jo was about to ask her daughter if she was messing with Stimpy's traps again when Caroline threw herself into Jo's arms and said, "I found Sara's body."

CHAPTER FORTY-SIX

It was close to three a.m., the dead hour. The Pavilion and bar had closed. Most of the lake community were tucked safely in their beds fast asleep, unaware of the news.

Caroline stood on the beach next to her friends. Their parents stood behind them. Mr. Roberts put his hand on Megan's shoulder. Mrs. Roberts bent her head toward Caroline's mother and murmured something about the emotional state of the drowned little girl's mother.

"She's in good hands," Caroline's mother assured her.

Cougar lay down near Adam's feet. The dog chomped happily on a piece of beef jerky. Since it was Cougar who found the little girl, the dog became a celebrity of sorts with the parents stopping to pat his head.

While their group waited for the underwater recovery team's watercraft to return with the body, Sheriff Borg peppered Caroline and the other kids with questions about what they were doing at the other end of the lake so late at night, and what was Stimpy's dog doing with them?

The twins explained they had been searching for Adam's fishing hole when Cougar found her. Adam mumbled something about his secret spot no longer being secret.

"And the dog?" the sheriff asked just as Stimpy approached from the pier.

Caroline opened her mouth, willing to take full responsibility, but Stimpy spoke up before she had a chance. He assured the sheriff he wasn't interested in pressing charges, although he was quite certain the kids not only stole his dog, but also released the snappers from his traps.

Caroline didn't believe Stimpy was letting them off easy because it was the right thing to do. No, he simply didn't want to look like the bad guy in front of their parents, who also happened to be paying customers.

Seizing the opportunity to get Cougar away from Stimpy once and for all, she said, "The dog should go to Adam." She glanced at Adam's mother, who didn't object. "You don't even take care of him," she said to Stimpy. "He's tied up all day and night. He's neglected and it's cruel."

"The law protects animals, too," Caroline's mother said, jumping in and sticking up for her. "Isn't that right, Sheriff?"

"That's right," the sheriff said.

"Why, you little—" Stimpy was cut-off when Heil appeared behind him and put his hand on his shoulder.

"Under the circumstances," Heil said, "what harm is there in letting the boy have the dog?" He made sure to look at each and every one of the kids as he spoke, his beady eyes roaming their guilty faces.

"Big of you," Caroline's mother said.

Caroline elbowed her. She didn't want her mother to make matters worse. It was no secret neither Stimpy nor Heil were friends of her family nor did the men give any indication that they'd like to be. Heil could easily tell Stimpy to press charges, to take the dog back, and the man would listen. Heil made the rules at the lake. He would always make the rules, whether anyone liked it or not.

Stimpy grumbled but was otherwise willing to let the dog go under Heil's orders.

"Can I keep him, Mom?" Adam asked.

"I don't see why not," his mother said.

Adam hugged Cougar tightly.

They turned their attention toward the lake as the recovery team's watercraft slowly made its way to the pier.

Heil walked away from the group, directing Stimpy to open the two large gates that lead to the beach. The SWIM AT YOUR OWN RISK sign rattled against the chain-link fence as though it were saying, *I told you so*.

The kids and parents parted as the coroner's vehicle backed onto the sand. Two men hopped out, opened the back doors, and pulled out a stretcher.

Sara's mother had been waiting at the pier. She released the most terrifying sound Caroline had ever heard. Caroline pinched her eyes closed and waited for the cry to end. She searched for comfort in the thought that at least Sara was finally with her mother. When she opened her eyes again, the men were loading Sara's body into the back of the van. The vehicle rolled off the beach in a hushed silence until it reached the parking lot, where the gravel crackled under its tires. It drove behind the Pavilion and up the hill onto Lake Road and out of sight.

Underwater recovery started packing their gear. One of the men explained Sara's body most likely surfaced sometime during the storm on that first night, a term they called *refloating*, and the wind had carried her to the south end of the lake. It was the reason they hadn't been able to find her sooner.

Once underwater recovery was packed and gone, Caroline's friends and their parents started making their way home. No one talked. There was nothing left to say.

Sheriff Borg tipped his hat at Caroline and her mother, pausing a long time to look over her mother's bruised face.

"It's a long story," her mother told him. "But you'll have to ask Dee Dee if you want to hear it. I'm sure she'll be happy to tell you all about it."

The sheriff continued staring at her mother as though he had more to say, but maybe under the circumstances he decided it could wait because he said, "Fair enough," and walked away. He stopped to talk with Chris's mother, Dee Dee. Chris and Johnny were with her. Caroline had just noticed they had been watching from the pier. Caroline couldn't help but think Johnny was with his new family, and it was her fault.

Her mother looked at the group on the pier, and Caroline wondered if she were thinking the same thing, if she blamed Caroline.

"I'm heading home," her mother said. "Are you coming?"

"In a minute."

Once her mother walked away, Johnny headed in Caroline's direction. He bumped her shoulder and motioned toward the south end of the lake. "You did good," he said.

She shrugged. "It was Cougar who found her."

"Yeah, but you're the one who brought the dog with you."

"I suppose." She paused and looked in the direction where the sheriff and Dee Dee were talking. She glanced back at Johnny. "I'm real sorry about what I did to you." It was the only other thing she could think to say.

"Forget about it," he said. "It's not your fault."

He was right. She was twelve years old and couldn't be held responsible for her parents' lies.

"It's funny," he said. "But I'm not really mad. I mean, it's messed up finding out Kevin's not my real dad, but it kind of makes sense. Now I know why things were always weird between him and me, you know?"

She nodded.

Johnny nudged her shoulder again. "I'm staying with Chris and his mom until the end of the summer. At least until I figure things out." He shrugged. "I wanted you to know."

Caroline looked at the ground and forced out the word *okay*.

"You're still my little sister, you know."

"Half-sister," she said.

"Technically, true." He wrapped an arm around her. "I'm still going to pick on you."

"Great."

He laughed and dropped his arm. "Well, I guess I'll see you around the watering hole." He started walking away.

"Hey, Johnny," she called.

He turned around.

"No halfsies," she said. "Brother and sister."

"You got it," he said and smiled his crazy silly smile that could break a million girls' hearts.

Gram was pulling out the last of the boxes in the back closet off the screened-in porch. She told Caroline she was determined to get through all the old junk and be done with it. She had been directing Caroline's mother all morning: *Pick up this box and set it out for the trash, carry this one to the car to donate, try not to break anything in this box and put it in the hall closet.*

Her mother didn't complain and did what Gram had asked her

to do. However, Caroline noticed every move her mother made was done with slow, careful steps, as though she were recovering from a bad fall. There were bruises on her mother's body to match the shiner on her face. Despite looking beat-up, her mother seemed, oh, Caroline didn't know, *better* somehow. There was something different about her, something Caroline struggled to name, but she didn't put much effort into it anyhow. She no longer felt as though it was her responsibility to figure her mother out. She learned maybe it was better to leave some things alone.

"I can help," Caroline said to Gram when she dropped another box onto the floor outside Caroline's bedroom door.

"No, you should be outside," Gram said. "Go on and have fun. You shouldn't be hanging around inside, not on a day like today."

When Gram left to get another box, Caroline closed her bedroom door, climbed out the window, and crawled into the arms of the willow tree. Her mother continued carrying boxes in and out of the cabin. She listened to the door creak open and bang closed. Every now and again Gram would call to have her mother lift something heavy.

Her father's truck was gone. He had told her late last night when she had returned to the cabin that he'd be on the road for awhile, and he had no idea when he would return. Something about the way he said it made her sad, although he assured her it had nothing to do with her or the fact that Johnny wasn't his. She didn't believe him nor did she try to stop him from leaving.

There was more stomping coming from the screened-in porch, and then the door slammed for the last time. Maybe her mother decided she had had enough and was taking off too.

"Caroline," her mother called. "Are you out here?"

"Over here," she said, and hopped down from her hiding spot.

She moved the long sweeping branches aside and emerged from under the tree where her mother stood waiting on the other side.

"I'm going for a drive," her mother said.

Of course you are, Caroline thought, but didn't say. She only nodded.

Her mother hesitated, as if she was deciding whether or not to say whatever else was on her mind. In another second she asked, "Do you want to come with me?"

The question surprised Caroline. Her mother had never asked her to come along before. A week ago she would've jumped at the chance to be with her. But now?

Now, Caroline decided, she didn't need to be.

CHAPTER FORTY-SEVEN

Jo felt as though she was seeing her daughter for the first time in a long time. There was something new about her, a maturity she hadn't seen before.

"Come on, come for a drive with me," she said. "I can't promise the radio station will play anything good, but I doubt the jukebox in the Pavilion is any better."

A hint of a smile touched the corners of Caroline's lips. "You're right about the jukebox," she said. "But I'm heading to the lake for the fishing tournament."

"Did you enter?"

"Not this year. I promised Adam I'd go and cheer him on."

"Oh," she said, somewhat surprised by her disappointment that her daughter had other plans. After all, she hadn't intended on asking her to come along. It was something that occurred to her at the last minute, that it was time to have the conversation she had been putting off. But nonetheless she said, "Well, if you promised Adam."

"I did promise." Caroline grabbed her bike from the yard.

It felt as though their roles had reversed overnight, and it was Jo begging with her eyes for her daughter to stick around.

"See you," Caroline said in a nonchalant way.

"Hey, Caroline."

Caroline stopped pushing her bike and looked over her shoulder.

"I'm coming back. You know that, don't you?"

"Yeah, Mom, I know."

"Do you?"

Caroline studied her, and Jo wondered what she saw: a mother who had lied to her, who had often run away for reasons Caroline had never understood. The longer her daughter stared at her, the more the guilt pressed down on Jo's heart.

"I guess," Caroline said finally. "I mean, I didn't always know if you would come back or not."

"I know. And I'm sorry about that." She walked closer to her, hoping she wouldn't jump on the bike and ride away. Although she supposed she couldn't blame her if she did. "I'm sorry about a lot of things."

Caroline shrugged, keeping her eyes on the ground by her feet.

"I know saying I'm sorry doesn't make up for everything. But I am sorry for not telling you and Johnny the truth. It was a mistake. I made a terrible mistake."

"Why didn't you tell us?" Caroline asked.

"Well," she said, wanting to give her an honest answer the best she could, but it was complicated. "I was young. And I was scared. Johnny's father . . ." She hesitated, unsure about saying Billy's name out loud.

"You mean Billy."

"Yes, Billy." She said it. "He'd drowned. And it was hard. For everyone. At the time I suppose I believed I was doing the right thing."

"And Dad agreed." There was a hard edge to Caroline's voice, but there was something else in her expression, a kindness she had inherited from her father.

"Yes." It had been Kevin's insistence on keeping the identity of Johnny's father a secret, putting distance between her and Billy's family as a way of protecting her when really he was only trying to protect himself. But she wasn't going to share this with her daughter. She wouldn't be responsible for tainting him in her daughter's eyes.

"You shouldn't have lied to us."

"I know." Jo reached for her.

Caroline drew back.

They were quiet; neither seemed to know what to say.

Jo was the first to break the silence. "Are you sure you don't want to come for a drive with me?" she asked.

"No." Caroline shook her head. "I gotta go," she said, and got on her bike.

Jo felt as though she had no other choice but to let her ride away. Her daughter no longer needed her as she once did. And Jo had no one to blame but herself. She turned toward the car. She wasn't three steps away when Caroline called, "Mom."

She turned back around. "Yes?" There was a hitch in her voice.

Caroline jumped off the bike and ran toward her. She fell into Jo's outstretched arms, and Jo pulled her close, hugging her tight. She continued to hold her, wanting to hold her, for as long as her daughter would allow.

Jo slipped behind the wheel of the old Chevy and started the engine. She rolled the windows down and turned on the radio before backing out of the yard. She took her time driving down the dirt road, dodging the potholes that had been there since the beginning of time, although she could've avoided hitting the bigger ones with her eyes closed. Nothing ever changed at the lake. Almost nothing.

She drove out of the colony and onto Lake Road. She continued down the hill that led to the Pavilion, but instead of heading toward the festival where Caroline and her friends had gathered, she made a sharp left turn and parked on the other side of the lake, far away from the crowd. She cut the engine and stared at the mountains covered in lush green trees. The water glistened under the bright blue sky. The sight was so beautiful, it took her breath away. It was something Kevin had said about her at one time.

He had to be out of the state by now, traveling west across country in his rig. She wondered how much time he'd have before he'd have to turn back around. It could be weeks, months, if he were lucky. With Patricia burying her daughter, there was no telling when she'd be ready to talk with the sheriff or how well she'd hold up as a witness.

Jo believed she had some time and in that time, she hoped she could find a way to forgive him. After all, she had come to terms with a few things about herself in the last twenty-four hours. She realized she was just as responsible as Kevin for Billy's death. She may not have been the one who had pushed him into the lake, but she had pushed him in her own way. She had manipulated him with her body, using her sex to control him.

She had been irresponsible and selfish, enjoying both boys' attention too much, rendering her incapable of choosing between them. She had been young and foolish thinking she could break the rules of love without anyone getting hurt. In the end, she not only hurt Billy and Kevin, but she hurt herself, too.

And Kevin had known all this about her. He had known her

better than she had known herself. And in spite of it all, he loved her anyway.

She reached for the cell phone because, after everything, he should've known this too. She typed: *I still would've married you.*

After hitting send, she sped away, the volume on the radio high, music blaring. She would drive as far as it would take to get her message through.